PAYBACK

A FRIEND IN NEED....

MARK DAVID ABBOTT

Copyright © 2020 by Mark David Abbott

All rights reserved.

No part of this book may be reproduced in any form or by any electronic or mechanical means, including information storage and retrieval systems, without written permission from the author, except for the use of brief quotations in a book review.

For all the faceless victims of Man's greed

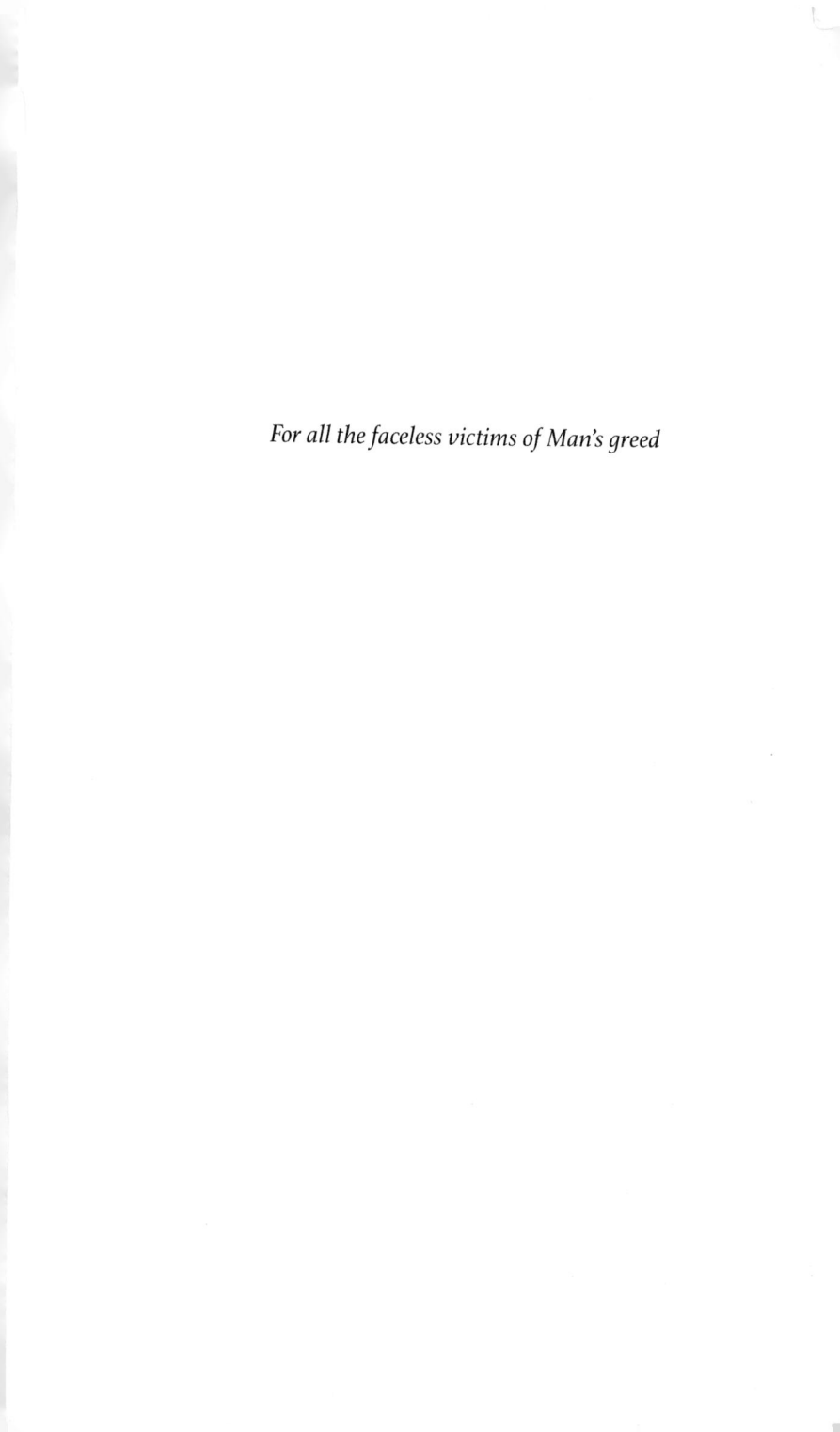

DO YOU WANT ADVANCE NOTICE OF THE NEXT ADVENTURE?

The next book is currently being written, but if you sign up for my VIP newsletter I will let you know as soon as it is released.

Your email will be kept 100% private and you can unsubscribe at any time.

If you are interested, please join here:

www.markdavidabbott.com
(No Spam. Ever.)

PROLOGUE

Hatay Province, Turkey, 2015

The girl thrust her hands deeper into her pockets in an effort to keep warm and hugged her arms closer to her body.

She looked up at the vast expanse of stars above her. It was a beautiful clear night, not a cloud in the sky, and the light from the moon bathed everything in a silvery glow.

It could have been magical, but for what lay ahead.

She tuned back into the murmured conversations around her—a mixture of languages, German, French, and English—but the volume was too low for her to make out anything, and besides, English was the only language in which she was fluent.

The man who called himself Abu Bakr came around the front of the SUV and stood in front of them. He was fat with a long straggly beard and a severely receding hairline. He spoke English with a thick accent she couldn't place. He pointed down the dirt track that ran along the fence line.

"Walk down that way for about five-hundred meters. There will be someone there. He will show you how to get through." He turned back to face them, looking at each of their faces one by one, his eyes resting on her for a moment longer than necessary. "Do you all understand?"

A low chorus of agreement and nods went through the group.

"Don't touch the fence except for where he tells you. It's electrified." He looked at them again to make sure they all understood before continuing. "Once you get through, run. Run as far as you can."

One of the men, a French speaker, spoke up, "Ow do we know where to go."

Abu Bakr grinned, his mouth opening to display a row of crooked teeth. "Don't worry. You will know. Someone will meet you. It's all arranged."

The girl gave a nervous smile to her companion and shifted her weight. She thought again about what she was doing. Was it the right thing? She had never been away from home like this before. She was scared, but... also excited. Another world was out there, waiting for her. A new promised land, a land where people could live as they were supposed to as it was written in the great book. And who better to go there with but the young man she loved, the man who had swept her off her feet back in the courtyards of the university, what seemed like just a short time ago. It had been a whirlwind, but everything she had imagined romance to be. He smiled back at her and laid a reassuring hand on her arm. She nodded and looked back at Abu Bakr, who was watching them with narrowed eyes. He looked away, his lip curling in a sneer, and addressed the group again.

"*Ma salaam.* Good journey. *Allahu Akbar!*"

"*Allahu akbar,*" the group repeated, a couple of men slapping each other on the back.

Abu Bakr gestured toward the track, "Now go."

The five men and one girl started walking in the direction he had shown. A high, chain-link fence lined the track on their left while to their right, fields of olive trees stretched off into the darkness. The group walked in nervous silence, the only sound from scuffed feet and pebbles rolling away.

The girl looked back over her shoulder, but Abu Bakr and his vehicle had already gone. There was no-one around. They were alone... at least that's what they thought.

A figure materialized out of the darkness, gesturing for them to hurry, and pointed toward the fence. As they neared, they saw someone had cut the fence, and the two sides were peeled back to make a hole just big enough for a body to pass through.

"Through there," the man hissed. "Hurry."

"The power?" asked one of the men in the group.

The man grinned. "Don't worry. It's cut. Now go."

One by one, the group eased themselves through the fence and waited for the others. The girl was last. She could feel her heart pounding in her chest. She took a deep breath and closed her eyes—it was now or never. She opened them and saw her companion kneeling on the other side of the fence, his hand reaching through the hole in the fence.

She nodded, crouched down, took his hand, and scrambled through the hole.

"*Yalla, yalla.* Run!"

"Which way?"

The man pointed into the darkness. "That way. *Allahu akbar!*"

"*Allahu Akbar!*"

1

John screwed up his face in distaste and glanced over his shoulder toward the cafe window. Just as he thought, it was the new guy.

He put the cup back down on the table and dabbed at his lips with a napkin before settling back in his chair. The coffee was over-extracted and bitter. He gazed across the street toward the tree-filled Jardim de Príncipe Real and sighed. There was no point in complaining on the guy's first day. He would learn.

John nodded at the elderly man walking past. *"Bom Dia."*

"Bom Dia," the man replied, his face creasing in a smile, the lines on his forehead and around his eyes, filled with stories from a long, well-lived life.

The sun burst through the clouds, bringing warm rays of light. John loosened the scarf around his neck, dropping it on the seat beside him. He sucked in a lungful of crisp spring air and reached for his coffee again. Apart from the coffee, life was wonderful.

He and Adriana had a nice apartment in the Príncipe Real district, a lovely neighborhood with cobblestoned streets, trees, and cafes and restaurants within easy walking distance. He glanced over at the car parked at the curb, a recent treat for himself. A 1970 Porsche 911 S in Bahia Red, the car he had dreamed about since he was a kid. She was beautiful and gave him a lot of pleasure, racing around the streets.

After the traumatic experiences in Oman and India, life was enjoyable again. Adriana loved her work and was enjoying being back in the country of her birth, close to her parents. John had settled in easily, was picking up Portuguese, and had been enjoying exploring Lisbon, seeking out great places to eat and drink. Their circle of friends had grown slowly, and the city was beginning to feel like home.

John was fortunate he didn't have to work, his shareholding in the Hong Kong listed Pegasus Land more than sufficient to provide him and Adriana with an extremely comfortable life. With all the time John had at his disposal, he had become fitter than ever before, lean and strong, full of energy and well-being. He was sleeping well. The occasional nightmares filled with repressed memories from the past were fewer and further between.

He reached for the coffee cup, then remembering the taste, changed his mind. He sighed. There was something wrong. He couldn't put his finger on it... He felt restless as if there was something lacking. It had been troubling him for a while, eating away at the back of his mind. It was why he had come out this morning and was drinking awful coffee, instead of one of his own at home. The walls of the apartment had felt as if they were closing in, and he needed to get out, to move around, to do... something. Perhaps he had too much time. It was ironic. When he had worked for a living, when he had been a wage slave, he had dreamed of free time, of being in control of every hour, not being bound by the clock and deadlines.

A presence beside him disturbed his thoughts.

"John *bom dia, como você está?*"

John smiled and reached out to shake the hand of Agostinho, the owner of the cafe.

"Bom dia Agostinho, estou bem, obrigado." He then gestured toward his coffee cup and made a face.

Agostinho placed a hand on John's shoulder and nodded, switching to English.

"I'll make it myself." He glanced toward the cafe and shrugged. "He's still learning."

John smiled. "It's okay."

"Give me a minute."

"Obrigado."

John sat back and continued his train of thought. People here were nice, friendly. His life was perfect, there was no reason to be dissatisfied, but if the truth be known, if he was completely honest with himself—he was bored.

2

The ground rocked with a heavy impact, and a fine mist of dust filled the air. Mahfuza pulled her daughter closer as they huddled under a blanket in the corner of the room. That was the closest one so far, the explosions getting closer and closer the past week. She looked down and placed a hand on her daughter's forehead. She was hot, a low fever, but there was little she could do. They hadn't eaten properly in months, and any medicines were solely for the use of the fighters. Mahfuza shivered and wrapped the loose end of her hijab across her face, covering her mouth and nose, and pulled the blanket tighter to keep warm. She closed her eyes and rocked back and forth, the motion the only comfort she could give her child.

It hadn't always been like this. There had been happier times in another world—a world filled with love and abundance, where people smiled and laughed, where food was plentiful. It seemed so long ago, and the thought increased the heavy feeling of despair that enveloped her. She wouldn't cry, there was no point. She had stopped crying a long time ago. She was here, and she must accept it.

Another explosion shook the building, and she winced, opening her eyes, and glancing down at the little girl in her arms as the sound of a jet fighter screamed overhead, but not a sound came from the child, her eyes open, staring blankly across the rubble-strewn floor, oblivious to her surroundings. Mahfuza leaned down and kissed her on the top of the head, continuing her rocking. She closed her eyes again, and her lips started moving.

"*Bismillaah ar-Raḥmān ar-Raheem. Alhamdulilah rab il alameen, Ar-Raḥmān ar-Raheem......*"

3

John felt a vibration in his pocket and shifted his position, so he could remove the phone as Agostinho returned with another cup of coffee.

"*Obrigado, Agostinho.*" John smiled and glanced at the screen. He raised his eyebrows, and his grin became wider. John nodded at the café owner, then answered the call.

"Steve."

"John, mate, how's it hanging?"

John chuckled. "I'm well, Steve. How are you?"

"Can't complain, mate. People keep having affairs, so I'm always busy."

"The glamorous and exciting life of a private eye."

"Yeah, you wouldn't think that after sitting in a car for twelve hours, drinking cold coffee, and pissing in a bottle."

John nodded, his thoughts going back to the times when he had done exactly that. He reached for his coffee and took a sip. Much better. He glanced across at Agostinho, who was clearing a nearby table and gave him the thumbs-up as Steve continued.

"How's life treating you? Still in Lisbon?"

"Yes. It's a great city. You should come and visit."

"Hmmm, maybe I will."

"You're always welcome, Steve. Adriana would love to see you again."

John liked Steve a lot. Despite meeting briefly, they had been through so much together, experiencing things that created a bond between them. In fact, if it hadn't been for Steve and his intervention in Oman, stepping in when the mercenaries hired by Surya Patil had attacked their desert camp, John and Adriana might not be alive today.

"How's she doing? Settled in with that newspaper? What's it called?"

"Público."

"Yeah."

"She's loving it. It was always her dream to do something like that."

"Well, send her my love, mate."

"I will."

There was a pause in conversation, and John heard a sigh on the other end. He frowned.

"Is everything okay, Steve?"

"Yeah, mate, it's just..."

"What?"

John listened to the silence. He almost thought the line had been cut when Steve spoke again.

"John, I need your help."

4

John wiped his hands on the dishcloth and draped it over his shoulder as he glanced toward the table, checking everything was laid out correctly. Good. He reached for the glass on the kitchen benchtop, swirled the ice cubes around, then took a sip. His gin and tonic was almost finished. Glancing at his wristwatch, he calculated Adriana should be home any minute, just in time for him to make a fresh one.

He took one last look around the kitchen, wiped a spot of liquid from the benchtop, then picked up his glass, and walked toward the bar. He retrieved a second glass from the cabinet just as the front door opened.

"Hi, baby."

John turned and smiled as Adriana removed her jacket, kicked off her shoes, and dropped her bag on the table by the door.

"Perfect timing." John held up the empty glass and raised an eyebrow.

"Yes, please." Adriana walked over, glancing at the dining table as she passed. She wrapped her arms around

John from behind and nuzzled her lips into his neck. John turned his head, and they kissed.

"Tough day?"

"No, no, just a long one." She continued to watch him over his shoulder, her arms still around him as he filled a copa glass with ice, then sliced an orange, slipping the orange wheel down the side of the glass before adding a generous serving of Botanist and topping it off with tonic.

"Here you go."

Loosening her arms, she took the glass, then a long sip, swallowing with satisfaction.

"Lovely, thank you." She placed a hand on his back, between the shoulder blades as John prepared a drink for himself.

"Something smells nice. What's for dinner?"

John turned and smiled. He held up his glass and clinked it against Adriana's.

"You'll see." He took a sip and licked his lips. "That's a damn good gin and tonic, even if I say so myself."

"It is." Adriana took another sip and moved away from the bar. "How was your day?"

"The usual." John shrugged. "Nothing exciting."

Adriana studied his face for a moment, gave a slight frown, then moved to the sofa and sat down. Slumping back in the chair, she rested her feet on the coffee table while John sat at the opposite end of the sofa. They remained in silence for a while, both content in each other's company, sipping their drinks and gazing out over the city as Adriana wound down from the tensions of the day.

John waited until Adriana had almost finished her drink before breaking the silence.

"Steve called today."

"Really? How is he? Still in Dubai?"

"Yes. He's good."

Adriana watched John stare at his drink, waiting for him to continue. She frowned.

"Something is wrong."

John's head jerked up, and he looked at Adriana in surprise.

"Yes. How did you know?"

Adriana gave a half-smile. "I know you well enough now, Mr. Hayes. What's the matter?"

John placed his drink down and turned, so he was facing Adriana, one knee on the sofa, his arm across the backrest. He looked down at the sofa, paused, then looked directly into her eyes.

"He needs my help. I have to go to Dubai."

5

Naeem Emwazi adjusted the AKM Assault rifle on its sling, so it hung down his back and climbed the narrow stairway to the first floor. He was tired, and each step was an effort. He had been awake for three days and badly needed sleep and food, but the single piece of flatbread he had folded in half and stuffed into the thigh pocket of his combat cargos was not for him.

Reaching the top of the stairs, he stepped over a pile of bricks and entered the dusty, rubble-strewn room. Light from the setting sun angled through the hole, where there had once been a window, and fell on what looked like a heap of cloth in the corner.

"Mahfuza," Naeem called softly.

The heap shifted with a start and took shape—a young woman, her face hidden by a black hijab, a blanket wrapped around her body, and in her arms another bundle.

Naeem stepped closer and knelt beside her. He reached out a hand, and with grime stained fingers, gently moved the blanket away to see the bundle below.

"Malak," he murmured. There was no response from the tiny girl. Her eyes remained closed, not a sound from her lips. He felt her forehead and sat back on his heels. "She's hot."

The girl's mother, Naeem's wife, nodded and pulled the baby closer.

Naeem lifted the flap of his pocket and removed the bread. He passed it over to Mahfuza, who snatched it with her spare hand and tore off a chunk with her teeth. She chewed hurriedly, swallowed before it was completely chewed, and took another bite. Halfway through the mouthful, she stopped chewing and asked, "Water?"

Naeem nodded and unscrewed the top of a battered plastic bottle and held it to her mouth so she could take a drink, taking it away after a couple of mouthfuls.

"Careful, it's all I have."

Mahfuza sat up and adjusted her back against the wall. She laid Malak on her lap and tore off a small piece of bread.

"Malak, baby, wake up," she whispered. Holding the bread near Malak's lips, she repeated, "Wake up, my darling. We have some food. Wake up."

There was no response. Mahfuza looked up at Naeem and shook her head.

"Let me try." Naeem moved closer, took the bread from Mahfuza's hands, and whispered to his daughter, "Malak, Daddy's home. Wake up, my baby." Again, the child didn't stir. Naeem dropped the bread in Mahfuza's lap and rubbed his face in frustration.

"Any news?" Mahfuza asked, a look of hope on her face.

Naeem shook his head. "Maybe tomorrow." He placed his hand on Mahfuza's leg. "Rest now, I'll try again in the morning."

He shifted sideways, unslung his weapon, and laid it on the floor beside him, then using his arm for a pillow, stretched out on the floor beside Mahfuza. Within seconds, he was fast asleep.

6

John and Adriana walked into the arrival hall of Dubai's Terminal Three and immediately spotted Steve's familiar figure in the crowd, his hand raised high in the air in greeting.

He wrapped his arms around Adriana in a bear hug, winking over her shoulder at John.

"Welcome to Dubai."

"Hi, Steve, good to see you again," Adriana gasped, struggling for air.

Steve released her and held her at arm's length, "You're looking as beautiful as ever." He nodded toward John. "This guy looking after you properly?"

Adriana chuckled. "He is."

"Good." Steve let go of her and reached out for John's hand. "Alright, mate?" He pulled John closer and turned the handshake into a hug, slapping John on his back with his free hand. "Thanks for coming."

"It's the least I could do, Steve. You are looking well."

Steve smiled and ran his hand down over his stomach. "Lost some weight, too."

"Yes, I was going to say. You are looking fitter and younger. Turned over a new leaf?"

"Ha, you'll see." Steve looked down at the two cabin bags they had brought with them. "This is it?"

"Yes, we travel light, and Adriana is only here for the weekend."

"Oh." Steve looked over at Adriana.

"Yes, Steve." Adriana nodded. "I have to be back on Tuesday. I couldn't get more time off."

Steve reached for the handle of her cabin bag and pulled it toward him. "Well, there's no time to waste then. Follow me."

Steve led them out of the terminal, through the parking building, and stopped beside a sparkling white Mitsubishi Pajero. Stowing their bags in the back, they climbed in together, John in the front, Adriana behind.

"You're staying with me. It's about thirty minutes from here."

"Are you sure it's okay? We're happy to stay in a hotel."

Steve looked at Adriana in the rear-view mirror as he replied, "Nonsense, when you're in Dubai, you stay with me."

Adriana smiled and settled back into her seat as Steve pulled out of the parking building and joined the flow of traffic. He took the E311 and settled into a steady cruise in the middle lane, heading southeast across the city.

John gazed out the window at the skyscrapers and cranes filling the skyline.

"Every time I come here, there seem to be more buildings. Construction never seems to stop."

"Yeah, mate, no shortage of money flowing into this place, not all of it clean. Every con-man, arms dealer, corrupt politician, dictator, and drug baron in the world has their money passing through this place."

John gave a half-smile. "Plenty to keep you busy then."

"For sure."

John turned to face Steve. "So, tell me more about this girl? You've been pretty vague so far."

Steve's eyes flicked to the rear mirror.

"He's told me, Steve," Adriana spoke up.

"Okay." Steve frowned, glanced in his side mirror, then indicated and moved into the next lane to avoid a slow-moving van.

"You said the girl is a relative? She's in trouble?"

"My niece, yes."

"Niece?"

"My older brother's daughter." Steve sighed, "Let's discuss it when we get home. It's complicated."

John nodded and turned his attention back to the passing landscape, a slight frown creasing his forehead. Steve wasn't giving the whole story, which worried him a little, but he owed Steve. The man had saved his life, and John would do anything to repay the debt. If that meant helping him out with a niece in trouble, so be it. Besides, he needed something to do.

7

After twenty-five minutes, Steve took an exit ramp as it looped around on itself in a massive circular interchange and joined a smaller road crossing over the highway. Large patches of sand interspersed with Industrial buildings lined each side of the road, and the traffic had reduced significantly. They followed the road for another fourteen kilometers until the sand and industrial buildings gave way to houses and trees.

Steve slowed for a speed-bump before turning left into the entrance of a tree-filled residential area. He paused while they raised the barrier, flicked a lazy wave at the security guard, then drove in. He took a right and followed the road as it curved past rows of palatial villas and lanes with names like Hibiscus Way and Poppy Lane. Unlike the surrounding area, it was lush and green, the road lined with trees, and the gardens filled with flowering plants and foliage. A pair of bright green parrots flew across the road in front of them, and a ring-necked dove stared back at them from a well-manicured lawn.

"I didn't expect to see this in the middle of the desert."

"It's cool, right? When they built this, there was nothing here. Every plant was brought in, and now it's filled with birds and squirrels. Nature is incredible."

"It is, despite our attempts to destroy it."

Steve slowed and pulled into the drive of a large white villa. A blue Mercedes convertible was parked in front of the double garage door.

"Home sweet home," he announced and switched off the engine.

"Nice. I thought you lived in an apartment, Steve?" John smiled. "The private eye business is obviously treating you well."

"I did. I haven't been here long." Steve grinned. "But there have been some changes in my life, which meant my bachelor pad was no longer suitable."

John raised an eyebrow, "You mean..."

A movement caught John's eye, and he looked toward the front door as it opened.

"Ha! You old devil!" John shook his head, opened the door, and strode across the drive. He paused in front of the lady standing in front of him, then with a big grin, stepped forward and gave her a hug.

"I can't believe it." He stepped back and shook his head. Turning, he looked back at a very happy Steve and a puzzled Adriana.

"Adriana, this is Maadhavi."

Maadhavi stepped forward and took Adriana by the hand.

"It's my pleasure to meet you, at last, Adriana." She winked at John. "William here told me a lot about you."

"William?"

Maadhavi laughed and turned to John. "You didn't tell

her?" Turning back to Adriana, she said, "When I met John in India, he told me his name was William."

Adriana raised an eyebrow at John. "Really?"

Maadhavi laughed. "Come, we have a lot to talk about."

The two men watched them enter the house, then John turned to Steve.

"I'm thrilled for you, Steve." Then he shook his head. "But what she sees in you, I don't know."

"Ha. No-one can resist my charm, mate." Steve slapped John on the back. "Let's take the bags in and have some lunch. I'm starving."

8

They enjoyed a leisurely lunch while Maadhavi explained how John had rescued her from the clutches of Surya Patil and helped her escape to Dubai to start a fresh life and rekindle her film career.

"I owe it all to you, John. Without you, I would still be stuck there in Bangalore,"—she gulped and looked down at the table—"living as the kept woman of that horrible man."

Adriana reached across the table and took Maadhavi's hand. They smiled at each other, although Maadhavi's eyes were moist.

"When did you find out my name wasn't William?" John glanced over at Adriana. "I wanted her to have plausible deniability if it all went wrong."

"Well, it didn't." Maadhavi smiled. "Google."

"Google?" Adriana asked.

"Yes, I Googled the news reports about the attack on..." She glanced at John.

"Charlotte." John shrugged. "It's okay." He smiled at Adriana but didn't say more. It was a few years ago, but the memories of the brutal attack on his late wife, Charlotte, by

Surya Patil's son in Bangalore, were still raw. He preferred not to dwell in the past, though. It never helped. He had done too many things he preferred to forget. He didn't even like to look too far into the future. Life rarely turned out as planned. The present was all that mattered, and right now, he had the woman he loved sitting next to him. He slid his hand onto Adriana's lap and gave her thigh a squeeze.

"More wine, anyone?" Steve broke the uncomfortable silence. He reached for the bottle of Sauvignon Blanc resting in the ice bucket. "Much as I don't like to admit it, those 'sheep shaggin' Kiwis know how to make wine."

"Steve," Maadhavi admonished him.

Steve gave a guilty grin at John, then topped up the glasses before upending the empty bottle in the bucket. He looked over his shoulder toward the kitchen,

"Marisel?"

"Yes, Sir?"

"Can you bring another bottle of the white wine from the fridge, please?" He turned back to the table and picked up his glass. "Here's to friendship,"—he smiled at Maadhavi—"love, and superb wine."

A chorus of cheers went around the table as Marisel, the Filipina housekeeper, placed a fresh bottle of wine in the ice bucket.

Adriana sipped her wine, then asked, "Maadhavi, you didn't explain how you met Steve."

"Yes, how did you two meet?" John asked. "Which part of discrete surveillance didn't you understand?" He turned to Adriana. "When Maadhavi fled Bangalore, I asked Steve to keep a discrete," he emphasized the word while looking meaningfully in Steve's direction, "watch over her."

"Well," Steve chuckled. "I rarely get to follow a beautiful Indian film actress around. You should see some of the ugly mugs I have to follow." He shrugged. "I couldn't help myself."

"It wasn't all his fault," Maadhavi interjected. "I noticed him on the second day. When I kept seeing him, I guessed he was working for you, John, so I approached him."

"I'm glad you did." Steve leaned over and kissed her on the cheek.

John shook his head. "Great private eye, you are. Perhaps you should think about another career?"

"Maybe you're right." He grinned at Maadhavi. "I'd happily be a house-husband."

"You'd be bored within a week."

"She's right." Steve nodded and winked at John.

"What type of movies do you do, Maadhavi?" Adriana asked.

"I work in the Kannada film industry, Adriana. Kannada is the language of Karnataka, the State in India where Bangalore is."

"And you can do that from here in Dubai?"

"Yes. I fly down whenever there's a shoot. We've even filmed scenes here in the Emirates. The film-going public loves a bit of Dubai glamor." Maadhavi took a sip from her glass. "Besides, I prefer to be here. I have more privacy... and him, of course."

"Well, I'm happy it all worked out for both of you." John raised his glass. "Cheers."

"Cheers."

"Now, how about you tell me why you needed me here?"

9

The four moved to the living room while Marisel cleared the table.

Steve topped up their glasses as the other three waited expectantly for him to begin his story. Sitting down in an armchair opposite John and Adriana, he took a sip from his wine glass, pursed his lips, then put his glass down and sat forward in the chair, his elbows resting on his thighs.

"My older brother, Thomas, has a daughter, my niece. Her name is... was Mia. She's twenty-four years old."

"Was?"

"She now goes by Mahfuza Fatima."

John and Adriana exchanged a glance.

Steve sighed and took a gulp of wine.

"Five years ago, she left Australia with her boyfriend on a trip to Europe. They arrived in Turkey, then crossed the border into Syria. To join the *Jihad*."

"Oh." Adriana's hand went to her mouth.

John narrowed his eyes, a feeling of apprehension growing within him.

"And?"

Steve stood and walked over to the French windows opening out onto the garden. He stood for a moment, staring out into the garden, then turned to face John.

"We need to get her out of there."

John glanced at Adriana, then Maadhavi, both waiting for his response.

"Ah... why now? She's been there for five years. What's changed?" He frowned. "Don't get me wrong, I know this sounds harsh, but she's an adult, she made a choice to go there and join ISIS or whatever they call themselves there."

"Yeah, she did." Steve sighed. "You're right." He ran his fingers through his hair. "She has a daughter, John. Not quite two years old. Her name is Malak. She doesn't want her to grow up over there. She wants her to have a proper life."

"Hmmm." John stared down at the carpet, his mind whirring away. What was the right thing to do?

"How do you know about all this, Steve?" Adriana asked.

"Her... husband," Steve said the word with obvious distaste, "called my brother. He... he... sounded desperate." Steve looked over at John. "I hate that bastard, John. He took Mia there. He destroyed our family, but..." He shook his head. "It's a child. My brother's granddaughter. My grand-niece, John."

John studied him, still not sure what to do.

Again, Adriana came to the rescue. "Do you know where they are?"

Steve nodded. "In Idlib province."

"Oh."

John looked at Adriana. "What?"

"Idlib province is one of the last remaining areas under

the control of the anti-government forces. There's a lot of fighting there right now."

"But they are the good guys, aren't they?"

Adriana gave a sad smile. "There are no good guys. We've been doing stories on the conflict. Nothing is as it seems... or as they lead us to believe."

John chewed his lip. "Where's your brother in all of this?"

Steve came back to his seat and sat down.

"He's in Melbourne, but he can't do anything. He's always had poor health, and when Mia left, it broke his heart. He's not physically capable of helping with anything like this."

"What about the aid organizations? Red Cross, people like that?"

"He's tried. There are millions of refugees in Syria. They can't help, even if they wanted to. They're overwhelmed, and besides, in their eyes, she and her husband are foreign fighters... terrorists. No country wants them back."

"So, if we get her out, what will you do then?"

Steve shrugged. "I'll worry about that then."

John rubbed his face and looked over at Adriana. She returned his gaze—even with concern etched across her face, she was beautiful. What if they had a daughter? What would they do if she was in the same situation?

John turned back to Steve.

"So, are you suggesting we go into a war zone, a country where we don't speak the language and rescue a mother and her daughter from under the noses of an army of battle-hardened *jihadis*, who love to behead westerners?"

"Ah, well, when you put it like that..." Steve winced. "It sounded easier in my head."

10

John and Adriana strolled along the narrow road that wound its way through the housing estate. The sun was low in the sky and threw long shadows across the street.

"The houses here are enormous, look at that one." Adriana pointed to a massive white villa behind an eight-foot-high wall.

John didn't answer, deep in thought.

"John?"

"Huh?"

Adriana tucked her arm in his and moved closer.

"Tell me what you're thinking."

"It's just... I don't know what to do." John shrugged and gave her arm a squeeze. "Before... the things I've done... the path was always reasonably clear, but now..."

"What do you mean?"

"Well, Oman, for example. You were in danger. I had to rescue you. There was no thinking about it."

John nodded at a neighbor walking their Labrador and paused until they were out of earshot.

"Then I had to go to India, I had to stop Surya Patil. If I hadn't, he would have continued to put your... our lives in danger."

"Yes, I agree." Adriana nodded. "But what about Thailand? I wasn't in danger, at least at first. You didn't even really know me."

"Hmmm." John thought back to the events when he had first met Adriana and had gone on to rescue Amira from her employer.

"After rescuing me and Amira, you found the Rohingya camp and had it closed down." She stopped walking and turned to face John. "You did that because it was the right thing to do. Because you are a good man."

"But Adriana, this girl is in a war zone. In the eyes of the world, maybe in my eyes, too, she is a terrorist. Her husband is a *jihadi*." He sighed. "The only reason I'm even thinking about it is I owe Steve my life."

"Yes, John, but that's not the only reason." Adriana reached up and placed her hand on his chest. "In here, you are thinking of the child. A child who doesn't deserve to suffer because of stupid decisions made by its parents."

John looked down into her eyes, the light from the setting sun highlighting the flecks of gold in her irises. Despite his misgivings, he knew she was right. He could never live with himself if that child suffered, and he had never even tried to help Steve bring it to safety. He exhaled and looked away. Anyway, only a few days ago, he was feeling sorry for himself because he was bored.

"Yes, you're right." He turned back, leaned down, and kissed her on the lips. "It will be bloody dangerous, though."

"I know," Adriana sighed and pulled him closer. "But maybe there's a safe way?"

"Hmmm, let's see. Come, let's go back and tell

Steve." They turned around and headed back the way they had come. "Honestly, I've absolutely no idea what to do."

"We'll work something out." She squeezed his arm. "If you have doubts, think about what you've done before."

"Huh, I appreciate your faith in me, but this won't be easy."

"No, but there's always a solution."

"I hope so."

11

Naeem had spent most of the day resting on the floor beside Mahfuza, getting up only to pray and leaving for a brief time in the late morning to find water and food, both in increasingly short supply.

He had been on the frontline for five days at a stretch and was exhausted. Fighting to keep control over the vital M5 highway had been fierce, the Syrian army and their Russian supporters unleashing everything on them. Every time Naeem and his brothers had regained ground, they had lost it shortly after in a back-and-forth squabble over the same pieces of ground. Another unit had finally come forward to relieve them, and he headed back to the shelter he had found for Mahfuza, to get some much-needed rest.

Hopefully, it would all be over soon.

He looked over at his wife and daughter, wrapped up in blankets against the cold. Things hadn't turned out the way he had planned all those years ago when they crossed the border. The dream of the Caliphate had collapsed, and he and his fellow fighters—men from all over the world who had been drawn to the ideal of the prophesied *Dar al Islam,* Land of the Muslim—had been reduced to fighting for a smaller and smaller piece of the country.

When little Malak had been born, she had been a gift from Allah himself, and he'd thought it a sign things would change, but he had been wrong. Staying in Syria, there was little to hope for. They wouldn't succeed, the forces against them too strong and the morale among his brothers decreasing by the day.

He'd seen so many killed and wounded, and many of those who survived had given up and surrendered. He, too, had been close to giving up when he had been called in by the *Amiat*, the Caliphate's secret police, just two weeks ago. He had been afraid at first, wondering why he had come to their attention. He was a good Muslim, had proven his loyalty to the Caliphate many times, first when he had served with the *Al Hisbah,* the religious police, then when he joined the frontline fighters of the *Al-Khansaa* Brigade.

When the *Amiat* had called him in, he thought someone had been spreading lies about him but was relieved to find it was nothing like that. Naeem closed his eyes, tuning out the background noise of explosions and gunfire, visualizing the meeting in his head. The *Emir* had told him he was being rewarded for his loyalty and had been chosen for the ultimate mission. He had come back from the meeting filled with a renewed purpose, his life holding meaning again.

He heard a noise beside him and opened his eyes again. Mahfuza was awake and watching him. He sat up and shifted backward, so he was leaning against the wall. She didn't smile, just stared, her face expressionless. She rarely smiled anymore. It was only when he had told her they should consider getting out and moving back to Australia, he had seen any emotion in her expression. She didn't believe him at first, but when he had given her the phone and she spoke to her father, she finally began to hope it was possible. He turned his wrist and looked at the cheap plastic Casio on his wrist. He would call her father again. Everything hinged on them getting out of Syria.

12

As they neared the house, they saw the diminutive figure of Marisel, Steve's Filipina housekeeper running toward them.

"Sir, Ma'am..."

"What is it?"

"Mr. Steve." Marisel paused for breath. "He wants you to come back quickly, he got a call."

Without another thought, John burst into a sprint, leaving Adriana and Marisel behind. He reached the house, running through the open doorway.

"Steve?"

"In here."

John followed the sound into the dining room, where Steve and Maadhavi were huddled around a phone lying on the table.

"My brother called. He had a call from Naeem, Mia's husband. The child, Malak, is not well. He gave me a number. We're trying to reach them, but I guess the signal is patchy."

John moved around to look at the phone screen. "Video call?"

"Yup."

John looked up as Adriana walked in, followed by an out of breath Marisel.

"Steve's trying to call her," he explained

"Okay." Adriana moved around, so she could see the screen as well.

"Just try a voice call first," John suggested. "It might be easier to connect."

"Yeah, good idea." Steve tapped on the phone screen. Nothing happened for a while, then the sound of the phone ringing came through the speakers. Steve looked up and nodded before staring back at the screen again.

"Allo?"

John saw Steve's lip curl in distaste.

"Naeem?"

"Na'am. Min hdha?" the voice said. "Yes, who's this."

"Speak in English," Steve growled. "You're fucking Australian."

There was a pause. "Who is this?"

"It's Steve, Mia's uncle. Where is she?"

"This is a Dubai number."

"I know where I am, where is Mia?"

"Mahfuza... she's here."

"Put her on."

They heard a muffled conversation, then a girl's voice.

"Uncle Steve?"

"Mia?" Steve's face softened.

"How did you get this number?"

"Your dad gave it to me. I want to help you."

"How?"

"I don't know yet. I'll work something out. But right now, are you okay? Are you safe?"

"Yeah... I'm okay... but Malak... she's sick. I don't know what to do."

Maadhavi placed a hand on Steve's shoulder as he continued.

"What's wrong with her?"

"She.... just sleeps, she won't eat... and I think she has a fever."

"Can you take her to a doctor?"

They heard a muffled boom.

"What was that, Mia?"

"It's nothing."

"Was that an explosion?"

"Yes, but not close. Don't worry, we're safe right now."

"Okay." Steve looked around at the others, a deep-set frown creasing his forehead. "Mia, can you get her to a doctor?"

"There're no doctors here now. They've all gone."

"Ask her if she can get her to an aid camp?" John murmured to Steve.

"Who's that?"

"It's my friend, Mia. Mia, can you get to an aid camp?"

"I tried. They gave me some medicine, something for her fever, but it's run out. They said they won't give me anymore. They... know I'm not Syrian. They said the medicine is for Syrians... not *jihadis*."

"Okay, Mia." Steve exhaled loudly. "I will try to help you. Don't worry, I'll work something out. Where are you now?"

They heard a muffled conversation, then, "It's a place called Sarmin, near Idlib."

"Okay, I'll work something out. I'll call you."

"Uncle Steve, the phone, we turn it off to save the battery. We can't always charge it. There's no power here."

"Damn. Okay, ummm..."

"Tell her we'll call her the same time tomorrow. To turn on the phone then," John suggested.

Steve nodded.

"I heard that... your friend."

"Yes, Mia. Can you do that?"

"Yes."

"Okay, now give the phone to Naeem."

Again, the sound of fumbling, then, "Hello."

Steve leaned closer to the phone, his hands on the table, the knuckles turning white as he clenched the table.

"Now you listen to me, you worthless piece of shit, you keep them safe. This is all your fault. If anything happens to them, I will personally come and rip your fucking head off with my bare hands."

There was silence for a moment.

"Did you hear me?"

"Yes... I'm not afraid. If Allah wills it, I will die at your hand, but... Malak, she deserves more... I'll keep her safe. *Inshallah*, we will speak tomorrow."

The call ended, and Steve straightened up, his fists clenched, his chest rising up and down. Maadhavi rubbed his back as he stared unseeing across the room.

"Steve."

Steve blinked and turned to John.

"I'll help you, Steve. We'll get her out, somehow."

Steve stared back, his eyes hard, his brow furrowed, then nodded slowly.

13

The four stood in silence, just staring at the now blank phone. John took control and spoke first.

"Marisel?"

"Yes, sir?"

"Can you make us all some coffee, please?"

"Yes, sir."

"Steve."

Steve looked up as if surprised they were there.

"Grab your laptop. I want to see exactly where she is."

"Yes, okay." Steve moved off while the other three pulled out chairs and sat around the table.

"What can we do?" Maadhavi asked, looking from John to Adriana and back again.

John pursed his lips and shrugged. "I don't know, Maadhavi. But one thing at a time." He looked up at Steve as he came back into the room. "We'll see where she is and try to find out what's happening around there."

Steve sat down beside Maadhavi and booted up his laptop as she placed a comforting hand on his shoulder.

"What was the name of the place?"

John closed his eyes as he thought. "S... S... Sarmin."

"Spelling?"

"No idea. As it sounds, I suppose."

John watched as Steve typed, stabbing at the keyboard with his index fingers. Steve frowned and then said, "Here we go." He swiveled the laptop around, so they could both see the screen, Adriana standing up and moving so she could look over their shoulders.

"Is that the Turkish border?" John pointed at the screen.

"Yeah."

"It's not far then. What do you reckon the distance is?"

Steve leaned closer. "Judging by the scale, forty, fifty kilometers?"

"Hmmm." John straightened up, his hands on his hips. "There must be someone there who can help get her out. So close to the border, there must be aid camps or at least someone on the Turkish side."

Steve pushed back his chair and leaned back, blowing out air between pursed lips and rubbed his head.

"Yeah, mate, but how do we find out?"

"I might be able to." Steve and John turned to face Adriana. "I'll call my office. We have freelancers reporting from there all the time. One of them should be able to help us, give us information on what it's like."

"Great idea." John smiled and placed his hand on Adriana's arm. "Can you reach them now?"

Adriana glanced at her watch. "Yes." She looked around for her bag. "I'll call the office."

"While she's doing that, we'll search the internet and find out everything we can," John suggested.

Steve nodded and sat forward, turning the laptop back to face him.

"What's the wifi here, Steve?" John pulled out his phone from his rear pocket.

"Magnum P.I."

"Ha, seriously?"

Steve looked up with a slight grin. "Yeah."

John smiled and tapped at his phone. "Password?"

Steve held out his hand. "Here, I'll do it for you, it's complicated." Steve took the phone, entered the password, then handed it back as Marisel arrived carrying a tray with four cups and a French press filled with coffee.

Steve, noticeably more relaxed now he had something to do, glanced at the tray. "Bring us some Tim-Tams too, Marisel. I'm starving."

"Tim-Tams?" John raised an eyebrow.

"He loves them," Maadhavi replied with a smile. She reached over and patted his stomach. "But he needs to cut back."

"Best biscuit in the world, mate."

"Must be Australian?"

"Of course."

14

Adriana walked back into the room, her phone in her hand. "I've got a contact. We can Skype him in half an hour. A photojournalist based in Istanbul. He goes into Syria regularly."

"Great. Coffee?" John gestured at the French press.

"No, thank you. I won't sleep."

"Can I get you something else?" Maadhavi stood up. "Wait, I'll make you something special." She left the room as Adriana pulled up a chair beside John.

"Give your phone to Steve, and he'll set you up with the wi-fi."

Adriana passed her phone over as John offered her a plate filled with rectangular-shaped chocolate biscuits.

"Try these. Best biscuit in the world, apparently."

Steve looked up from her phone. "You'll love it."

Adriana took a bite. "Hmmm, not bad, Steve."

"See." He handed her phone back. "I told you so."

John poured a coffee for Steve and himself, took a bite of a Tim-Tam, and screwed up his face. "Too sweet for me." He passed it to Adriana.

He took a sip of coffee, then gestured at his phone.

"It says here, the region she's in has been experiencing heavy fighting." He looked up at Steve, "That would explain the explosion we heard."

"Yeah, I read that, too. The Syrian Army is advancing toward Idlib, which is the closest sizable town near Sarmin."

John leaned back in his chair, cradling the coffee cup in his hands.

"You know, I've not paid much attention to what's been going on there, just the headlines now and then. We need to get as much information as possible before we can decide what to do."

"Well, hopefully, my contact can help," Adriana replied. "We can call him soon. He was just heading back to his apartment when I messaged him."

"Okay, let's wait until we've spoken to him. He may have some ideas on who can help get her out."

Maadhavi walked back in with two cups, passing one to Adriana. "Try this."

Adriana took the cup and moved it back and forth beneath her nose, inhaling the fragrance from the steaming cup.

"What's this? It smells wonderful. Cardamom?"

"Yes." Maadhavi grinned. "Try it."

Adriana took a sip and looked up, her eyebrows raised. "Wow."

John chuckled. "*Masala chai.* India can't function without it."

"It's delicious. I've had a *chai* latte before, but this is so much better."

"Yes." Maadhavi nodded as she sipped from her cup. "What they give you in the cafés in the west is nothing like a proper homemade *chai*. I crush the cardamom myself and add lemongrass."

"You must teach me."

"Of course." Maadhavi smiled and reached over to squeeze Adriana's hand.

John glanced at his watch. "We have about fifteen minutes. Let's see what else we can find out before the call."

15

The screen flickered, and a face appeared, a youngish man, close-cropped hair, a deep crease in his forehead, black smudges under his eyes. He appeared to be in a living room, a bookshelf behind him and the edge of a map pinned to the wall could just be seen in the edge of the screen.

"Craig?"

"Yes, and you must be Adriana?" His voice had a slight Scottish burr.

"Yes. Thank you for agreeing to speak to us." Adriana stepped back from the screen. "I have some others here with me. John, Steve, and Maadhavi."

"Hi."

"Hi, Craig."

"Did João explain why we were calling?"

"He did. There's a girl and her child you want to get out of Syria."

"That's right, and we wanted to get some information about what's going on there and maybe some ideas on how to get her out."

Craig sighed. "It won't be easy." He reached for something off-screen, and his hand came back holding a packet of cigarettes and a lighter. He tapped out a cigarette and lit it, took a puff, then blew a cloud of smoke up and to the side. "Do you know where she is?"

"Craig, John here. She's in a place called Sarmin, just southwest of Idlib."

Craig's frown grew deeper, and he took another drag from his cigarette. "I know the area. There's been a lot of fighting there. Not a safe place to be."

"Who's fighting who?"

Craig gave a half-smile. "How much do you know about the war in Syria?"

They all shook their heads.

"Not much," John replied.

"Okay. It's complicated..."

"Just give us the easy version as it relates to where she is."

Craig nodded, blowing smoke into the air.

"Forget anything you've read in the press about it being a freedom struggle. It may have started like that for some people, but in reality, it's all about regime change. On one side, you have the Syrian Government. On the other, you have groups of Islamist rebels."

"ISIS?" Steve asked.

"No, not officially." Craig shook his head. "ISIS, ISIL, Daesh, whatever you want to call them, controlled the southeastern part of Syria, but they've been effectively driven out. In Idlib province, you have several factions operating under the umbrella of Al Qaeda."

"Al Qaeda? But I thought the bad guys were the Syrian Government?" a puzzled Steve asked.

Craig stubbed his cigarette butt in an ashtray just out of shot and shook his head.

"When you've seen what I've seen over the years, you'll realize there are no good guys or bad guys. It's war."

John leaned forward. "So, this place, ahh Sarmin, is under the control of Al Qaeda?"

"Technically H.T.S., *Hay'at Tahrir al-Sham*. Before that, they called themselves the *Al Nusrah* Front. But yes, the name changes, but it's still Al Qaeda."

John nodded slowly. "And they are fighting the Syrian army."

"Yes, they are up against the Syrian Army, which is backed by Russia."

"Russia?"

"Assad invited Russia to help him in driving out ISIS and Al Qaeda from Syria. They've pretty much succeeded. Idlib province is one of the last remaining areas under rebel control."

"So, where does Turkey come into it? Before this call, I read online, the Turkish Army is engaged in fighting, too."

Craig picked up the cigarette packet again. "This is what I meant about complicated." He tapped out another cigarette. "The Al Qaeda aligned forces are supported by Turkey and other NATO members, including the U.S."

John looked across at Steve, his eyebrows raised.

Craig continued, his cigarette held unlit between nicotine-stained fingers. "All these western powers used the uprising during the Arab Spring to push forward their idea of regime change, so they could gain control of Syrian oil and destroy Iran's only ally in the Middle East. They, with the help of Saudi Arabia and Qatar, funded, trained, and supported Al Qaeda and ISIS as a means to get their own ends. But..." He paused to light the cigarette. "Now it's not going their way, they've stepped back, leaving Turkey to shoulder the brunt of the action."

"But why would Turkey want the Islamists to succeed? Isn't Turkey a secular nation?"

"Yes, Adriana, and so was Syria. But the current ruling party is a Muslim Brotherhood party, and they have the same political ideology as Al Qaeda. They would love an Islamic State next door."

"Nightmare."

"Yup, ahh, John." Craig puffed on his cigarette. "It's unlikely to be sorted out anytime soon. Not while there is money to be made and power to be gained. Meanwhile, we have over three million people in the Idlib region alone who are suffering, who have lost their homes, and have nothing to eat. It's a shit show if you'll pardon my French."

Silence fell as they digested this depressing information while Craig smoked his cigarette.

Steve spoke first. "So, what do we do about Mia?"

"Mia is the girl? Who is she to you?"

"My niece."

"Shit. I'm sorry."

Steve just nodded.

Craig rubbed his face with his free hand. "Look, I will be honest with you... Steve?"

"Yeah, mate, Steve."

"Steve, you can try the aid agencies, I'll give you some contacts, but it's unlikely they can or even will help you. There're millions of people there who need their help. People who belong there. Your niece, she's, I'm guessing by your accent, Australian?"

"Yeah."

"Why is she there? I'm guessing she's not an aid worker. Journalist?" Craig didn't wait for an answer, "No, I would have heard about her. My guess is she joined the *Jihadis*, am I right?"

"Yup," Steve sighed.

Craig nodded slowly. "No-one will help her. She shouldn't be there. Even though our governments are supporting these rebels behind our backs, they are officially terrorist groups. H.T.S. was declared a terrorist organization back in 2017. If she's involved with them, you won't get any sympathy from anyone. No government in their right mind will help her out."

"So, you're saying I should ignore my niece and her daughter and leave them there to die?" Steve raised his voice.

On the screen, Craig held his hands up. "Hey, I'm just letting you know how it is. There's no point in me sugar-coating it."

"Fuck." Steve thumped the table and stepped back from the laptop. Maadhavi placed a hand on his shoulder, and he shook it off. "Fuck," he cursed again, then walked out of the room.

John glanced at Adriana, then pulled out a chair and sat down in front of the laptop, Adriana moving to stand behind him.

"Craig, I'm sorry. It's his only niece."

Craig had lit up another cigarette. "Yeah, I'm sorry too. It's a shitty position to be in, but there's no point in giving him false hope."

"No, you're right." John looked down at the desk for a moment. "What if we go in and get her?"

Craig stared at John, then took a long puff on his cigarette.

"Have you ever been in a war zone before?"

"No."

"Any military training?"

"No."

"Do you work for the government?"

"No."

"What's your background, John?"

"I'm... an ex-banker."

Craig shook his head and gave a wry smile.

"And Steve?"

"An ex-cop. He's a private investigator now."

"No chance."

"I'm very resourceful. So is Steve."

"Sorry, John, but you are dreaming."

16

John rubbed his face with both hands and turned his head to look up at Adriana. She placed her hand on his shoulder and gave him a reassuring squeeze. Through the window, they could see Steve sitting out on the patio, Maadhavi sitting close beside him, a comforting hand on his leg.

Turning back to the screen, John sighed.

"The girl has a daughter. I think she's only about two years old... she's sick."

"Look, John, I wish I could say something to help, but it's brutal over there. You can't just wander in and travel around. Do either of you speak Arabic?"

"No."

Craig studied him through the screen. John matched his gaze until Craig looked away and tapped the ash from his cigarette.

"Craig, I will back Steve every step of the way on this. I owe him, and I don't mean just a favor. He saved my,"—John glanced back to Adriana—"our lives once. It's the least I can do."

Craig nodded and leaned back in his chair, crossing his arms. He looked to his right as if looking out a window. John could see him thinking, weighing a decision.

"Let's say you can get across the border. I might be able to help you. I know a guy, but you can't get in through Turkey anymore. It's impossible. They've built a wall along the whole border. It's three meters high and in places, two meters thick. There are minefields and regular patrols." Craig lit up another cigarette. "I always cross from Iraq. I fly to Erbil in Iraqi Kurdistan, then drive down to the border. My guy might get you across there. It's not patrolled as much."

John nodded as he typed notes into his phone.

"Once you are in Syria, you'll have to cross the entire country from East to West. First through Kurdish controlled territory, then Syrian government territory. In the government area, you've got the Syrian Army, the Russians, the Iranians, and Hezbollah. There are checkpoints everywhere." Craig puffed away on his cigarette. "If you make it to the rebel-held area around Idlib, you've got the Turks and H.T.S. If the Turks don't get you, the H.T.S. will. And they don't take kindly to westerners interfering in what they're doing. You could end up on YouTube with a black bag over your head and a knife at your throat."

John felt Adriana's grip on his shoulder tighten.

"If you survive all that, there are air and drone strikes, IEDs, and booby traps." Craig flicked ash from his cigarette and leaned forward. "John, I've seen stuff you can't imagine, by both sides. I can't sleep at night." He waved his cigarette at the screen. "My only wish is I live long enough for these bloody things to kill me instead."

John stared over the top of the laptop at the wall behind it, chewing on his lip. It sounded impossible, but he couldn't let Steve down. Steve had looked after him; he should at least try. He looked back at the screen.

"Okay, so now tell me the difficult parts."

Craig studied his face for a moment and then broke into a grin.

"You're a crazy bugger, John. Okay, this is what we'll do. You sleep on it, think it over. If you still want to go ahead, I'll put you in touch with my guy. He's a smuggler. He'll get you over the border. It'll be expensive and don't trust him completely. He's a slimy bastard and may sell you out to the next highest bidder given the chance. Once over the border, you'll be on your own. So, let me know what you decide. The good news is, right now, there's a temporary truce being negotiated between all the sides, so there may not be much fighting going on. Let's hope it lasts while you're there."

"Thank you, Craig. I appreciate it."

"Good luck, John. Send me your number. If I think of anything, I'll call you. In fact, I'll message you a link right now. It's a live map us journos use to see what's going on and who controls what. It's updated daily, so I'll think you'll find it useful."

"Thanks a lot, Craig."

Adriana leaned forward. "Thank you, Craig."

"You're welcome. Say hi to João for me."

"I will. Goodbye."

The screen went blank, and Adriana wrapped her arms around John from behind, kissed the top of his head, then rested her chin on his head as they both stared silently at the wall in front of them.

17

John walked out onto the rear patio where Steve was sitting, staring out over the swimming pool. Beside him, Maadhavi looked up and smiled, then spying the glass in John's hand and the bottle of beer, she nodded and stood. She leaned down, placed a kiss on Steve's head, then, with a nod at John, walked back into the house.

John sat down and handed the bottle of beer to Steve.

"Cheers."

Steve nodded and sat forward. Leaning his elbows on his knees, he took a long pull on the bottle, then wiped his mouth with the back of his hand.

"I can't leave her there, John."

"I know."

"You know, my ex-wife and I never had kids..." Steve shook his head. "We didn't plan it that way. It just never happened." He glanced at John. "It was probably for the best. Our marriage didn't last. Imagine having kids as well."

John nodded and sipped his drink, allowing Steve to talk it through.

"But Mia, she was the closest thing I had to a daughter. I still remember holding her in my arms when she was born." Steve's voice caught in his throat. "She was so tiny, she could fit on my forearm." He stared down at the ground, the beer bottle dangling in his fingers. "She used to spend her school holidays with us. I'd take leave, and we would go camping, fishing. Just the two of us. She'd tell me things she could never share with her parents." He sipped from the bottle again. "Then she met that fucking lowlife piece of shit." He shook his head. "She changed, John. She withdrew, spent less time with me, started dressing differently. I should have done something." Steve sighed and took a swig from his bottle.

"But I had my own issues, the divorce,"—he waved around the garden—"moving here. We lost touch. The day I found out she was in Syria was one of the worst days of my life. That shitbag of a boyfriend... if I could get my hands on him, I'd rip his fucking guts out." Steve drained the bottle and placed it on the ground beside his chair and sat back, then turned to look at John.

"I'm not leaving her there. We all make wrong decisions in life, make mistakes, choose the wrong partners, but that doesn't make us bad people. She's a good girl, John, and she will always be the daughter I never had. I'll never be able to live with myself if I don't try to save her."

John swirled the ice cubes around in his glass, listening to the tinkle of the ice. Taking a sip, he held the liquid in his mouth, savoring the flavor of the gin on the tastebuds at the back of his mouth, then swallowed.

"It won't be easy."

"I know."

"We could die."

"We?"

John grinned. "You didn't think I would let you do this by yourself, did you?"

Steve reached over and clasped a giant hand on John's shoulder.

"I hoped you'd say that. That's why I called you." His eyes misted, and he gripped John's shoulder hard and gave him a shake. "Thanks, mate. I mean it."

"Well, I never bought you that beer after you helped me in Oman." He shrugged, "It's the least I can do." John stood. "Come, we can plan tomorrow after a goodnight's sleep. Let's get another drink and see what our beautiful ladies are up to."

18

John slept fitfully that night. After a big dinner and three or four large gin and tonics, he had fallen asleep as soon as his head hit the pillow but had woken hours later drenched in sweat, his heart pounding, and filled with a sense of unease. After that, he couldn't get back into a decent sleep, tossing and turning. Every time he closed his eyes, his head filled with images of blood and sand. In the end, he gave up and laid, staring at the ceiling. Eventually, he reached over to the bedside table and picked up his G-Shock. The luminous dial read five fifteen, and it was still dark outside, the sun not due to be up for another hour and a half.

John turned his head and looked over at Adriana. The ambient light filtering through the window was just enough to make out the details of her features, her thick mane of raven hair framing her face against the crisp white pillow. Her breathing was deep and steady through slightly parted lips, and he envied her ability to sleep so soundly. He rolled onto his side, propping himself up on one elbow and gazed at her. Even in the faint light, he could make out the fine lines of her face, the high cheekbones, her long eyelashes, her nose. She was perfect.

He would do anything for her, in fact, he had—risking his own life for her, more than once. She was everything to him, and he was happier than he had been in years—since he lost Charlotte. Charlotte had also made him feel this way. He felt a heavy sensation in his chest. Was he making a mistake? He was going to risk losing the woman he loved by taking on the most dangerous task he had ever faced. Was it worth it?

John's heart started pounding again, and he sat up, swinging his legs over the side of the bed. He needed to do something. He padded quietly across the room to his open suitcase lying on the floor. Carefully and quietly, he removed his running gear and got dressed. Picking up his running shoes, he tiptoed to the door and let himself out. Once outside the house, he slipped on his running shoes and headed onto the street. Running always made everything seem better, and he needed to burn off the adrenaline already coursing through his veins. He started slowly, allowing the blood to circulate and warm his joints. The air was cool and silent, the only sound from a few birds who, like him, couldn't sleep. A cat paused as it crossed the road, looking at him curiously before scampering for the safety of a flower bed.

John completed a full loop of the housing estate, but it wasn't enough, he was only just getting warmed up. He headed toward the exit, waved at the sleepy Pakistani security guard manning the gate, ducked under the barrier, and headed out on the main road. He increased his pace, breathing rhythmically through his nostrils, emptying his mind, focusing on the flow of air over his top lip and the rhythmic pounding of his feet. After a few kilometers, the effort melted away, his body running by itself, just a witness as if observing his body from without. He increased his speed, faster and faster until he was flying along, and his whole being filled with joy. There was no past, no future, no fear, no desire, just the present moment. He ran for thirty minutes before turning back and returning the way he had come as the sky lightened, a faint glow on the horizon signaling the sun's awakening.

Spotting the entrance to the housing estate in the distance, he increased his pace, now sucking air in through his mouth, but it was still effortless, his body reveling in the primal joy of movement. He reached the barrier and slowed, reducing his pace to a jog, then a walk, his hands on his hips as he caught his breath. He continued up the road for a few hundred meters before turning back and entering the housing complex. The guard grinned with approval and gave him a thumbs-up as he passed. John walked back along the street, signs of life now more apparent as households slowly woke and began their day. A pair of bright green parrots squawked noisily as they swooped low overhead, and a neighbor raised a hand in greeting as their dog peed on the tire of an Audi parked in their driveway.

Despite the lack of sleep and the tension of the day before, John felt at peace, the endorphin rush making him feel almost invincible, able to tackle anything the universe threw at him. As he pushed open the front door, he felt more confident than at any time since Steve had first contacted him. It was time to work out how he would rescue Steve's niece.

19

Mia stirred, blinked her eyes open, then sat up with a start. She looked down beside her at Malak, sleeping on the blanket beside her, and touched her forehead; she was still hot. She heard a faint noise beside her, and she looked over to see Naeem kneeling on the floor, his eyes closed, hands raised in prayer as he performed *namaaz.*

She watched him perform the rituals but had no desire to join him. She didn't pray much anymore, not in the formal sense, not like Naeem. There was little point. She doubted God cared which way you faced or how many times a day you prayed—not when people were dying every day.

She shuffled back until she was leaning against the wall, gently picked up her daughter, holding her with one arm as she pulled the blanket up around them. It was cold, and she could see vapor from her breath rising in the early morning light.

Naeem finished his prayers and opened his eyes. He nodded at her, then looked around for his boots.

"I've left some water for you," he said as he laced them

up. "I'll try to find some food." He stood up and reached for his weapon leaning against the wall, slung it over his shoulder, then reached into the pocket of his leather jacket and removed the phone. "Here take this. There is still some battery charge. Don't turn it on until it's time. I don't know when I can charge it again."

"You're not coming back?"

"I don't know." Naeem shrugged and looked out the hole in the wall where the window had once been. He turned back to look at her and scratched his scraggly beard with his right hand. "I'll find food now, but I have to go back to the front. I can't leave my brothers."

"Brothers? What about your daughter?"

Naeem sighed and looked down at the bundle in Mia's arms. He stepped forward, kissed his fingertips, then placed them on the child's head.

"I'll be back with food. *Inshallah.*"

Mia closed her eyes and rocked her child back and forth. Despite everything, she didn't want Naeem to leave her alone. She retreated into the protective shell she had built for herself—just her and Malak. The outside world didn't exist, didn't matter.

20

John and Steve sat together, staring at the laptop screen.

"So, if we fly to Erbil, then it's over two hundred kilometers to the border crossing at Faysh Khabur." John tapped on the keyboard. "Hmmm."

"Probably at least a three-hour drive, then who knows how long it will take to cross the border. And that's if we do it legally."

"That's right." John leaned back in his chair and crossed his arms. "Then it's over six hundred kilometers across the whole of Syria from here,"—John leaned forward and pointed at the screen—"to here."

"Shit." Steve exhaled noisily

"Yeah." John continued to stare at the screen, then looked up as Marisel walked in with a tray. "Oh, thank you, Marisel."

"Is Madam up yet, Marisel?" Steve asked.

"I think so, sir." Marisel nodded as she placed the tray with two cups and a French press on the table beside them. "Shall I prepare breakfast?"

Steve gave a questioning look at John.

"Yes, I'm starving. Adriana's just having a shower. She'll be down soon."

Steve nodded and smiled at Marisel, then reached for the French press, depressed the plunger, and poured two cups of coffee. He handed one to John, then added two teaspoons of sugar to his own. He noticed John watching and grinned.

"Don't tell Maadhavi. She's trying to get me to cut down."

"It's good to know someone is taking care of you." He took a sip of his coffee. "Are you happy?"

"Very." Steve stirred his coffee, then dropped the teaspoon onto the tray. "She's a wonderful woman, John. My life is so much better with her in it."

"Good, I'm happy for you both. Everyone deserves to be happy."

"Yeah, mate." Steve sipped his coffee, then licked his lips and placed the cup back down on the table, staring out the French windows into the garden. "It's been a long time since I've been happy. My divorce, in fact, the last few years of my marriage..." He turned back to John and grimaced. "Not fun, mate, not fun at all."

John said nothing, allowing Steve to continue.

"That's why I came here. I needed to get away from it all, to start afresh. Somewhere no-one knew me." He grinned. "And this city is full of work for an ex-cop."

"So..." John chose his words carefully. "Now this,"—John gestured to the laptop with his spare hand—"will be dangerous. Is it worth risking,"—he gestured as if encompassing the entire house—"all this? What if you never see Maadhavi again?"

Steve looked down, turning the coffee cup around and around on the table, then looked up.

"What kind of man would I be if I left Mia and her child to die over there... if I didn't at least try,... just because I feared losing my happiness and comfort? I couldn't do it. My entire life would be a lie, John."

John stared down at the dining table surface. He took a deep, slow breath, then exhaled.

"Yeah. I know."

The men sipped their coffee in silence, lost in their own thoughts until a sound by the door made them look up to see Adriana watching them.

"Well, don't you two make a happy pair this morning?"

21

Later that morning, after a large breakfast and Marisel had cleared away the plates, they sat around the dining table. A fresh pot of coffee sat on the table next to a laptop, a couple of notebooks, and pens.

"Look, Steve, going into Syria should be our last resort. We need to make sure we've exhausted every other channel first."

Steve raised both his hands.

"John, I know that's the sensible thing to do. Don't think we haven't tried. My brother and I have been working on this for weeks before I called you. The Australian government doesn't want to have anything to do with them. She's a terrorist in their eyes."

"She's a mother with a child," Adriana protested.

"I know, but they don't see it that way. They are worried about what the public will think if they allow,"—Steve made quotation signs with his fingers—"members of ISIS into the country, just because they are Australian." He shrugged, "It's an election year."

"Red Cross, UNHCR?" John asked.

"John, we've gone through this already. No-one is interested. They've got bigger things to worry about."

John nodded and drummed his fingers on the table. He looked up at Adriana, then across to Maadhavi.

"What do you think about this, Maadhavi?"

"John, I've seen what Steve has gone through in the past few weeks. He's tried everything. I don't see what else he can do."

"And if he goes into Syria?"

Maadhavi paused, turned her head to look at Steve, and gave him a sad smile.

"Of course, I don't want him to go, but..." She turned back to face John. "I know what she means to him. I can't hold him back. It wouldn't be fair." She looked down at the table and frowned, a faint quiver in her lip, "I love him, and I have to respect whatever decision he makes." Looking up, she continued, "There are two lives at stake here. It's not right for me to be selfish."

Steve reached across and gave her hand a squeeze.

Maadhavi looked at Adriana. "You understand, don't you?"

"I do." Adriana half-smiled in support, but her eyes remained concerned. "I don't want John to be in harm's way, but I know he, too, can't stand by and do nothing." She smiled at Steve. "And I know what Steve has done for us. It's the least we can do."

"Yes, he told me what happened in Oman."

"We wouldn't be here today if it hadn't been for Steve."

Steve looked down, uncharacteristically embarrassed as Adriana continued.

"So, yes, it will be dangerous, but it's the right thing to do." Adriana turned to John and placed a hand on his thigh.

"I'm canceling my flight back. I'm staying here. I'll help in whatever way I can."

"But your work?"

"You really think I can go back to the office while you and Steve are doing this? Besides, I convinced João to let me work from here, and hopefully, there'll be a story in it for the paper." She looked at Steve. "That's if you don't mind, Steve?"

"No worries. Just make me look good."

John smiled, leaned over, and kissed her on the neck.

"I love you," he murmured in her ear

"Right." Steve clapped his hands. "We've got work to do."

22

They spent the rest of the day researching as much as possible about the conflict in Syria while Marisel kept them supplied with coffee and food. Adriana worked the phone, contacting as many journalists covering the region as she could. The dining table resembled a conference table at a startup, with laptops, phones, and pieces of paper strewn everywhere. By late afternoon, they were tired and dejected. Steve pushed back his chair and went to stand by the window, his hands in his pockets. John looked up, glanced over at Adriana, then leaned back in his chair.

"What's up, Steve?"

Steve shook his head and turned to face them. He looked at them all one by one and sighed.

"I'm sorry I dragged you into this. It's looking hopeless."

"Hey, Steve, don't give up. We'll find a way."

"Yes," Adriana agreed. "There's always a solution."

"That's right." John massaged his eyes with his fingertips. "Remember what we did together in Oman when all seemed lost." He smiled, "We've proven we are an excellent team. We'll work something out." He glanced at his watch. "What time did we say we'd call Mia?"

"Six."

"Good. We have an hour. Let's take a break, relax for a bit. Sometimes, we need to step away from the problem to find a solution." John looked around the table. "I think we've done enough research for one day."

"Yeah, you're right. I could murder a beer."

John fixed gin and tonics for himself and the ladies while Steve grabbed a beer from the fridge, and they all moved outside to the patio. The air had cooled, and the sun threw long shadows across the pool. The trees were filled with birds, chirping and squawking as they returned home from a day of foraging, and the smell of food cooking wafted through the patio doors as Marisel prepared dinner in the kitchen. It was a peaceful setting, at odds with the turmoil in each of their heads.

John was halfway through his gin and tonic when he sat up straight, a wide smile lighting up his face.

"I've got an idea."

Maadhavi, Steve, and Adriana waited for him to continue.

"Let's say we can get across the border. We all know moving around inside Syria could be a major problem. From what we have learned, there are checkpoints everywhere."

Steve nodded.

"What if we pose as journalists? Don't they get to go everywhere?" He looked at Adriana. "Can you get us some press passes?"

Adriana shook her head. "It's not that easy."

"Okay, talk me through it. How does it usually work?"

"To enter a country as a journalist, you need to first get a press visa. Then you'll need to get accredited with the government of that country as a journalist, so you can get a press card. You'll need sponsorship letters from your news agency, maybe an employment contract, letters of recommendation, all officially stamped. Even if João agreed to do it, it's too complicated and time-consuming. Once we have all the documents, we would have to send them all to the Syrian Government for approval. We don't have the luxury of time."

"Shit." John sat back in his chair and frowned at the swimming pool. After a minute, he stood up. "I need another drink. Anyone else?"

Maadhavi and Adriana shook their heads while Steve waved his empty beer bottle in the air.

John walked into the kitchen and smiled at Marisel, who was busy at the stove.

"Smells good, Marisel."

"Thank you, sir."

He grabbed a bottle of beer from the fridge, popped off the top using a bottle opener stuck to the fridge door, filled his glass with ice from the freezer, then moved to the bar cabinet in the living room. He picked up the bottle of gin and frowned at the label. Not the best, but it would have to do. The second one was always better. He would need to educate Steve on what a quality gin was. John poured a generous measure into his glass, then reached for the bottle of tonic. His hand stopped halfway as another idea formed in his head.

23

John walked out onto the patio with the drinks. He passed the bottle of beer to Steve, raised his own drink in a toast.

"I have a better idea."

Before he could say anything, Steve's phone rang.

"One sec." Steve removed the phone from his pocket and glanced at the screen, frowning.

"What is it?" John asked.

Steve looked up. "Mia." He tapped on the screen to answer the call.

John checked his watch. It was still half an hour before they were scheduled to call. He frowned and watched Steve's face.

"Hello? Mia... wait, I'll put you on speaker." Steve tapped the screen, then held the phone out so all could hear.

"Uncle Steve?"

"Yes, I can hear you. Is everything okay?"

The boom of an explosion and the rapid rat-tat-tat of gunfire came through the phone's tiny speakers.

"Shit," Steve cursed. "Mia?"

"Yes... I have to leave here." Another explosion. "The fighting is getting closer.... it's... no longer safe here."

"Are you okay? Malak?"

"She's a little better. She is awake but still has a fever."

Steve gave a worried look at John.

"Where will you go?"

"I..." Her voice was cut off by the sound of gunfire, closer than before. "I don't know. I'm waiting for Naeem. He is at the front with the others. When he comes, we'll try to find somewhere else to stay."

"I'm coming to get you, Mia."

"How, Uncle?"

"We have a plan."

John raised an eyebrow but said nothing as Steve continued.

"Don't worry, but keep safe. We need some time."

"Okay, but... please come quickly, Malak, she..." There was another muffled boom. "I'll call tomorrow." The phone went dead.

"Mia, Mia..." Steve took the phone off speaker and held it to his ear. "Mia, Mia." He held the phone out and tapped redial. "Shit."

The phone failed to connect. He tried again, still no luck. He looked at John, his forehead creased.

"What do I do?"

"It's probably just the phone system is down, Steve."

Steve nodded but didn't look convinced. He stood staring at the ground, the phone in one hand, his beer bottle in the other.

"I have to go there," he said almost to himself.

"Steve, look at me." John raised his voice. "We'll get her out, but we have to be sensible about this. We can't just rush over there without a plan."

Steve looked at John, then Maadhavi and Adriana.

"John's right, baby," Maadhavi agreed. "You need to plan properly. It's dangerous there."

Steve nodded slowly, his eyes locked with Maadhavi and sighed.

"Yeah, you're right." He looked behind him for his chair and sat down, dropping the phone on the coffee table in front of them. Remembering the beer in his hand, he took a swig and massaged his eyes with his left hand.

"Look, Steve, I have an idea." John stood in front of him. "Craig said he can give us a number for a guy who can get us across the border. We don't waste time with visas. We'll get him to smuggle us in and out as he suggested."

"Okay." Steve stared up at John, his mind whirring away. "But what about moving around inside Syria? Checkpoints?"

"That's my idea. We fake the press credentials and pretend to be reporters. Do you really think the guys manning checkpoints can tell the difference between genuine documents and fake ones?"

Steve nodded slowly, his forehead slowly relaxing.

John turned to Adriana. "Can you get us examples of what we need?"

"I think so. At least a soft copy."

"Good. That will have to do." John turned back. "We'll take a look at it and see if it's something we can knock up on the computer."

"I've got a better idea." Steve grinned for the first time since the call. "I know a guy."

24

Mia turned off the phone and slipped it inside her pocket. The last explosion seemed to have knocked out the phone network. She looked down at Malak. Her eyes were open, but she looked back at her mother without recognition. Mia gently rocked.

"It won't be long, my darling," she whispered. "Soon, we'll be in Australia, where the skies are blue, there's plenty of food and water, and it's quiet." She flinched as another explosion rocked the building, sending dust flying in the air. Mia covered Malak's face and continued rocking. "The beaches, Malak, they are beautiful. Long, with golden sand and clear blue water sparkling in the sun. People are happy there, Malak. Everyone smiles, everyone talks to each other. You'll love it, my baby. Not long now." Mia said the words more for her own reassurance. She wasn't sure if Malak would understand.

She heard footsteps on the stairs and tensed. Naeem hadn't said when he would be back. She slid herself across the floor into the darkest corner and pulled Malak closer. The footsteps got closer, then a man stepped into the room.

He was dressed like the fighters—camouflaged pants, running shoes, a hooded tracksuit top—his beard was long and unkempt, eyes sunken deep into their sockets, and he cradled an AK47 in his arms. Mia's breath caught, and she shrank back against the wall, trying to make herself smaller. The man didn't see her at first, his eyes adjusting to the darkness in the room, but when he did, he raised his weapon and pointed it in her direction.

More footsteps and three more men dressed in the same fashion entered the room. They stared at her, and one stepped forward and crouched down. He stared at her face with dead eyes, then down at her body. He wiped his mouth with the back of his hand and grinned, exposing a mouthful of dirty yellow teeth. Mia closed her eyes, clenched her teeth, and started praying.

She heard a noise and then her name.

"Mahfuza."

Opening her eyes, she saw Naeem push through the men and walk toward her. He walked around the man with yellow teeth and stood in front of her.

"Mahfuza, we have to leave. We're pulling back."

Mia didn't move. She looked past Naeem to the man who was still leering at her.

Naeem held out his hand. "Come. We have to move fast."

Mia ignored his hand and pushed herself up off the floor with her spare hand, holding Malak close to her with the other. She looked around the floor but didn't know why. She had nothing, only her daughter, the clothes on her back, and the blanket wrapped around them.

The crouching man stood up at the same time, his eyes never leaving her face. Mia looked away and moved closer to Naeem. He stepped to one side, adjusted his AKM, then pushed her toward the door with his left hand.

The other men led the way out the door, and Mia paused and looked back. Naeem stood chest to chest with Yellow Teeth, staring him down. The other man sniggered but didn't back down.

"Naeem," she called, and he glanced toward her. He gave one more look at Yellow Teeth, then followed her out the door.

As Mia reached the ground floor, she heard muffled voices, and when she stepped onto the street, in the falling light, she could just make out a group of women huddled together while more fighters stood guard.

"Go with them," she heard Naeem mutter behind her.

"But..."

"Now," he growled and pushed her forward.

She stumbled, clutching Malak close, then stepped toward the other women. They regarded her with little interest, their faces devoid of expression. Their hair was unkempt, their faces dirty, and like her, they were dressed in a mishmash of unwashed clothes.

"*Yalla!*" called out one of the fighters, and the others pushed the women down the street.

Mia looked around for Naeem but couldn't make him out in the darkness.

25

Steve indicated and pulled off the main road onto a side street, leading behind a row of commercial buildings. He pulled the Pajero to the curb and switched off the engine.

"Here we are."

John looked around but couldn't see where they needed to go. They were in the old part of Dubai, an area called Bur Dubai, on the wrong side of the creek. It was so far removed from the glitz and glamor of Dubai most people see, they could have been in another country.

"Where?"

"You'll see." Steve grinned as he opened the door.

They climbed out, and John waited on the pavement until Steve crossed around the front of the vehicle.

"Follow me." Steve led John along the pavement, then turned into the loading bay of a darkened four-story building. Discarded packing crates and polystyrene stacked in one corner were the only sign the building was occupied. Steve walked up the loading ramp and knocked on an unmarked door. He knocked three times, waited, knocked twice, paused, then three times again.

"Really?" John asked.

Steve winked. "Nah, mate, I'm just yankin' your chain." He turned and banged on the door with the ball of his fist. He looked up at the security camera above the door. "Ramesh, open the bloody door."

After a moment, the door cracked open, and a bespectacled young Indian man peered out. He saw John first, frowned, then looked at Steve.

"Oh, it's you," he said as if he hadn't already seen him on the camera. He opened the door wider, and Steve and John stepped inside, the auto-closer closing the door behind them.

They followed Ramesh down a long, grimy corridor lit by fluorescent strip lights to another unmarked door, then into a windowless room. Ramesh walked over and sat in a large leather swivel chair and turned it to face both of them.

"Who's your friend?"

John stepped forward and held out his hand. "John."

Ramesh frowned slightly, hesitated, then shook John's hand. He then pushed his glasses up his nose with his index finger and peered at Steve.

"What do you want today, Steve? Another security badge, a hotel name tag?"

"I'm well, thank you, Ramesh, thanks for asking."

"Yeah." Ramesh dismissed his comment with a wave of his hand.

John studied the man sitting in front of him. He was thin, perhaps in his late twenties, and despite being Indian, his skin was pallid as if he didn't spend much time outdoors. The room was stuffy, smelled of stale food and farts, and was filled with the electric hum of computers and other unrecognizable electronics stacked in racks along each wall.

"Steve told me you are very skilled in producing documentation."

Ramesh looked back at John and shrugged.

"In fact, he said you are the best in the business."

"Did he now?"

John's flattery had the desired effect, just as John intended.

"What do you need? Please tell me it's something more interesting than the library cards Steve usually wants."

"Library cards? You cheeky bloody curry muncher. I have a good mind to get you sent back to Madras."

"It's Chennai, Steve. Read an atlas." Ramesh winked at John. "Ignore the Aussie. They can't even play cricket properly. Now, what do you need?"

John smiled and handed over a memory stick.

"Take a look at this. Can you make these?"

Ramesh plugged the memory stick into his computer and clicked around with the mouse. He stared at the documents on the screen before swiveling his chair around, so he could face John. He studied his face for a moment.

"Syria?"

John nodded and handed over a slip of paper.

"This is my name, and these are the dimensions and the type of paper." He took a small envelope from his pocket and handed that over as well. "Some passport photos, various sizes. Use whatever you need. Can you do it?"

"I can do anything."

"He's a cheeky bugger, but he's good," Steve admitted grudgingly.

"Are you feeling okay, Steve? Running a fever?" Ramesh asked.

"Yeah, must be. Probably food poisoning from one of those samosas you gave me last time."

"Hey, my mom made those." Ramesh turned back to John. "When do you need it by?"

"Yesterday. Whatever Steve normally pays you, we'll double it."

"It'll be done by the morning."

"We need two sets. One for me and one for Steve."

Ramesh blinked and glanced at Steve. "You're also going?"

"Yup."

Ramesh pursed his lips and nodded slowly.

"Okay, I've got Steve's photos. I'll text you in the morning when they're done."

"Thank you." John leaned forward and held out his hand. "I appreciate it."

Both men turned for the door.

"Wait."

"What now?"

"How are you getting in?" Ramesh asked John, ignoring Steve.

John glanced at Steve, who nodded.

"Across the border by land."

"I'm assuming you don't have visas?"

John shook his head.

"Bring your passports tomorrow. I'll have a visa stamp for both of you. You'll need it." He gestured at the screen. "This probably won't be enough."

"You can do that?"

"I can do anything."

"Thank you, just add it to the bill."

"I will, and John…"

"Yes?"

"Keep an eye on the Aussie. I need someone to eat my mom's terrible samosas."

26

They used the thirty-minute drive back to Steve's house to brainstorm.

"Let's start from the beginning. Craig's smuggler is based in Istanbul. Entry into Turkey is easy. We can get visas online. We'll fly into Istanbul, meet this guy, then, depending on what he can do, fly into Iraq, and cross the border there. But it will all depend on this smuggler contact of Craig's."

"Makes sense." Steve nodded, his eyes on the road as they cruised along in the center lane.

"Assuming he can get us across the border safely, I would guess at night, we have the day to get down to Idlib, pick her and the child up and back to the border to cross over again, probably the next night."

"Sounds good."

"So, let's think about what we need," John continued. "We're posing as journalists, so we need to look the part."

"I've got the cameras I use for stakeouts, so I'll go as a photographer."

"Good. I'll go as a reporter. I'll get some notebooks, pens..."

"You'll need a laptop, mate."

"Yeah, but I don't want to carry ours in case someone takes it off us. I'll get another one."

Steve glanced at John. "I know a place that sells second-hand ones. Don't take a new one, it won't look right."

"I should write all this down..."

"There's a notebook and pens in the glove box."

John took out a dog-eared notebook and a pen, found a blank page, and started writing. "Notebooks, pens, second-hand laptop."

"Bulletproof vests."

"Shit, yes." John chewed on his lip. "Can we get them here?"

"I'll make some calls."

"We should write Press on them in big letters."

"Phones?"

"Yes. Let's get a couple of burners as soon as possible. I don't want to phone the smuggler with my own number. We must check if we can get signal there."

"We can do that in the morning." Steve glanced in the mirrors, then took the exit for the E311. "What about transport inside Syria?"

"Hmmm." John stared out the windshield as he tried to think of a solution. "I don't know. Maybe the smuggler knows someone?"

"Maybe."

"To be honest, I'm reluctant to depend on one person, especially someone we don't know. Let's think about it. Maybe we can find a taxi driver once we're over the border. If we offer enough cash, I'm sure we'll find someone." John scribbled on the notepad. "Cash. U.S. dollars."

"I have some in the safe at home." He glanced over at John. "By the way, I'm covering all the expenses for this. She's my niece, it's the right thing to do."

John waved a dismissive hand. "Hey, don't worry about it."

"No, I mean it, John. It means a lot to me you've come to help me. I'll never forget it, but the expenses are on me."

"Steve, we're in this together. Let's not talk about money. We'll sort it out later. The most important thing is we get your niece and her daughter out of there, and we all come back safely."

Steve slowed for the exit and pulled off the highway onto the side road.

"Thanks, mate."

He stayed quiet until they had pulled up outside his house. Switching the engine off, he looked out the windshield at the closed double garage door while John studied his notes, trying to think of anything else they would need.

"We'll need someone with us who can speak the language," John said after a while.

Steve turned to face John but didn't comment.

"I'm assuming your Arabic hasn't improved since the last time we met?"

"No." Steve frowned and shook his head.

"Then we'll definitely need someone. It will be much easier if we can have someone deal with the locals for us in a way they can understand."

Steve took a breath, then exhaled noisily.

"But who?"

John drummed his fingers on his lap. "Anyone here you can use? Someone you can trust?"

Steve thought for a while and then shook his head. "No,

not someone I can trust or who would be willing to do something this dangerous."

"Hmmm, okay. We'll think about it." John clicked open his door. "Let's go see what the girls are up to."

He stepped out, closed the door behind him, and walked to the front entrance of the house. He waited on the step, watching Steve lock the car and walk around toward him. He grinned as an idea struck him.

"Mansur."

Steve frowned. "Who?"

"Oman."

Steve's frown turned into a smile as he remembered.

"The Bedouin?" He nodded agreement. "He's our man, and he's nearby. Do you think he'll come?"

"We won't know if we don't ask."

27

The camel groaned as it knelt down, forelegs first, then rear, and dropped to the sand. Mansur patted it on the neck. "Good girl."

He checked the water trough was full, glanced over at the other two camels already bedded down for the night, then stood with his hands on his hips, looking up at the sky. Not for the first time, he wondered about the vast expanse above. He identified the familiar constellations of Ursa Minor and Camelopardalis and spied the blinking lights of a jetliner as it crossed high above the desert, heading south to somewhere in Africa.

The stars had always fascinated him, ever since his father taught him how to navigate across the desert at night. He'd spent many a night wondering if there were other worlds like this, out there among the blinking stars. He glanced down at his watch. Enough star gazing. He wanted to get back home to see the girls before Warda put them to bed. It had been a long day, the resort fully booked, and he had been busy since late afternoon, taking guests up and down the sand dunes. He was tired, and so were his camels.

"Tusbih ealaa khayr waihlam saeida," he called out. "Goodnight and sweet dreams."

He turned and walked across the sand to the house he occupied with Warda and his two daughters. Light streamed from one of the windows, and he could smell the smoke from the cooking fire, along with something more delicious. His stomach growled, and he realized he hadn't eaten since morning. Just as he reached the house, he heard his cell phone ring. Reaching into the pocket of his *dishdasha,* he pulled out his phone and peered at the number showing on the cracked screen. Dubai? Who could it be?

"Allo."

He frowned as a voice spoke to him in English, then his face lit up in a smile as he realized who it was.

Hearing his voice, Warda came out of the house and looked at him with a question on her face. Mansur held up his hand and signaled for her to wait. For the next few minutes, he listened, nodded, and asked a couple of questions, all the while Warda watched him, wondering why he was speaking in English. Five minutes later, he ended the call and stared at his wife.

She waited for him to say something, but curiosity got the better of her.

"Man kan hatha? Who was that?"

"Mr. John."

"Mr. John?" Warda looked puzzled for a moment, then recognition crossed her face. "Ahh, Mr. John. But why?"

"I must go to Dubai."

"Dubai?"

"I'll explain everything inside, *habibi.*" Mansur guided his wife back inside the house. "But first, let's eat. I'm starving."

28

Steve looked up as John walked in.

"Did he agree?"

"He did." John placed his phone on the coffee table. "He'll be here by tomorrow evening. He said he'd drive up."

Steve did a quick calculation. "Should take him around seven to eight hours."

"Good. You better let Ramesh know we need another set of documents. Mansur said he'd message a photo of his passport."

The phone buzzed and moved across the table.

"That'll be it now." John picked it up and glanced at the messages. "Yup. We can start booking flights first thing in the morning." He looked at the photo album on Steve's lap.

"What are you looking at?"

"Mia when she was a kid." Steve flipped a page, then looked up at John. "She was such a cute kid and sharp as a tack." He turned another page, running his fingers over each photo. "She did so well at school." He shook his head. "Such a bright future ahead of her, then... she met that prick." He balled his hands into fists and closed his eyes.

John moved closer and put his hand on Steve's shoulder. "Don't worry, we will get her out of there."

Steve opened his eyes, relaxed his fist, and nodded.

"I need a beer, do you want one?"

"No, thanks, I'm good."

Steve closed the album and stood up.

"Hey, you'd better send Mansur our location too. Much easier for him to find us."

"Will do." John shared the location, then leaned back in the chair and stared at his reflection in the darkened panes of the French windows. It was all beginning to come together, and despite the danger of the task ahead, he was feeling a buzz of excitement, something he hadn't felt in a while. He saw Adriana appear in the reflection and felt her hand on his shoulder. She leaned down and kissed him on the top of the head and with her other hand, passed him a gin and tonic.

"It's not Botanist, I'm sorry. Steve obviously isn't a gin guy."

"No." John turned and smiled up at her. Her hair was pulled back in an untidy bun, emphasizing her cheekbones. His heart did a little jump as not for the first time, he marveled at how beautiful she was. The excitement he felt a moment before ebbed away, replaced with a kernel of fear. If things went wrong, he might never get to see her again.

"What's the matter?"

"Nothing." John shook off the thought and smiled. "I was just thinking about how much I love you."

Adriana smiled back. "I love you too. Now come, dinner is ready. It smells delicious. Marisel's a superb cook."

"She is. Maybe we should ask her if she wants to come to Lisbon?" John winked and took a sip of his drink.

"I wouldn't do that to Maadhavi." Adriana held out her hand, and John stood, leaning forward to kiss Adriana below her ear. "I've got a surprise for you."

"A surprise?"

"You'll find out tomorrow," he smiled and allowed himself to be led into the dining room.

29

Mia stirred, changing her position to ease the pain where her hip bone pressed against the concrete floor. She opened her eyes, forgetting for a moment where she was. The room looked familiar, but everywhere she had stayed in the last few months looked the same—a concrete floor strewn with rubble, windows devoid of glass, and no furniture or anything else to suggest who the previous occupants had been. She lifted her head and looked around. There were bodies sleeping on the floor with her, huddled together for warmth, and the memory of the previous night came flooding back.

It had taken them over three hours to walk the ten kilometers from Sarmin to the once-bustling market town of Idlib, although there was little left now to recommend it. They had stopped often, taking shelter when the sound of fighting appeared to be close. There were rumors of a ceasefire, but it didn't seem to be in effect yet. They couldn't afford to use light, for fear of being spotted by enemy aircraft or artillery. They stumbled and staggered along, some women weak and taking support from the others, but they got little sympathy from the fighters who herded them along, getting more and more impatient as the night wore on. Once in Idlib, they roamed the streets for another hour until they chose a building to sleep in.

The women collapsed, exhausted on the second floor of an abandoned building, and went to sleep as the fighters melted away into the night.

Mia looked down at Malak, who was still sleeping, her breath short and shallow. She felt her forehead, still hot, then with the corner of the blanket, wiped away the congealed mucus from under her nostrils. She sat up and noticed one woman watching her, an older lady, her hair covered in a headscarf.

Mia nodded, not sure what language to use. Despite her five years in Syria, she still wasn't fluent in Arabic, but from the little she had heard them speaking the previous night, they appeared to be speaking another language.

The woman said something, but Mia didn't understand. The woman tried again, then realizing Mia didn't comprehend, she pointed at Malak and mimed putting food in her mouth.

Mia shook her head.

The lady rummaged in a bag and reached over, her hand open, three green olives nestling in her palm.

"*Shukraan.*" Mia took them from her.

The woman motioned putting them in her mouth, chewing, then moving them from her mouth to the baby's.

Mia nodded her understanding. She stroked Malak's face, whispering, "Wake up little darling, wake up. Mummy has some food for you."

Malak's eyes blinked open, and she pulled her arm out from under the blanket and rubbed her nose. Mia placed an olive in her mouth, separated the flesh from the seed, and spat the seed into her spare hand. She continued chewing the flesh, ignoring the growling of her stomach. She hadn't eaten since the previous morning, only a piece of old bread. It was all she could do not to swallow the olive. She spat the olive paste into her hand, then laid Malak on her lap. With the fingers of her right hand, she took the paste from her left and held it close to the little girl's mouth.

"Eat now, my baby, yummy yummy." Malak's mouth opened slowly, and Mia pushed the food inside. "Good girl. I'll give you some more." Mia glanced up at the woman and nodded her thanks before chewing on another olive. A younger woman sat up, and the older woman leaned toward her and murmured something in her ear.

Mia began to feed Malak the second olive when the younger lady spoke.

"English?"

Mia looked up in surprise. The only person she spoke English with was Naeem. "No," She shook her head. "I'm Australian."

The younger woman translated. The conversation woke the others, and they stirred and sat up, rubbing their faces, and stretching.

"Why are you here?" the young lady asked.

Mia frowned, "Here?"

"In Syria."

Mia looked down at Malak and pushed a little more olive paste into her mouth.

"My husband."

The young woman narrowed her eyes, "Husband? Your real husband?"

Mia nodded. She heard the women talking amongst themselves.

"He is... one of them?" the woman gestured toward the window. "*Al Qaeda?*"

"Yes."

Her answer seemed to displease the women, whose conversation became more animated. She looked down, not wanting to maintain eye contact. It was just her and Malak.

"*Al Qaeda,* they are *shaytan*... how do you say?" The woman paused, thinking of the word.

Mia looked up. "The devil."

"Yes."

Mia looked around at the women facing her, their faces filled with sadness, creased with worry and despair. Women who had given up any hope of finding happiness. She nodded.

"I know."

"Then why you come? Why you marry your... husband?" The last word spoken as it if was a curse.

Mia looked down at her daughter, the only thing left in her life she loved. *Why had she come?*

30

Mia had just finished a class at Melbourne University and was walking across the South Lawn when she first saw him.

It was one of those beautiful early spring days, warm but not too warm, filled with the promise of the summer to come. The students were making the most of the pleasant weather after a dreary winter, shedding layers of clothing and reveling in the sun's rays.

He was walking toward her with a group of friends. She had seen him before but not paid him much attention. He was just another guy on campus, but that day was different. He locked eyes with her as he passed and smiled, and her heart skipped a beat. For some reason, she could think of nothing else for the rest of that day and the next.

They met again a couple of days later, and this time, he spoke to her. His name was Naeem, a second-generation Lebanese Australian, and he made her laugh. They began to see each other regularly. He was happy, full of life, and made her feel special.

His parents had fled North Lebanon in the eighties,

making a home in the North Melbourne suburb of Darebin. Naeem had been born there, and not once did he seem any different from the other Australian boys she knew. He played footy with his mates, enjoyed going to the pub at the weekend, and surfed in the summer. It was only later he changed. She didn't notice at first, but by then, it was too late —she was head over heels in love with him and worshiped the ground he walked on.

It started with another student, a boy in one of his classes. He was also Middle Eastern, she never did learn from where exactly, but he convinced Naeem to join him at the mosque in Preston. Naeem stopped going to the pub, started commenting on what she was wearing, and seemed to be increasingly angry with the world.

Their time alone together was spent with him talking about the beauty of Islam, the wisdom in the holy Quran, the benefits of life as a Muslim, and she soaked it in. She wore a headscarf when they were together, and he taught her how to pray—anything to spend time with him. He told her he would call her Mahfuza, which meant 'protected' in Arabic, and he would always be around to protect her. She loved the idea, but it remained a secret between the two of them. She'd never had a boyfriend before, and the thought of losing him terrified her.

Then one day, he announced he was going to Turkey, and he wanted her to go with him. She was thrilled, she'd never been overseas before. In fact, she had only been out of the state once, when her parents had taken her to Sydney for a long weekend.

Naeem arranged everything—the visas, tickets, and the itinerary—all she had to do was convince her parents. They weren't sure at first, but she eventually persuaded them, promising she would keep in constant touch. And she did, excited calls every day about the wonders she had seen—the Hagia Sophia, the Grand Bazaar, the mighty Bosphorus teeming with river traffic. It was exotic, noisy, colorful. She had loved it, never imagining such a magical place existed.

Then he convinced her into crossing into Syria. The romance began to wane that day, and every day since, until now, there was nothing left. Syria wasn't the paradise he had promised. It was all a lie—he had tricked her. The light had gone from her life... until Malak was born.

Mia looked down at her daughter, Malak, her little angel. She smiled and touched her daughter's cheek with her fingertips. Looking up, she realized the other women were still waiting for her answer.

Why had she come? Why did she marry him? Why was she still with him? Despite her unhappiness, she still didn't think he was as bad as the other men, the fighters. Coarse, brutal men, who thought women were sub-human; in fact, thought any non-believer was sub-human. No, he wasn't like them, but he wasn't the same Naeem she fell in love with. She missed that Naeem, the happy-go-lucky boy with the dazzling smile.

Mia looked at the woman who had questioned her and pointed to her heart.

"Love." She shook her head sadly. "I did it for love."

31

The women talked among themselves, occasionally shooting glances in her direction. She couldn't understand a word they said in a language she'd never heard before. Only one woman appeared to speak English as they had all looked to her for a translation.

Mia studied their faces and their clothes, trying to put a label on them as if knowing who they were would restore some order in her life. They were of varying ages, from mid-teens to middle-aged, and they shared similar features as if all from the same ethnic group. Their clothing was a rag-tag assortment of sweaters, cardigans, and long skirts. Unusually, not one wore a hijab or abaya, only covering their hair with a simple headscarf.

Malak licked her lips, having finished the small pieces of olive, then for the first time in days, called out.

"Mama."

Mia smiled, leaned forward, and kissed her on the forehead as the women stopped talking and stared. One lady, perhaps the oldest in the group, slid forward and held out her hands. Mia looked down at Malak again, not sure, then slowly passed her over. The older woman broke into a smile and held Malak close, rocking back and forth, murmuring something in her language.

"What is her name?" the English speaker asked.

"Malak."

"Angel." The woman nodded, her eyes on the child. "In our language, we say *Melek*." She said something to the other women that made them excited, and they all gathered around the child. "I used to believe in angels." She shrugged. "But now..."

"Where are you from? I don't understand your language."

The woman regarded Mia for a moment and said, "Iraq."

"Iraq?" Mia frowned. "How did you end up here?"

The woman said something to the others in her language, and they sneered, shaking their heads, some waving their hands. She turned back to Mia,

"You really don't know?"

Mia shook her head.

"We are Yazidis. You know?"

"No."

"These men,"—she gestured toward the door—"men like your husband," she spat the word like it was a curse. "They came to my village... they killed all the men, my father, my brothers." She paused and looked down at the floor. When she looked up, her face was blank, her eyes empty, devoid of emotion as if she was narrating something that happened to someone else,

"They made us line up... without clothes. They looked at us... touched us... asked if we were... virgins." She nodded at two of the girls who must have been all of twelve or thirteen years old. "The young ones, they are worth more. Women like me?" She shrugged. "For them we are old, used, not worth as much. But... they rape us, anyway."

Mia winced. "I'm so sorry."

The woman stared at the wall over Mia's shoulder, then snapped back to the present.

"Then they took us and sold us to other men, men who used us, then sold us again. They marry us, rape us, then sell us. Over and over." She narrowed her eyes, "How many husbands have you had?"

The question puzzled Mia. "One."

The woman sneered and again said something to the other women. She pointed at one of them, a girl of around fourteen.

"Shayma has had five husbands." The girl wouldn't meet Mia's eyes, gazing down at her fingers as she toyed with the end of her blanket.

The woman pointed at the older lady holding Malak. "My mother. She is fifty-eight." She looked back at Mia and held up three fingers.

Mia shook her head. She knew the fighters treated women as second-class humans, but she had never known the reality of it. Naeem had kept her isolated for most of her time in Syria, and she had resented him for it. She had been unhappy and incredibly lonely until Malak was born, but now, she understood why he had kept her alone.

"The last man who... took me... he was old and fat..." Her voice trailed off. "He beat me with a belt..."

Mia swallowed and leaned forward to take the woman's hand. She held it in both of hers, and they sat quietly, listening to the murmured voices of the other women as they watched Malak. After a while, the woman took her hand back.

"My name is Nadia."

"Mahfuza... I mean, Mia."

Nadia raised an eyebrow.

"Mia is my real name. How do you know English?"

"I learned at school. I was good at my studies. My father wanted me to become a doctor." Nadia sighed. "So long ago now."

"I wanted to be an architect."

Nadia smiled. "Only Allah, *subhanahu wa-ta'ala,* knows what is planned for us."

Mia tilted her head to one side. "Nadia, all of you are Muslim. Why did the men do that to your village?"

"They don't like our Islam." Nadia sighed and raised her hands and shoulders in a half shrug. "We are different, our beliefs are different. We believe in angels, too." She smiled. "Malak. But they think we worship *Al Shaytan...* the devil." She scoffed, "Those men are the *Al Shayateen*. They are the real devils."

32

"So, unlike English tea, we boil the tea leaves in with the milk."

"Only milk?"

"No," replied Maadhavi as she gave the pot a stir. "Half milk, half water."

"And the spices?" Adriana asked as she watched.

"Yes, cardamom and ginger, but I also add lemongrass like this." Maadhavi chopped a few leaves of lemongrass and added them to the pot.

"It smells so good."

A movement caught their eye, and they both looked out the window as a cream-colored Land Cruiser pickup pulled into the driveway. It was battered and dusty, the bull bar and snorkel hinting at a hard, practical life.

"Who's that?"

Maadhavi shrugged, "I don't know. We're not expecting anyone."

The door of the pickup opened, and a tall, well-built man got out. His crisp white *dishdasha* accentuated his deeply tanned skin behind dark sunglasses and a richly embroidered Omani *mussar* tied around his head.

"Wait, it can't be?" Adriana murmured.

The man reached inside to remove a bag, and when he stood up again, he removed his sunglasses.

"Mansur!" Adriana exclaimed.

"Who?"

"Come with me." Adriana rushed for the front door.

"Marisel, keep an eye on the *chai*," Maadhavi called over her shoulder as she followed after her.

Adriana opened the door and stood on the top step as Mansur approached.

"Miss Adriana." He broke into a broad smile.

Adriana briefly puzzled over the appropriate way to greet the Bedouin, who had helped save her life in Oman, eventually opting to hold out her hand. Mansur dropped his kitbag on the ground and clasped her hand in both of his.

"I'm so happy to see you again."

"So am I, Mansur." Adriana beamed. "So am I. How is Warda? Farida and Saara?"

"They are all well. The girls are growing fast."

"I'm sure."

Mansur's eyes flicked over her shoulder.

"Oh, Mansur, this is Maadhavi."

Mansur let go of Adriana's hand and shook Maadhavi's. "Nice to meet you."

"Mansur is a wonderful friend of ours from Oman. He saved my life."

"Welcome to our home, Mansur, please come inside."

Mansur bent down and picked up his bag.

"John told me he had a surprise for me. I would never have guessed you were coming."

Mansur smiled, his teeth flashing white against his tan. "He called me yesterday."

"Come on in, John and Steve are inside."

Adriana led him inside and down the hallway into the dining room.

"Look who I found."

John and Steve looked up from the dining table covered in maps, notebooks, and two laptops.

"Mansur, so good to see you." John stood, clasped Mansur's hand, and pulled him into a hug, kissing him on both cheeks in the traditional Arab way. "We really appreciate you coming at such short notice."

"It is my duty, Mr. John."

"Mate!" Steve rounded the table. "Good to see ya."

The two men hugged, but when Mansur moved to kiss him on the cheek, he pulled back.

"Nah, I don't do that, mate." Steve clasped both his arms. "Thanks for coming. It means a lot." Steve turned to Maadhavi. "Remember, I told you about Oman? This is the guy."

Maadhavi nodded and smiled.

"So, Mansur, I have you to thank. If not for you, we wouldn't all be together."

Mansur looked embarrassed. "Perhaps, Miss Maadhavi, they haven't told you the complete story. If it wasn't for Mr. John and Mr. Steve, my wife would not be alive today." He turned to both the men. "I owe you both a great debt."

"It was nothing, Mansur." John patted him on the upper arm. "What's important is you agreed to come and help us. Please, take a seat. Are you tired?"

Mansur pulled out a chair. "I'm okay. I stopped twice to rest."

"How long was the drive?"

"About eight hours."

"Do you want to freshen up, Mansur?" Maadhavi offered.

Mansur turned toward her and smiled. "No, thank you."

At that moment, Marisel walked in carrying a tray.

"Ah, perfect timing, Marisel." Steve gestured toward Mansur. "This is Mansur. He will stay with us. Can you make up the spare room for him?"

"Yes, sir." Marisel nodded and gave Mansur a smile. "Welcome, sir."

Mansur smiled back. "Hello, Marisel."

Maadhavi poured a cup of *masala chai* and passed it to Mansur, before pouring cups for the others.

They spent the next few minutes in small talk, catching up with everything that had happened since they had parted ways in Oman.

John finally placed his cup back on the tray and cleared his throat.

"Mansur, I explained briefly on the phone what we're planning to do, but I'll go over it again." John glanced at Steve. "Steve's niece and her young daughter are in Syria. Not just in Syria, but in Al Qaeda held territory. We are going there to rescue her. The child is not well, so we need to move fast." John paused and looked from Mansur to Adriana and Maadhavi and back again.

"It will be dangerous. We don't have permission from the government to be there, and we're going right into the middle of a war zone." John paused again, thinking of the right words. "We'll have the Syrian Army and the Russians on one side, the Al Qaeda forces and the Turkish Army on the other, not to mention the drones and fighter planes of the U.S. and UK overhead." John paused again and looked down at his hands.

"Mansur, you have a wife and two daughters. We appreciate you have come so far, and I know you've already agreed to help, but I want you to think again very carefully about whether you want to come with us." Mansur moved to protest, and John held up his hand. "Mansur, forget about any debt. Think about your family. If you decide not to join us, neither Steve nor I will think any less of you." John looked up at Steve. "Am I right, Steve?"

Steve nodded.

Mansur placed his cup on the table.

"Mr. John, it's because I have two daughters of my own, I agreed to help you. If my daughters were in this situation, I would also want all the help I could get. I'm coming with you."

John smiled. "Thank you, Mansur."

"Yeah." Steve's voice caught, and he swallowed. "Thanks, mate."

"Right, let's do a quick run-through of our plan, then Steve needs to borrow your passport for an hour or two."

33

The five of them sat around the table, staring at the phone, willing it to ring.

It was ten minutes after six, and Steve had already tried calling three times, but the phone hadn't connected.

"Maybe the battery is flat," Maadhavi suggested helpfully.

Steve nodded slowly but didn't take his eyes off the phone.

"The phone system could be down too, Steve," John added. "It is a war zone."

They sat quietly for another five minutes until Steve let out a long sigh and turned to John.

"What do we do?"

John looked from him to Mansur and back again.

"I say we still go ahead. Nothing's changed. We keep the phone on and try calling her at one-hour intervals. We proceed as planned and head to Turkey. We take each day as it comes." He looked at Mansur. "Do you agree?"

"Yes."

"Steve?"

"Yeah, you're right."

"Okay, I've booked the three of us on the Emirates flight to Istanbul tomorrow. It gets in at six in the evening."

"Three of you?" Adriana interjected, looking at Maadhavi and then John.

"Yes. It's too dangerous for you both to come."

"No way, John, am I staying here while you head into Syria. Maadhavi and I will come as far as Turkey and provide whatever support you'll need from there. Right, Maadhavi?"

"Yes," Maadhavi agreed. "I'm not staying here."

"But..." Steve protested.

"No arguments, Steve," Maadhavi replied sternly. "Adriana and I are coming."

John studied Adriana's face for a moment as she matched his gaze, not looking away. Finally, he nodded once and half-smiled.

"Right, I'd better make some more bookings."

Steve stood up, scowled at Maadhavi, and walked out of the room. John winked at Adriana before smiling at Maadhavi.

"Don't worry, he'll come round. He's worried about you, that's all."

"I can hear you," came a voice from the other room.

John grinned and picked up his phone.

"I'm calling Craig. We need his smuggler contact."

34

Mia woke early, just as the sun's rays filtered through the window. She sat up, rubbed her face, and looked around at the sleeping bodies huddled together on the floor.

The night had been relatively quiet. Quiet but for the distant sounds of gunfire and bombing, but the women had got so used to it, they all slept right through.

Naeem hadn't returned, and apart from the one guard stationed at the door on the ground floor, neither had the other men. The women were relieved. They explained to Mia that when the fighting was heavy, it had two benefits. It kept the men away, and there was always the possibility they would be killed and wouldn't return. For Mia, it was different. Although Naeem was no longer the man she had fallen in love with, she still feared for his safety and was always relieved when he returned. Apart from Malak, she had no-one else here, and she benefited from his protection, as these women's stories had proven.

The women had talked for most of the previous day and into the night, recounting their brutal experiences since being kidnapped from their villages, some of them from Iraq, some from Yazidi settlements in Northern Syria. None of the women cried or seemed to feel sorry for themselves. They told their stories without emotion, distancing themselves from their feelings. Perhaps it was their way of protecting themselves, but Mia was horrified.

The last few years for her had been tough, but nothing compared to what these women had gone through. As much as she'd grown to resent Naeem for bringing her to Syria and destroying any chance of happiness, she had to respect that he had kept her protected from most of the harm that could have come her way.

Later in the evening, when their stories were over, Mia told them of her childhood in Australia, and the women, in turn, talked about happier times before the war. The women shared what little food they had among themselves, although most of it seemed to go to Malak, who, although still running a fever, was more active than she had been in days.

When the sun set, Mia had become restless. She had to speak to Uncle Steve but was reluctant to let the other women see she had a phone. She still wasn't sure how much she could trust them, and the phone was her only link to the outside world. She couldn't afford to lose it, especially when Uncle Steve was so close to saving her and Malak.

Mia looked at Malak, curled up in the blanket. Her breath was still irregular, and her sunken cheeks betrayed the lack of food they had endured over the past couple of months. Her little angel deserved so much more. She needed to let her uncle know where she was. He was her only chance of giving Malak the life she deserved.

She slowly slid her feet toward her and got to her feet. Carefully and quietly, she stepped over the sleeping women and made her way to the door. Pausing in the doorway, she looked back, but no-one showed signs of stirring. She started down the stairs, paused on the first-floor landing, and listened—nothing. She continued down, then stopped as she heard a noise from below. Dropping to a crouch, she peered around the stairs. The guard was awake. Damn.

She stood and slowly went back up the stairs to the first floor, keeping close to the wall, careful not to kick or stumble on any rubble. On the first floor, she entered the room the women had been using as a toilet, wrinkling her nose at the smell, and moved cautiously to the far side of the room, away from the door and the window. She wanted to avoid any chance of sound carrying to the sleeping women above or the guard below.

Lifting her *abaya*, she reached inside and removed the phone from where she had tucked it inside the waistband of her knickers. Powering it on, she waited while the phone searched for a signal, hoping the network had been restored. The battery was low, and she hoped there was still enough credit on the phone to make a call. Naeem usually charged the battery and added money at one of the few shops remaining open in the district, but she didn't know when she would see him again. Two bars, good. She pressed redial and waited for the phone to connect.

35

Steve's phone rang in his pocket, and he scrambled to answer it before it stopped ringing. Pulling it out, he glanced quickly at the screen then answered.

"Mia?"

"Yes, Uncle, we are safe."

Steve heaved a big sigh of relief. "Where are you now? Why are you whispering?"

"I don't want the others to hear. We are in a building in Idlib, near the vegetable market."

"Good, good. The others?"

"Some other women are here with me."

"Okay." Steve glanced toward the door where John was leaning on the doorframe, having heard the phone ring. He gave a thumbs-up and continued. "We are coming, Mia. We'll be there soon. Maybe in two days."

"Okay." There was silence for a while.

"Mia?"

"Yes, I... thank you."

"Keep your phone on tomorrow."

"Uncle, I can't. There's very little battery left. I have nowhere to charge it."

"Damn it." Steve screwed up his face and rubbed the top of his head. "Okay, I'll call you tomorrow evening at seven. Turn the phone on then."

"Okay."

"How is Malak?"

"She's... okay, Uncle."

"Good. Keep safe. I'll be there soon."

"Okay, bye."

"Bye, Mia."

The phone went dead, and Steve looked up, smiling for the first time that day.

"She's okay. She's moved to Idlib."

"Great news." John nodded thoughtfully.

"Yeah." Steve looked down at the items strewn on the floor of the bedroom. "Have you packed?"

"Yes, we're done. Don't forget your camera gear. It's important we look the part."

"Done. Have you packed the phones?"

"Yup. Phones, notebooks, laptop." John drummed his fingers on the door frame. "I wish we'd got the bulletproof vests, though."

"We should be able to get some in Istanbul."

"Yeah, Craig said he would try. I just hate leaving things 'til the last minute."

"We'll be alright."

"Hmmm." John turned to leave, then turned back. "Craig is trying to set up a meeting with the smuggler this evening at our hotel."

"Good. So, we're all set." Steve grinned. "Tell everyone to be ready to leave by eleven-thirty. We can eat at the airport."

"Done, and hey,"

"What?"

"Don't shave. Let's see how quickly we can grow a bit of facial hair. Best not to be the only clean-shaven men in Syria. We don't want to stand out too much."

36

John finished loading the luggage in the rear of the black Mercedes Vito and closed the door. Walking around to the front, he climbed into the driver's seat and glanced over his shoulder.

"Everyone comfortable in the back?"

"Yes," Maadhavi and Adriana chorused. "Very comfortable."

"Do you think we have enough seats, mate?" Steve piped up from the back. "This seats nine."

"Well, no-one wants to sit next to you, Steve." He winked at Mansur, sitting beside him. "That's why I got you a row to yourself."

"Yeah, thanks, mate."

John slipped on his seatbelt, checked the mirrors, and pulled out into the traffic, just as his phone buzzed on the dashboard.

"Can you check that for me, Mansur? I'm expecting a message from Craig."

Mansur picked up the phone and glanced at the screen.

"He says he'll meet you in the hotel bar at eight-thirty with his contact."

"Good." John checked the time on the dashboard. "It's about thirty-five minutes from here to the hotel, so we'll have about fifteen minutes to check-in before he arrives." He glanced in the rear-view mirror at Steve. "Steve, I reckon you and I meet them together without Adriana and Maadhavi." He moved his head so he could see Adriana. "I don't want this smuggler guy to know you are here. We don't know who he is, so the less he knows, the better."

Adriana nodded. "Ok with me, Maadhavi?"

"Okay, for me, too." Maadhavi added, "I can do with a freshen up before dinner, anyway."

"Good." John indicated and pulled into the next lane to avoid a slow-moving lorry. "Mansur, I want you in the background as backup. Go to the bar before us and find a table where you can watch. Pretend you don't know us. Just sit there and observe."

"Okay, Mr. John."

"Mansur, you'd better wear something less conspicuous. You'll stick out like dog's balls in that outfit," Steve added from the back row.

"Steve." Maadhavi frowned at him as John stifled a laugh.

Mansur frowned and repeated slowly, "Stick out like dog's balls..." He looked to John for an explanation.

"What he means, is in your *dishdasha* and,"—John glanced at Mansur's headdress—"*mussar,* you will be very noticeable. Especially in a bar." He looked away from the road again and smiled at Mansur. "You had better change into some western clothing."

"Yes, I will." Mansur stared out the window, a slight frown on his forehead, his lips moving soundlessly. He began to smile, then chuckled. The chuckle turned into laughter, and he turned in his seat to look back at Steve. "I understand now." He gave him a thumbs-up, a big grin on his face, then turned back to face the front.

"Like a dog's balls, that's a good one."

37

John and Steve walked into the hotel bar and looked around. The bar was half full of travelers and businessmen, and in the far corner Mansur sat by himself, facing the room, a glass with an umbrella in front of him. John was relieved he had changed into something less noticeable and looked like a traveler from somewhere in the Mediterranean.

"Over there," Steve said as he saw a hand being raised. They spotted Craig sitting at a table in front of a large man with his back to them. They walked over as Craig stood up and reached out his hand.

"Good to meet you, at last, Craig." John shook his hand. He had a firm grip and looked thinner than on the video call, his face drawn and tired.

"You too, John, Steve."

They turned to face the man sitting opposite him, who was studying them with small cynical eyes set in a corpulent face. His hair, greying at the temples, was slicked back, and his thick mustache twitched as he regarded them without warmth, weighing them, figuring out where they stood in the scheme of things.

"This is Mehmet. Mehmet, John and Steve."

Mehmet didn't stand, just nodded, so John held out his hand. Almost reluctantly, he leaned forward in his chair and took John's hand, a loose handshake, his hands soft and fleshy. Steve didn't bother, just nodded, and moved around him to sit down.

John and Craig sat down as well, and Craig waved for the waiter. "What do you want to drink?"

"I'll have a beer," Steve replied.

Craig nodded and turned to the waiter who had appeared by his side. "One beer, another Glenmorangie,"—he glanced at Mehmet, who nodded—"a raki," then turned to John. "John?"

John turned to the waiter. "Do you have Botanist?"

"Yes, sir."

"Good. Large Botanist and tonic, lots of ice, slice of orange, please."

"Yes, sir."

John felt Mehmet staring at him, and he gave him a smile. "I'm particular about my drink."

Mehmet nodded slowly. "You are English, no?"

"Yes."

"And you?" Mehmet turned to Steve.

"Australian."

"You are not Muslim," he said as a statement, not a question.

Both men shook their heads, and Mehmet frowned, his eyes almost disappearing between the fleshy folds of his face.

"Then why you want to go to Syria?"

John glanced at Craig. "You didn't tell him?"

"No, just that you wanted to go there."

John turned back to face Mehmet as the waiter arrived with their drinks. He waited until the waiter was out of earshot, using the time to think about how much he should tell him. He didn't know the guy and wasn't getting great energy from him. He pulled his drink closer, swirled it around, and held it up.

"Cheers..."

"Cheers."

Mehmet took a sip of his raki, then put the glass back on the table. He tapped out a rhythm on the tabletop with his index finger as he waited for John's answer.

"We want to find someone."

The tapping stopped. "Who?"

John glanced at Steve.

"A girl."

"Ha," Mehmet snorted and looked around the table. "I can get you girls here. Beautiful girls. Why you want to go there?"

Steve banged his bottle of beer on the table and sat forward. He leaned toward Mehmet and growled, "The girl is my niece."

Mehmet raised an eyebrow and looked from Steve to John and back again. "Your niece?"

"Yes."

"Oh." He raised both hands in a placatory gesture. "Sorry." He took another drink. "And where is this... niece?"

Steve looked at John, and John gave a slight shake of his head. "I... we don't know yet."

Mehmet pursed his lips. "You don't know," he repeated, one eyebrow raised. "What is she doing there? Journalist? Like Craig here? Aid worker?"

"No, she..."

"She made some wrong decisions, and she needs help to come back. So, we are going to get her," John interjected.

"Ah." Mehmet nodded slowly. He ran his tongue along his bottom lip. "I see."

"Craig said you could help get us across the border?"

"Hmmm."

Steve shifted in his chair. "Well, can you?"

Mehmet's eyes flicked from John to Steve. "It will be expensive."

"How much?"

"Twenty thousand U.S. dollars."

"What?" Steve spluttered on his beer. "You cheating son of a…"

"Steve." John held up his hand. He fixed his gaze on Mehmet. "Mehmet, we can't afford that."

Mehmet shrugged. "I have expenses; I have to pay people to look the other way."

"Yeah, and buy yourself more gold rings," Steve muttered.

"Steve…" John admonished him.

"Gentlemen, let's keep things civil," Craig attempted to play peacekeeper. "Mehmet, there must be something you can do to help these gentlemen?"

"Nothing I can do." Mehmet shrugged and turned out his bottom lip. "It's a war zone."

"Mehmet, do you have a family?" John asked.

"I do." Mehmet narrowed his eyes.

"Children?"

"No."

John nodded slowly. "Steve doesn't have children, either, but his niece is like a daughter to him."

"And?"

John leaned forward in his chair, his eyes fixed on Mehmet's.

"Imagine being in his position. You have a daughter, and she is in danger. She's in a war zone, fearing for her life. The only one who can help her is you."

Mehmet said nothing, the only sign he was thinking about it a twitch of his mustache.

"Now, imagine your daughter has a baby, a granddaughter you have never seen. A granddaughter whose health is failing, and if nothing is done, will probably die along with your daughter. What would you do, Mehmet?"

John sat back in his chair, crossed his arms, and waited to see if he had struck a nerve.

Mehmet stared down at the tabletop as he played with his glass, turning it around and around with his gold ring clad fingers.

Looking up, his eyes darted around the table, looking at each man before settling back on John.

"Okay." He pointed a fat finger at John. "I deal with you. Because of the... special circumstances, I will not charge you my fee, only my expenses. Ten thousand U.S. dollars."

Steve snorted, and John shot him a warning glance.

"Five thousand."

"Seven. Upfront in cash."

"Half now, half when we are across the border."

Steve made to protest but stopped when John shot him another look.

Mehmet stared at John, his mustache twitching, "Done. When?"

"Tomorrow."

Mehmet sucked air in through his teeth.

"Okay. Take my number from Craig. Call me at ten tomorrow morning. I will give you instructions."

"Thank you." John reached forward and held out his hand. Mehmet looked at it as if wondering what it was, then reached forward and shook it.

"I will give you a discount for the return journey?" he asked before letting go.

John smiled without mirth. "That's generous of you."

Mehmet released his hand and stood up. He nodded at Craig, glanced at Steve, then back at John.

"Call me tomorrow."

"I will, oh, and Mehmet?"

"Yes?"

"There will be three of us."

"Three?"

"Three."

Mehmet frowned again, then nodded and turned for the door.

The three men waited until he had left the bar before Steve exploded.

"What a prick."

John gave a slight nod across the bar to Mansur, who pushed back his chair and walked out, then turned to Steve.

"He might be, but we need someone to help us."

"But, John, seven grand?"

"Steve, don't worry about it. I'll cover it."

"But..."

"No buts, Steve. It's okay. Besides, I didn't want to haggle too much. We need to leave some profit in it for him; otherwise he's bound to sell us out."

"Good thinking, John," Craig said. He picked up his whiskey, knocked back the contents, and signaled for the waiter. "Same again, gents?"

"Yeah," Steve replied. "I didn't enjoy the last one."

"John?"

"Not for me, thanks." John held his hand over his glass. "How well do you know this guy, Craig?"

Craig exhaled. "Not well. I just know he's heavily involved in cross border traffic. He smuggles people out all the time and sends weapons in." He shook his head. "To be honest, I don't trust any of these guys. For them, money is more important than human life, but given the short notice and the lack of legal options for you, he was the best I could think of."

"He'll have to do. As you said, we have little time and few options." John waited while the waiter delivered Craig and Steve's drinks before continuing, "Did you have any luck with bulletproof vests?"

"Yes, I'll drop them off in the morning."

"Thank you."

"You told Mehmet, three people. Who's the third?"

John glanced toward the door. "Here he is now."

38

"He got into a black Mercedes, I have the registration number."

"Good. Alone?"

"No, he had two men with him. One had been in the bar." Mansur nodded to a table near to where they were sitting. "He sat over there. The other was sitting out in the lobby. Big guys. Looked like bodyguards."

"Thank you, Mansur, please grab a chair."

Mansur sat in the seat Mehmet had occupied.

"Craig, this is Mansur. He is the third man."

"Mansur, nice to meet you." Craig reached across the table and shook his hand.

"Mansur, once this is over, you should come and work for me," Steve joked and punched him on the arm. "You did well."

Mansur smiled shyly.

"Can we get you a drink, Mansur?" offered Craig.

Mansur held up his hand and shook his head, "Thank you, no."

"Mansur, it looks like we can cross over tomorrow. The

man we just met will give me the arrangements tomorrow," John explained.

"Okay."

John turned to Craig.

"Now tell me, Craig. What's it like over there? What should we expect?"

39

Craig shook his head, reached for his drink, took a large swig, then placed the glass back on the table.

"It's not pretty." He looked at each of the men in turn. "I think what you are doing is admirable, I would do the same if it was my daughter, but..." He shrugged. "It's bloody dangerous."

"We're expecting that."

Craig studied John's face. "Yes, I'm sure you are. Okay, let me put it this way. From the minute you cross that border, you will not know who you can trust. Who is a good guy, and who is a bad guy. They are all good guys, all bad guys. It depends on your luck." He took another sip of his drink, warming to the subject. "You've got multiple anti-government factions in the area she's in, all affiliated to Al Qaeda. Some of them genuinely feel they are fighting for freedom from Assad. Others are just Islamic extremists who dream of a caliphate."

John decided he would need another drink and signaled for the waiter.

"You will also have the Turkish Army. They are easier to deal with, but my point is, you will be crossing checkpoints, not just around Idlib but every step of the way once you set foot in the country and have to justify your reason for being there."

"Understood."

Craig waited while John's drink arrived before continuing.

"How will you communicate?"

John tipped his head toward Mansur. "Mansur speaks Arabic."

"Good. Arabic and English will be sufficient for dealing with the Syrian Army, the Russians, and the Kurds. If you cross the front line, you will have the Turks and the rebels to deal with. Again, Arabic and English should get you by. You mentioned before you are going as Press?"

"That's right. Doable?"

"You'll need documentation. You can't just wander around with a notebook."

John reached into his pocket and removed a laminated plastic card in a leather holder and handed it over.

"I have this, letters of invitation, and everything else you said we'd need."

Craig examined the card and nodded his approval.

"How did you get this? Adriana?"

John glanced at Steve, who gave a subtle shake of his head.

"It's best you don't know."

Craig stared back at John, then grinned. "Okay." He picked up his drink and knocked back the rest of the whiskey. "I'll throw in some Press badges for the bulletproof vests before I bring them over. I've got some extra in the flat. You just Velcro them to the front and back."

"Thank you."

"Now remember, a vest will not be enough to protect you if it turns to shit, and it turns to shit really quickly. If bullets start flying, your instinct will be to run. Don't! Nothing attracts attention more than someone running. Drop to the ground and find something substantial to hide behind. And I mean substantial. Rounds can cut through most things like paper. Stay down, stay hidden until you have an escape route."

John glanced at Steve, who looked increasingly nervous.

"Take money but keep it hidden. Bribery can help at a checkpoint but only use it as a last resort. Remember, you are supposed to be legitimate journalists. Take notes, photos, look like you are supposed to be there, but be careful what you photograph. Try to avoid pointing your cameras at the fighters. Some love their photos being taken, but others can get really angry and will turn on you in seconds."

Steve exhaled loudly. "I need another beer."

Craig smiled in sympathy.

"Just keep your wits about you and always be calm and polite at the checkpoints. These guys want you to know who's in charge. If you do all that, you should be okay."

"Yeah." Steve waved for the waiter.

"Do you have transport once you are across?"

"Ah... no." John cleared his throat. "I assumed we might find a taxi, someone to drive us from the border."

"Yes, there are plenty of guys who will do that for you. You will see them hanging around, depending on where Mehmet makes you cross. Pay them well and win their trust. They're pretty good at getting you through checkpoints."

"Good, thanks."

"I..." Craig stopped, his eyes on something over John's shoulder, his mouth hanging open.

John turned to see what he was looking at, and his frown turned into a grin as Adriana and Maadhavi, both dressed to kill, entered the bar. He turned back, noticing that most of the conversation in the bar had stopped.

"Craig, why don't you join us for dinner?"

40

After a large breakfast, they all gathered in John and Adriana's room. At exactly ten o'clock, John dialed the number Craig had given him. It rang twice before a gruff voice answered.

"Alo?"

"Mehmet? This is John."

"Yes, John. Good morning. It is all organized. I want you to fly down to the town of Cizre. The nearest airport is Sirnak, and there's a flight just after one. Book yourself into a hotel there and text me the hotel name. My associate, Hemin, will call you. He will take you across the border tonight."

"He is reliable?"

"John," Mehmet scoffed. "You doubt me? He is my best man. He makes the trip many times already."

"Thank you, Mehmet."

"Oh, and John. One of my men is waiting in the lobby. You pay him half now and the balance to Hemin once you are over the border."

John pursed his lips. He didn't like to part with the

money before they had even left, but he didn't have any other options.

"Okay."

"İyi şanslar."

"I'm sorry?"

"Good luck."

The phone went dead. John stared at the blank screen for a moment.

"All okay, mate?"

John looked up and smiled at Steve.

"Yes, all good. We have to get a flight down to Sirnak and book into a hotel there. One of his men will meet us and take us across the border tonight."

"That's good, then," Steve replied. "Why the frown?"

"We have to pay half the fee now to his man in the lobby."

"Hmmm."

"What if he doesn't go ahead with it?" Adriana asked.

John thought for a moment. "Well, then we are down three and a half grand. We have no-one else, so I say let's do it, but Steve, it's your call."

"Yeah, okay. We'll pay him. It could take us days to find someone else."

"Okay. Mansur, can you go down to the lobby and hang around? Just keep an eye out for any trouble. Steve or I will be down in five minutes with the money."

"Okay." Mansur nodded and walked out of the room.

"Steve, do you want to go, or shall I?"

"I'll do it, mate."

"Okay. We'll book flights and a hotel. We don't have much time."

"I'll do the flights," Adriana offered.

"And I'll look for a hotel," added Maadhavi.

"I'm not even going to insist you two stay here. I know I'd be wasting my breath."

Adriana grinned at Maadhavi.

"But..."

Both women turned to look at John.

"I don't think you should come on the same flight."

Adriana straightened and put her hands on her hips.

"Why?"

John shrugged. "I don't know. I just feel it's better, the less these guys know about us, the better. Mehmet knows we'll be on the one o'clock flight. I'm sure he will have someone there, watching it. It's better he only sees me, Steve, and Mansur."

"I agree." Steve looked at Maadhavi. "I think it will be safer, honey."

Maadhavi looked questioningly at Adriana, who nodded.

"Okay, I'll book us on the next flight after yours."

"Good."

"I'll head down and pay the man," Steve said as he headed for the door.

"Good luck. Mansur will keep an eye on you."

Steve waved over his shoulder and closed the door behind him.

"I think it's better to make two hotel bookings as well. Keep you and Maadhavi separate from ours."

"Okay."

The two women grabbed laptops and started typing away.

John walked over to his bag and pulled out the second-hand laptop Steve had picked up in Dubai. He booted it up, opened Google Maps, and zoomed in on the border closest to Cizre. Now, where would they be crossing?

Payback

41

The captain had announced preparation for landing when Steve spoke up. The three of them were sitting together in coach, Mansur by the window, Steve in the middle, John in the aisle seat.

"John, I want to ask you to do something for me."

John blinked his eyes open. He hadn't been sleeping, just thinking, trying to plan for all eventualities.

"Sure."

"If...." Steve cleared his throat. "If anything happens to me, please see that Mia is looked after."

John elbowed Steve. "Hey, nothing will happen. Why are you thinking like this?"

"No, it's just..."

"Thinking like that won't help any of us. We're going in, straight to Idlib, pick her up, and coming straight back again."

"Yeah."

John didn't like allowing thoughts like this to take shape, so he sought to change the subject.

"You need to think about what you do once she is back

here across the border. How is her child, will she need medical treatment? Where will you take them?"

Steve nodded as he stared at the seatback in front of him.

John glanced past Steve to look at Mansur, who was listening to the conversation. He didn't look worried at all, and John wished he had the same composure. Despite what he was telling Steve, he was concerned, too. He had never been in a war zone, and although he had done many dangerous things in the past, nothing compared to what he was about to do. But he couldn't let the others know what he was thinking. If they all started doubting their success, the mission was a failure before it even started.

"Look, Steve, everything has worked out so far. I'm a firm believer if you are not supposed to do something, roadblocks are thrown up in your path to guide you in a different direction. So far, there have been no roadblocks. We can do it."

"Mr. John is right," Mansur spoke for the first time. "Allah... God will always guide you. You just need to see the signs."

Steve looked at Mansur and gave a half-smile. "Thanks, mate." He looked back at John. "Thank you both. I really appreciate what you are doing for me. I'll never forget this. When this is all over... I owe *you* a beer this time."

John grinned. "So, then we'll be even." He looked at Mansur. "But what about Mansur? He doesn't drink."

"Ah yeah, sorry, mate. Some coffee?"

Mansur grinned. "It's okay, Mr. Steve. It is my honor to help you."

Steve nodded, swallowed, and looked away. Mansur went back to looking out the window, and John leaned his head against the headrest. He thought back over what Mansur had said.

He didn't believe in God, Allah, whatever you liked to call it. Too many shitty things had happened in his past to believe in an all-seeing benevolent being, but when he thought back over the things he had done, there were signs of some sort of a guiding hand. Maybe it was intuition, a sixth sense, or even his subconscious drawing on the vast storehouse of information it had accumulated over his life, guiding his conscious mind in the correct course of action. Whatever it was, right now, there was nothing telling him that what they were doing was wrong. He had to keep faith and keep moving forward. There was no turning back now.

42

"Do you see him?"

"Yeah."

"Mansur?"

"The grey pickup?"

"Yes."

"Do you think he's watching us?"

John threw the last of the bags in the back of the minivan and closed the door.

"Well, he's had eyes on us since we came out of the terminal."

The three men climbed into the van, Steve up front with John, Mansur in the back. John entered the address of the hotel into the phone, handed it to Steve, and started the engine.

"Let's see if he follows us."

He pulled out of the carpark, turned onto the exit road leading from Sirnak Airport to the main highway, and headed off.

"Mansur?"

"Wait... Yes, he's left the parking, too."

John glanced at Steve. "I thought he would have someone follow us."

"Yeah, good job you suggested the girls travel separately."

John nodded, his eyes back on the road. He didn't think there was anything to worry about, just Mehmet being prudent, but he knew they would have to keep on their toes.

John joined the D380 heading southeast and glanced in his mirror.

"Still there?"

"Yes, Mr. John. About four cars back."

For just over fifteen minutes, they followed the highway through a sun-scorched patchwork of fields and villages. John kept just under the speed limit, Steve providing the directions while Mansur kept an eye on the vehicle following them. As they neared Cizre, they took the road skirting the town to the west and south before joining the E90 heading north.

"Look at that!" Steve pointed out his window.

"What?"

"That wall." Steve tapped on his window. "Is that the Syrian border?"

"Looks like it."

"Shit. We're so close." He turned to look at John. "It's actually happening."

"Yup." John nodded, his eyes back on the road.

"The wall is massive. How the fuck are we getting across that?"

John glanced in the mirror at the vehicle following them.

"I guess we'll find out soon enough."

The E90 crossed over the River Tigris before taking a turn to the south. John took the exit road just after the turn and a minute later, pulled up outside their hotel, the pickup staying with them all the way. If there had been before, there was no doubt now the vehicle had been following them.

It was the only decent hotel in a town battered by the Turkish government's crackdown on its predominantly Kurdish population five years earlier, but it had a five-star rating and was next to the river. Anyway, they weren't planning on being there long. John pulled up in front and climbed out. He walked around to the back, opened the door, and smiled at the bellhop who had come rushing down the steps.

"Welcome, sir."

"Thank you." He handed over the keys and turned to Steve and Mansur. "Get us checked in. I'll join you in a minute."

"Where are you going?"

John didn't answer, already heading toward the pickup he had seen pull up further down the road. As he approached, he saw the look of surprise on the driver's face. John stepped onto the road, blocking the vehicle's path, and walked around to the driver's window and tapped on the glass. The man inside reluctantly wound down the window. John put on his biggest smile and stuck his hand through the window.

"I'm John. You must be Hemin?"

43

Mia was secretly pleased to have company. She had spent months alone, just her and Malak, waiting for Naeem to come home, sweating through the summer, shivering through the winter, always hungry, always fearful he wouldn't come back from the front.

Now at least, she had someone to talk to, someone to take her mind off the always present hunger and boredom.

Some of the older women tried to go out to find food, but the young fighter guarding the door wouldn't allow them to leave. They pleaded with him but gave up when he turned the barrel of his AK47 on them.

The hours passed in stories—of childhood, of a better time before the war—the women taking turns holding Malak and sharing what tiny morsels of food they had saved with her. The younger girls had only known the war and couldn't imagine a time when people weren't fighting or hungry.

As the shadows lengthened across the room, Mia thought about turning the phone on again and calling

Steve. She glanced at her watch, a present from her mother on her eighteenth birthday. It seemed so long ago now. It had been years since she had seen her, and only since Malak had been born had she even reconnected with them. She still had around thirty minutes before the agreed time to call and hoped there was still enough battery for the phone to start up. The fighting had been fierce in the last few days, despite the rumored ceasefire, and Naeem hadn't had enough downtime to seek out a building with a generator, so he could recharge it.

What was he doing now? She turned her head toward the window and realized the constant sound of shelling in the distance was absent. She heard something else, men's voices in the street, and she stiffened, as did the other women. She heard a shout, a man's name being called, then a minute later footsteps in the building. The women separated, moved away from the center of the room toward the walls, pulled their scarves over their heads, and wrapped their clothes around them. The almost cheerful atmosphere of minutes before completely dissolved, replaced with apprehension. Mia took Malak from one of the women and cradled her in her arms, then shuffled her butt along the floor until she was in the corner.

The steps and voices got nearer, then men appeared in the doorway. One by one, they filed in, leaned their weapons against the wall, and flopped down on the floor, exhausted —all except one, the man with yellow teeth. He stood in the doorway, looking around the room, his eyes running over each woman until they finally settled on Mia. She gripped Malak tighter and tried to get closer to the wall behind her. Yellow Teeth sniffed, his eyes boring holes in her. His mouth widened into a leer, and he took a step closer, unslinging his AKM. He held out the weapon, and a man on the floor beside the door took it from him. Mia's heart started pounding in her chest, her jaw clenched tight. She looked to her side for help, but the other women had their gaze averted, careful not to attract attention to themselves. They had all been through this before, there was no escaping it. Yellow Teeth licked his lips and walked across the room to stand over her, his hands on his hips, looking down at her. His eyes were wide, and his breathing was erratic.

Mia looked away, hugging Malak close to her chest, looking down at the floor. She heard more footsteps, and another pair of boots appeared beside those of Yellow Teeth's. She flinched, closed her eyes, then heard a familiar voice.

"Malak, wake up, Papa's home."

Her eyes blinked open, and she saw Naeem crouched in front of her. Exhaling with relief, she looked over his shoulder to see Yellow Teeth glaring down at them. Naeem pretended he wasn't there and shifted his position, so he was between Mia and Yellow Teeth. Yellow Teeth cleared his throat, spat a big glob of phlegm on the floor, then turned away. He barked an order, and the other men cleared a space for him against the far wall. Walking over, he sat down, still glaring in their direction while Naeem reached out and stroked Malak's face with grimy fingertips.

"Everything is okay, Papa is here," he murmured, then looked up into Mia's eyes, and gave a subtle nod.

44

John walked back to the front of the hotel, where the two men were still waiting.

"All okay?"

"Yeah, he was Hemin."

"Why was he following us?" Mansur asked as he watched the pickup pull out into traffic and drive off.

"Mehmet told him to keep an eye on us." John watched the vehicle disappear up the road. "He seems like a good guy. Much better than Mehmet, anyway. He actually apologized, said he was just following orders."

"Good, so what's the plan?"

John looked around and made sure there was no-one in earshot. Two men walked past, deep in conversation, and the bellhop had already gone inside with the bags. He lowered his voice, anyway.

"We leave at two-thirty a.m. He'll pick us up in the side street there." John nodded toward the street that ran along the side of the hotel, near the entrance to the parking garage. "He said to dress warmly and wear dark clothing."

"Okay." Steve slapped Mansur on the back, "Don't wear your *dishdasha.*"

"I know." Mansur grinned. "Dog's balls."

The three of them chuckled, the mood lightening. John checked his G-Shock.

"Let's get settled in. The girls won't be here until around seven-thirty. Let's eat well and get some rest. It will be a long night. We'll meet again just before seven in my room. We need to let Mia know we are coming, and she needs to let us know exactly where we can find her."

John tried to sleep, but his mind was racing, and he had given up after a while. Instead, he spent the time researching Idlib, looking at photos and maps online to try to get an idea of what to expect. It was a small agricultural town once famed for its olive oil but now only occupied the news as one of the last strongholds of the Al Qaeda backed H.T.S. John skimmed through the photos of bombed-out streets and destroyed buildings, feeling increasingly worried about the task ahead. He wondered if he had bitten off more than he could chew but quickly forced the thought back down. He had been in tough situations before, times when he had almost lost hope, but he had pushed through and succeeded. He had to hope this would be the same.

There was a tap on the door, and he checked his watch, five to seven. He slid off the bed and opened the door to see Steve and Mansur waiting in the corridor.

Standing aside to let them in, he noted the strained look on Steve's face.

"Did you get some sleep?"

"Nah."

"Mansur?"

"No, I was watching TV."

John waved to the single chair and the bed. "Make yourselves comfortable."

Mansur took the chair while Steve perched on the corner of the bed. John sat on the bed and leaned against the headboard while Steve dialed Mia's number.

"Put it on speaker."

Steve tapped the screen, and they waited for the call to connect.

Nothing happened.

Steve tried again.

Nothing.

He looked up at John.

"It's not going through."

"Keep trying. Could be a network issue."

Steve tried again... and again, but nothing happened.

"Fuck," he cursed, then threw to phone down on the bed. "What do we do now?"

"It's okay, Steve. There could be many reasons. No network, her battery flat..." John glanced at Mansur, then back to Steve. "We'll keep trying every hour."

Steve sighed, stood, and paced in front of the bed.

"What do we do? What if we can't get hold of her before we leave here? We don't know where she is. She doesn't know we're definitely coming." He threw up his hands in frustration. "Shit, fuck, shit!"

John let him vent. Steve was right. What if they couldn't get in touch with her? Would it be a wasted journey? He looked at Mansur, who had been watching calmly.

"What do you think, Mansur?"

Mansur brushed imaginary lint from the legs of his pants, took a deep breath, and said, "I think we should still try."

Steve stopped pacing and looked at him.

"How will we find her?"

Mansur shrugged. "I don't know, but if we stay here, we will never find her." He glanced at John, then back at Steve. "Mr. Steve, we are doing something good. He will show us the way."

"He? Oh..." Steve stood with his hands on his hips, staring at the carpet, then nodded.

"Okay, if you guys are happy to still proceed..." He looked up. "We've already come this far, so let's do it."

Mansur nodded. "I'm in."

They both turned and looked at John.

John chewed his lip. After what he had seen on the internet, he wasn't so bullish, but he couldn't let his friend down. Hoping he wasn't about to make the most stupid decision of his life, he nodded.

"I'm in."

45

"Who is he?"

"He calls himself Abu Mujahid," Naeem murmured as he rocked Malak. "He's my new commander after Abu Qasim was martyred."

Mia glanced across the room to where Abu Mujahid was sitting cross-legged on the floor, cleaning his weapon by the light of the single solar-powered lamp whose light failed to reach the corners of the room.

"He scares me."

"Hmmm. He fought in Iraq before coming here." Naeem nodded slowly, his eyes fixed on his baby daughter. "He's a bit crazy. He believes Allah has made him bulletproof."

"You knew about these women? Before?"

Naeem sighed. "Yes."

"They are slaves, Naeem."

"They are *Al Sabayah*. Prisoners of war." Naeem shrugged, "It is allowed."

"Allowed?" Mia looked at him in disbelief. "Allowed?" she asked again. "By whom? And besides, they are Muslim."

"They are Yazidi, not true Muslims. They are *kuffaar* and worship the devil."

Mia struggled to keep her voice down as her temper rose. She tried another tack.

"But what gives them the right to take women as slaves, to rape them? Some of them are only twelve or thirteen years old."

"They are a gift from God." Naeem sighed. "It is written. Allah, *subhanahu wa-ta'ala* says so. 'Successful are the believers who guard their chastity, except from their wives or that their right hands possess, for then they are free from blame.' We possess them, so it's allowed."

"And you believe this?" Mia's voice rose.

"Quiet." Naeem glared at her. "It's in the book."

"What has happened to you, Naeem? This is not the Islam you taught me. What happened to loving all, to doing good? The book also says, 'Do good; indeed, Allah, peace be upon him, loves the doers of good.' What about that? And the Prophet, peace be upon him, himself said, 'A man's true wealth is the good he does in this world.' Do you really think keeping young girls as slaves is doing good?"

Mia could see a vein pulsing in Naeem's neck as he glared at her.

"We are doing good. By expelling the *kuffaar* from this land. These..."—he jerked his head toward the Yazidi women—"are our reward."

"Is that what I am to you? A reward?"

"No." Naeem looked away. He glanced around the room again, at the men resting on one side, the women huddled together on the other. "You are the mother of my daughter."

"And if I didn't have a daughter?"

Naeem didn't answer, his eyes back on Malak's face, rocking her gently.

Mia sank back into angry silence. She couldn't believe how much Naeem had changed. He was so different when they met back in Australia. It seemed unreal as if she had imagined the entire thing. She again searched her heart for any trace of the love she held before, but it wasn't there. She was used to him, and she relied on him to keep her safe, but love? No way. She had to leave him. Thank Allah for Uncle Steve. She couldn't stay in a relationship like this or live in a place where human life was considered worthless if you dared to believe in something else. Uncle Steve. Oh no!

She looked at her watch again, and her heart sank. In all the activity of the fighters arriving, she had forgotten about Steve's call. It was well past the time when she was supposed to have turned the phone on.

"Naeem," she whispered.

He looked up from Malak.

"Uncle Steve was supposed to call. But..." Her eyes darted around the room. "I can't turn the phone on."

Naeem widened his eyes in warning and shook his head. "No, don't let anyone find out about the phone. Especially Abu Mujahid." He chewed his lip. "Don't worry. We'll find a way."

Naeem flinched at a sound behind him. He turned to see a fighter standing up. The man stretched, then walked over to the women. He looked down on them for a moment, then reached out his hand and grabbed one of the girls. Mia searched for her name; Nour, she was seventeen. He pulled her away from the others and dragged her to her feet. She didn't make a sound, didn't fight back, just allowed herself to be pulled along like a rag doll. He pushed her out the door and upstairs, to a chorus of jibes and sniggers from the other men.

Mia shuddered. Whatever she now thought of Naeem, at least he had kept her protected from this sort of thing.

"Why can't we be alone again? Like before. Why are these men here?"

"Keep your voice down." Naeem shot her an angry look, looking over his shoulder to make sure no-one had heard. Looking back at Mia, he continued, "It's not like before... we are..." He lowered his voice. "Losing. The Russians are coming. We all have to stick together now."

"What do you mean losing?"

"Why do you think we have to run in the middle of the night? Almost all the territory we won has been taken back by the government forces and the Russians." He looked down at the baby in his arms and whispered, "Soon, we will have nowhere to go."

"Then what will happen to us?"

Naeem didn't answer at first. When he spoke, it was a whisper, "That is why we have to leave."

Mia watched him as he stared at Malak. The sooner Uncle Steve came and got them, the better.

They stayed like that, both watching Malak sleep as one by one, the men stood and took a woman from the room, only to return a short while later, their smiling faces in complete contrast with the downcast, shamed looks of the women. The women took it without complaint, without protest, like zombies, retreating into themselves.

The only one who didn't partake was Abu Mujahid. He sat cradling his now clean AKM in his lap, and every time Mia looked up, she could feel his eyes boring into her as if he was waiting to pounce.

46

John nuzzled his face into the fold of Adriana's neck, where it joined her shoulders and held her close. She smelled of lavender and musk. Would this be the last time he would see her? He pulled back a little, so he could see her face, a tear trickling from the corner of her eye as she returned his gaze.

"Be careful, John. I want you back in one piece."

He smiled and wiped the tear away with his finger. Leaning in, he kissed her lips. Despite the smile on his face, his heart was heavy. He didn't want to leave her, but he'd made a promise. A promise to a friend who had put his own life on the line before for John, and there was no way John could let him down.

"I'll be back before you know it," he reassured her and hoped it was true. "Keep the phone on, text me, but don't call. I'll call you whenever we're in a safe place."

"Okay." Adriana sniffled.

"If all goes to plan, we will be back in two to three days. Reserve an extra room in our name for Mia and her child."

Adriana nodded, her eyes still holding his.

"As soon as I know when and how we are getting back, I will text you. I might need you to bring the minivan to pick us up. Can you do that?"

"Yes."

"Good. I know you can." John smiled and brushed a lock of hair away from her face with his right hand. "The key is with the concierge. The van is in the basement parking. It's a silver Mercedes Vito just like the one we had in Istanbul."

"Okay."

John let go of her waist and checked his watch.

"Okay, I have to go now." He leaned forward and kissed her again. "Get some sleep. Before you know it, we'll be back, and it will seem like none of this has happened."

Adriana gave a sad smile and wiped her nose with the back of her hand.

John turned, picked up the backpack leaning against the wall, and opened the door. Stepping outside, he saw Steve doing the same. He nodded in his direction, then looked back at Adriana standing in the doorway. She wrapped the hotel robe tighter around herself and stepped forward and kissed John again.

"Good luck."

"See you soon." John smiled and turned before she could see the tears in his eyes.

John walked down the corridor toward Steve and smiled at Maadhavi, who also stood in the doorway.

"Bye, Maadhavi."

She swallowed and gave a half-smile.

John looked back over his shoulder, saw Adriana still standing there, and gave her a wave. He walked ahead and waited by the lift for Steve to finish his goodbyes. The lift pinged just as Steve approached.

"Did you get hold of Mia?"

Steve shook his head, his forehead creased with worry.

John frowned. He stepped into the lift and turned around, Steve followed him in, and the doors closed behind him.

"Mansur?"

"He's gone down already."

"Good."

"What do we do, John? If we can't get hold of her?"

John looked down at the floor of the lift. What was the right thing to do, the sensible thing? The sensible thing would have been to stay at home. He looked up.

"We keep trying, Steve. We've come this far. We'll keep pushing forward." He slapped Steve on the shoulder. "Stay positive, Steve. This will work."

Steve exhaled loudly but didn't look convinced. John wasn't so sure, either.

"Send her a text once we're in the car. Tell her all is going well, and we will be there tomorrow night. If she had no signal or the battery was flat, she'll get it once the phone is working again."

"Yeah..." Steve sighed.

"Come on, Steve. We can do this."

He nodded and gave a tight smile.

The two men rode the lift down to the basement, stepping out into a dimly lit car park. Mansur was waiting for them, dressed as they were in dark cargo pants, jackets, and trekking boots. They each carried navy blue ballistic vests with Press stuck to the front and back with Velcro, and Steve carried a camera bag with a camera body and two lenses.

John looked at both the men.

"No second thoughts?"

Steve and Mansur shook their heads.

"Right, let's go then."

They walked three abreast up the parking ramp and out onto the road. The air was cool and quiet, and the road empty apart from the pickup idling by the curb. They walked over, hoisted their bags into the back, and pulled a tarpaulin over them, then climbed into the double cab, John up front with Hemin.

"Good morning, Hemin."

"Good morning." He smiled, flashing white teeth under a luxuriant mustache. He shifted in his seat, turned so he could face the back, and studied the two men sitting behind him. He seemed to be satisfied with what he saw and nodded a greeting.

Both men nodded back but stayed silent. Hemin turned back to the front and looked at John expectantly.

John gave him a nod.

"Let's go, Hemin."

47

Adriana stood in the doorway, her heart in her throat, as John walked toward the lift. She understood why he had to go. Steve had saved their lives back in Oman when they didn't even know him. Now, as a friend, when he asked for help, there was no way John could have turned down the request, but it didn't make things any easier to watch the man you love walk off into a situation from which he may not come back. Adriana blinked away tears as she saw Steve give a last kiss to Maadhavi and walk after John. The two men disappeared inside the lift, and Maadhavi turned to go back into her room.

"Are you okay?" Adriana called out.

Maadhavi looked up and gave a sad smile. Her eyes moist, she wiped her cheek and nodded.

"Do you want to come and stay with me? I don't think I will sleep much."

"Thank you." Maadhavi reached inside the doorway, removed the key card from the slot, and allowed the door to close. She walked down the corridor to Adriana's room, and

Adriana stepped aside to let her enter. Closing the door behind her, she followed Maadhavi into the room.

"Would you like a drink? I think there is something in the minibar."

Maadhavi shook her head. "No, thank you." She looked around, and Adriana waved toward the bed.

"Make yourself comfortable. It will be a long night."

Maadhavi climbed onto the bed and leaned against the headboard, pulling the covers over her legs.

Adriana climbed in beside her, and they stared at the wall at the foot of the bed.

"How do you do this?"

"What do you mean?" Adriana looked over, unsure of Maadhavi's meaning.

"I mean, wait for John, knowing he is doing something so dangerous? When... he came to India... when he saved me." She looked up at Adriana. "You knew what he was going to do?"

Adriana nodded slowly.

"Not everything." She reached over and held Maadhavi's hand. "It had to be done. Surya Patil was an evil man. He tried to kill John and me. He had to be stopped. Otherwise, we would never have been able to live in peace."

"I know all that, but..."

"Was I worried? Yes, of course, I was." Adriana smiled. "It was terrible. I couldn't sleep properly for days." She squeezed Maadhavi's hand. "But John and Steve aren't ordinary men. John has dealt with things you can never imagine. Maybe one day, he'll tell you. Steve, too. If it wasn't for him, John and I would be buried in the desert in Oman. If anyone can do this, it's them. I'm worried, too, but what's the alternative? We make them stay with us in safety because of our own fears and let his niece and her daughter die in

Syria?" She shook her head. "That would be selfish, and it would destroy the spirit of the men we love. They would regret it for the rest of their lives and probably resent us. I couldn't do it."

"Yes, I know you're right, but..." Maadhavi gulped, "If anything were to happen to Steve, I don't know what I would do. I've... I've only just found him."

"Don't worry." Adriana gave a reassuring smile. "Nothing is going to happen. Now tell me all about how you met Steve."

48

They headed southeast along the E90, which roughly followed the route of the River Tigris. The roads were empty, only the occasional goods vehicle trundling along in the slow lane or passing in the opposite direction. John lowered his window a little to savor the cool night air.

He turned his attention to the man sitting beside him. Perhaps in his late thirties, he had the weather-beaten face of someone who spent a lot of his life outdoors. His handshake had been strong and firm, and he exuded a feeling of confidence. Right or wrong, John had liked him instantly, in complete contrast to his boss.

"Do you do this a lot?"

Hemin glanced at him, then looked in the mirror, studying the men behind him, deciding how much to say.

"I have done it before, yes."

They drove in silence for a while, then Hemin asked, "Why do you want to go there? I saw your vests. It says Press, but..." He glanced sideways at John. "I don't think you are press."

"Why not?"

Hemin snorted. "Press don't need to enter Syria illegally. They cross the border at the normal crossing."

"Mehmet didn't tell you?"

"No."

John remained silent. Perhaps there was a reason Mehmet hadn't told his man why they were crossing.

Hemin kept quiet for a while.

"You are not fighters. I've seen the fighters, they are different." He glanced in the rear mirror again, then looked at John. "Who are you?"

John didn't know what to say. He felt he could trust the man but was reluctant to give too much information. Steve saved him from making a decision.

"Hemin, right?" Steve leaned forward and spoke from the back. "I'm Steve. My niece is over there with her baby. Her baby is sick. We are going to rescue her. We have nothing to do with any government, Al Qaeda, or ISIS, or whatever it's called in these parts. We just want to bring a young girl and her daughter to safety. Do you understand me?"

Hemin frowned and nodded slowly, his eyes alternating between the road ahead and the image of Steve in his rear-view mirror.

"The girl is like a daughter to me, so if you or your boss are planning any monkey business, and you prevent me from saving her life, I will come back here and rip your balls off and stuff them down your throat." He sat back in his seat, scowling at the back of Hemin's head.

Mansur leaned across and whispered, "Monkey business?"

"I'll explain later."

John turned to look at Steve with raised eyebrows. He

wasn't sure how to tell him to calm down without actually saying it, but Steve seemed to understand. He took a deep breath, exhaled slowly, then stared out the window into the darkness.

John turned back to the front and watched the road, hoping Steve's outburst wouldn't have a detrimental effect. A sign for the Iraqi border flashed past on his right, and he hoped they were heading in the right direction.

"How old is the girl?" Hemin asked after a tense couple of minutes.

"Twenty-four," John replied.

"And the baby?"

"Maybe eighteen months."

Hemin shook his head and muttered something in Turkish. His eyes moved to the rear-view mirror.

"You can trust me. Don't worry."

49

They followed the highway for twenty minutes, at one point passing a long line of semi-trailers parked along the side of the road.

"They will cross into Iraq in the morning," Hemin said by way of explanation. "The border gate is about fifteen kilometers ahead."

"Is that where we are going?"

Hemin grinned and shook his head. "Wait and see."

"Hemin, there is something I don't understand. The Turkish government is supporting the fight against the Syrian government?"

Hemin raised one hand off the steering wheel at the same time as he shrugged. "It's complicated."

"Hmmm, everyone seems to say that."

Hemin glanced across at John.

"These matters are beyond people like you and me. These are the games of our leaders." He shook his head and went back to looking at the road ahead. "The Syrian people are good. We have traded with them for thousands of years. But..." He sighed. "Power, money, greed..."

"Religion," added John.

"No, no, no," Hemin protested vehemently. "What is happening there is not about religion. Religion is the... how do you say? Tool. The fight in Syria is about oil, money, control."

John was beginning to like Hemin, confirming his earlier impression. This simple working man, dressed in farmer's clothes, knew a lot more about what was really happening than so many so-called educated people.

"Who do you think is fighting the Syrian government? Freedom fighters? No, it is Al Qaeda, Daesh. And who do you think is funding them, training them, supplying them with weapons?"

"Turkey."

"Not just Turkey. America, England, Saudi Arabia. All the people who tell us Al Qaeda and Daesh are our enemies."

"How do you know?"

Hemin laughed. "I've seen it with my own eyes."

John chewed his lip and stared out the window. He wasn't surprised. He already knew the world was a shitty place. He turned back to Hemin.

"But isn't Assad's government a bad government?"

Hemin shrugged. "Whose government is good? I think you are English, no?"

"Yes."

"Can you honestly say your government is good? That it has never done any wrong? How many countries has it been involved in, peacekeeping?" He said the last word with a sneer. "Look, no government is perfect, but at least there was peace in Syria." He exhaled noisily, his eyes darting to the rear-view mirror, and back to the road in front. "How many people have to die because of the games of our leaders?"

"So, why do you do this?" Steve asked from the back.

Hemin's eyes met Steve's in the rear-view mirror.

"This?"

"This." Steve gestured around the car. "Taking people across the border. Smuggling."

"You are judging me?"

"Maybe."

John turned in his seat and gave Steve a warning look.

"It's easy to judge from afar, but if you live here, you will see it's not so simple." Hemin slowed. "If we go straight, it's the crossing into Iraq, but we go this way." He took a narrow and unlit exit road leading off into the countryside.

"In the old days, before the war, a long time before the war, we used to go back and forth." He pointed up the road. "Ahead is the river. On the other side is Syria. But the borders are all political. This side and that side is Kurdistan. I am Kurdish. Half of my family lives here, the other half there. But there is nothing over there now. Only death and destruction. I take food, medicine."

"That's all you take?" John asked.

Hemin paused. "No." He glanced at John, then back at Steve. "No, it's not. But the other... things pay for the food and medicine."

"And Mehmet?"

Hemin didn't answer immediately. John saw his eyes narrow a little, then relax as if Hemin was thinking of what he could say.

"He is my boss," came the eventual answer. "He... arranges things."

They sank back into silence, and Hemin concentrated on the road ahead. There was nothing to see, no lights, very few buildings, just the narrow asphalt road in the twin beams of light from the pickup.

They had driven for ten minutes without seeing anyone when they spotted headlights approaching ahead. Hemin slowed a little, and John noticed his grip tightening on the steering wheel. The lights got nearer, then flicked to full beam. John shielded his eyes with his hand, and Hemin cursed as he turned his head to the side, trying to preserve some of his night vision. He slowed even more, then the sky lit up with the red and blue strobe of police lights.

"Shit," John cursed, and the three men sat up straight as Hemin pulled to the side of the road.

"It's okay. I will speak to them."

John clenched his jaw and looked back at Steve and Mansur, both men tense and upright.

Hemin wound down his window as the vehicle pulled alongside. A powerful flashlight switched on, and the beam played over them, so bright, they had to look away. The flashlight switched off, and once the spots cleared from his eyes, John could see the occupants, two lean, hard-looking men in uniform. Their hair was cropped close to their scalps, and their eyes were wary.

Hemin spoke rapidly in Turkish, the driver of the car nodding while his partner stared at John. John's pulse rate was climbing rapidly. Would it all end here? On the side of a road in the middle of rural Turkey? He willed himself to relax; they had done nothing wrong yet. They had visas for Turkey and were just out for a night drive through the countryside. The driver looked over Hemin's shoulder at John, sending his heart rate sky high again. John forced a smile and nodded a greeting. The policeman studied John's face for a moment, then nodded back. He asked Hemin a couple of questions, then turned to his partner and said something. As he turned back, Hemin reached out a hand through the window, and John thought he glimpsed something in Hemin's hand. The policeman shook his hand, and when he let go, made a fist, and quickly dropped it below the window. He said something, gave a nod to Hemin, then drove away. John exhaled slowly and realizing his fingertips had been digging into the seat cushion, relaxed his grip. He leaned forward, so he could see in the wing mirror and watched the red taillights disappear up the road.

Sitting back in his seat, he looked over at Hemin. Hemin grinned, released the handbrake, and pulled out onto the road. John looked back over his shoulder at Mansur, calm as ever, and gave him a nod, while Steve puffed air out through pursed lips.

"Fuck me."

Hemin glanced in the rear-view mirror.

"I told you that you could trust me."

"Yeah." Steve leaned forward and slapped him on the shoulder. "Thanks, mate."

"Australian?"

"Yeah."

"Good people."

"I'm beginning to like you, Hemin."

Ten minutes later, Hemin slowed and turned right, across the road onto a dirt track which led off the road into a field. He pulled to a stop and switched off the engine.

"Come."

They climbed out of the pickup and stretched their backs and legs. Darkness surrounded them, and the sky above hung low and thick like a blanket. The only sound came from the river and the ticking of the cooling engine.

"Take your bags and follow me. We cross here."

The three men grabbed their bags and vests and

followed Hemin down a dirt path. John hung back and pulled out his phone. He closed one eye to preserve his night vision and shielded the light from the phone screen with his hand. He opened his messaging app and shared the location with Adriana before slipping the phone back into his pocket, then moved to catch up with the others. They walked slowly and cautiously, mindful of keeping their footing in the darkness. After about fifty meters, they reached the riverbank, the water flowing slowly past in inky blackness. A stone pier glowed pale in the ambient light, and Hemin led them onto it, then knelt down and pulled on a rope tied to an iron ring set in the stone. They gathered around him and watched as he pulled a small boat toward the pier.

"In the old days, we used to cross here," he explained in a low voice. As the boat bumped against the pier, he looked back. "I can take two at a time."

John looked at Steve. "I'll go first with Mansur."

"Okay."

John climbed into the boat, sat down, then reached up as Mansur passed him his backpack and two vests.

As Mansur prepared to climb into the boat, Hemin asked, "Mansur?"

"Yes."

"Where are you from?"

Mansur glanced at John. John gave a slight nod.

"Oman."

"You speak Arabic?"

"Yes."

"That is good. It will be easier for you all over there."

Mansur climbed in and sat beside John while Hemin passed the rope to Steve, then climbed in and sat facing the two men. He removed two oars, fitted them into the oarlocks, and nodded at Steve. Steve threw the end of the rope into the boat and watched as the boat headed across the river.

The water was slow-moving and calm, and it seemed only a moment before John saw the other bank approaching, another stone pier catching what little moonlight filtered through the clouds. Hemin headed a little upstream of the pier, glancing over his shoulder now and then to check his direction, then stowed the oars and allowed the flow of the water to bring the boat back down and alongside the pier. It bumped gently against the stonework, and he reached out and grabbed hold of an iron ring, pulling the boat close to the pier.

"Okay," he murmured, and John stood carefully, hoisted himself up onto the stonework, then turned to take the bag and vests from Mansur. Mansur climbed out after him, and they both turned to look at Hemin.

"Wait here. I'll be back soon," he said quietly. "Don't worry. It is safe here." He gestured for them to crouch down. "But stay low."

Using the ring, he pulled the boat out into the flow of water and effortlessly, with the skill of someone who had done it many times before, turned the boat around and disappeared into the blackness.

John stood and looked around. Just like the other side, there was nothing to be seen, just a dirt track leading up and over a slight rise. There was silence all around, nothing but the gentle lap of water against the stonework. He removed his jacket, picked up his vest, and slipped it on before putting his jacket back on over the top. Mansur copied him, then they stared into the blackness, waiting for Hemin's return.

"There he is."

John strained to see, but his vision was never a match for Mansur's. He had discovered that back in the Omani desert when the Bedouin had seen things well before they were visible to John.

A moment later, though, he saw the boat appearing out of the darkness and watched as Hemin guided it across the current and alongside the pier. He threw the rope to John, who pulled the boat close and held it against the pier as Steve passed his camera bag and vest up, then climbed out. Hemin followed him out, securing the boat to the iron ring as Steve donned his bulletproof vest.

Hemin moved closer to them, then pointed along the pier and up the dirt track that led over the rise.

"Follow that track for about two kilometers. Don't take any turn, just go straight. You will reach a village. They are honorable people. You will be safe there. Ask for a man called Ferhad Hussein. Tell him my name." Hemin turned to Mansur. "He doesn't speak English, only Kurdish and Arabic."

"Okay."

"He has a taxi. He will take you where you need to go."

"Idlib?"

"Idlib?" Hemin raised an eyebrow and shook his head. "No, that's not possible. He can probably take you as far as Manbij. That's still in Kurdish territory, but... be careful. Idlib province is not a good place right now."

"We know." John reached into his pocket and pulled out a wad of notes he had prepared earlier. He held it out to Hemin. "Thank you, Hemin."

Hemin took it, pulled out his phone and with the light from the screen, checked the notes. He then licked his thumb and counted them. Satisfied, he looked up.

"Thank you."

John reached out and shook him by the hand.

"Thank you, Hemin."

Hemin held onto his hand.

"How will you get back?"

John hesitated; he liked the man but wasn't sure if he could trust him completely. Erring on the side of caution, he replied, "We have a plan."

Hemin studied John's face, then nodded slowly.

"Give me your phone."

John frowned.

Hemin smiled. "It's okay, I will give you my number."

John reached into his pocket, passed over his phone, Hemin entered his number, then handed it back.

"If you need anything, anything at all, you call me. Okay?"

"Thank you, Hemin."

Hemin turned to Steve and held out his hand. "Good luck, Aussie. I hope you are successful."

"Cheers, mate."

To Mansur he said, *"Toroh wo terjah bel salama.* Come back safely."

"Inshallah. God willing."

Hemin turned and climbed down into the boat while John untied the rope. Hemin turned his wrist and looked at his watch.

"Sunrise will be in two-and-a-half hours." He pointed up the track. "Over that hill are some trees. Wait there until the sun comes up, then go to the village. It will take you thirty minutes." He turned to look back across the river. "Don't wait here. Sometimes, the police check this crossing."

John tossed the rope into the boat.

"Thank you again, Hemin."

Hemin nodded and pushed the boat out into the current while the three men stood nervously on the pier and watched him disappear into the darkness.

50

"Right, let's get out of here." John hoisted the backpack onto his back, waited for Steve to do the same, then led the way up the track away from the pier. There was just enough ambient light for him to pick out the track, but only just. He kept to the side, close to the trees, although there was no sound of life from anywhere. He walked slowly, placing his feet carefully. The last thing he needed to do was turn an ankle before they had gone anywhere. Pausing briefly to look back, he saw Steve and Mansur following quietly behind him, keeping a two-meter spacing between them and also keeping close to the side of the track.

The moon broke free from the cloud cover, and for the first time, John could see the river they had crossed. Twin beams of light from a vehicle traced the road on the Turkish side, and in the distance, he could just make out the black silhouette of the Zagros Mountain Range. Turning back to the track, he continued walking, eager to get out of sight of the road. The men crested the rise and followed the track as it divided plowed fields. Once out of sight of the road, John stopped and waited for the others to catch up.

"Let's rest up here until first light." He nodded to the side of the track. Stepping carefully between the plowed furrows he led the way to a small clump of trees about fifty meters from the track.

Easing off his backpack, he smoothed out a patch of ground with the toe of his boot and sat down, Steve and Mansur doing the same. John unfastened the top flap of his pack, pulled out a flask of coffee he had brought from the hotel, and unscrewed the top before taking a sip and passing it on. It was only lukewarm, but it would have to do. He tilted his wrist and peered at the luminous face of his G-Shock.

"We've got about two hours. Why don't you get your heads down and rest? I'll take the first watch. Mansur, I'll wake you in forty minutes."

Mansur whispered his agreement and stretched out on the ground, using his arm as a pillow. Almost immediately, his breath slowed and deepened as he fell asleep.

Steve remained sitting.

"Not sleepy?"

"Nuh."

John peered at him through the moonlight. "Are you okay?"

"Yeah... no, not really." Steve exhaled, "I've still not heard from Mia."

"You sent the text?"

"Yup."

"It's still too early. Don't worry, Steve. She'll be asleep now. You should, too."

"I can't mate." He jerked his head toward Mansur. "I wish I could be as relaxed as this guy."

"Huh." John smiled in the darkness. "He does seem pretty chilled." John stowed the flask back in his pack. "Maybe it's his faith?"

"Inshallah?"

"Yeah. If God wills it." John made a face. "It seems to work... for him at least. No need to worry because it's all God's will."

"Hmmm."

John heard the cynicism. "You don't believe?"

"No." Steve paused. "I don't think so. I see Maadhavi praying in the morning to that one with the elephant head..."

"Ganesha."

"Ah, yeah. Well, anyway, it seems to give her peace, but no, not for me."

"Well, it's certainly giving Mansur some peace."

"Yeah, the bugger is cool as a cucumber. How about you, John? What do you believe?"

"Me?" John shook his head. "No, I don't think there's a god. There's too much shit going on in the world." He sighed and shifted, so he could remove a pebble from under his thigh. "I think people just want a reason for their problems. What if there's no reason?"

"Yeah, maybe you're right."

"Who knows? But one thing's for sure. If we sit around here, waiting for God to help us, we will be disappointed. It's up to us and good people like our friend Mansur here." John smiled in the darkness, "Anyway, better get some rest, Steve. It's going to be a long day."

"Yeah, I'll try." Steve stretched out, resting his head on his pack. "See you in a bit."

John nodded, forgetting Steve couldn't really see him. Staring across the field, he thought about what he'd said. He meant it. Sitting around, hoping some greater being would help them rescue Mia and her daughter was a fool's errand. When he looked back over all the things he had experienced in his life—danger, loss, death—it was his own willpower and determination that got him through... and good people. John believed in good people. Mansur and Steve were good people, and he liked to think Hemin was another one. He had been so far, but time would tell. In life, as long as you met more good people than bad people, you were ahead. God had nothing to do with it.

51

John's eyes were beginning to droop when his watch pinged. He reached over and shook Mansur, the Bedouin waking immediately. He sat up, nodded at John, and looked around.

"Anything?"

"All quiet."

"Good. Sleep now."

"I will." John stretched out, adjusted the pack under his head, and within seconds, he was fast asleep.

It seemed like only a minute later when he felt a hand on his arm. Opening his eyes, he looked up to see Steve kneeling beside him.

"It's time."

John sat up and looked across the fields. The sky had lightened, turning grey as the sun began its appearance. He spotted movement and saw a rabbit dart from beneath a tree and bound across the furrows before disappearing into the ground. An owl hooted from the branches, and elsewhere, birds began their early morning chorus. John sensed Mansur stirring and looked over and smiled. Reaching behind him, he pulled his pack forward and removed the flask, taking a swig before passing it on.

"Cold, but the caffeine will help."

He got to his feet and bent forward, hearing the pops and cracks of his spine, then twisted side to side and shook his legs out. Steve passed the flask back, and John stowed it away, before hoisting the pack onto his shoulders. He retrieved his phone and sent a quick text to Adriana. *All okay. In Syria. Heading to Idlib. See you soon.* Slipping the phone back in his pocket, he looked at Steve and Mansur.

"Ready?"

The two men nodded, and John led the way across the field toward the track, the going much easier now they could see. They headed along the track toward the rising sun, the sky turning from grey to red and orange.

The sunrise call to prayer from a distant mosque carried across the fields, mingling with the chirping of birds and the distant barking of dogs as the area began its day. As they walked and the sun rose, they warmed up, and it wasn't long before they had stripped off their outer jackets, exposing their bulletproof vests with Press emblazoned across the front and back. Steve stopped and removed a camera from his bag and slung it over his shoulder, completing the look, while John looked on approvingly. Steve looked the part, although that early in the morning, there was little sign of life from the farmhouses and huts they passed.

The road followed a ridgeline with fields stretching out to their right and the land sloping away to their left toward the river, the slopes more lush and greener than those on the right side of the road.

The buildings became more frequent the closer they got to the village until the fields disappeared from sight, and the houses closed in around them. A man approached from the opposite direction, took a quick look at them, and averted his eyes as he passed. They were strangers, and it was safer to avoid them.

The three men reached a junction, and not sure where to go, John suggested, Mansur go and enquire about Ferhad Hussein and his taxi. He and Steve shrugged off their backpacks and leaned against the wall while Mansur crossed the street to a tiny bakery. John angled his face toward the sun, feeling the warmth on his face, and kept one eye on Mansur while Steve fiddled with his camera and tried to look casual.

After a few minutes, the baker stepped out of his shop onto the street and pointed down the road. Judging by the hand signals, John guessed he was giving Mansur directions. A minute later, Mansur returned with a big smile and a handful of flatbread.

"We'll find him down that way." Mansur nodded in the direction the baker had pointed, then handed them each a piece of bread. "Try this. He just made it."

The bread was soft and still warm from the oven, and the three men chewed away as they walked down the road.

"How was he?" John asked. "Suspicious?"

"No," Mansur said through a mouthful of bread. He swallowed and continued, "He asked who we worked for, so I told him we work for the BBC, and he accepted it."

"Good. Let's hope it continues. But next time if someone asks, tell them we work for the Portuguese newspaper, Público. Our story has to match our press passes."

"No problem." He pointed toward a street on their right. "This way."

They walked on for another five-hundred meters until they entered a village square where, at the far end, an ancient Olive tree provided shade for a line of yellow taxis. Mansur walked ahead and peered inside each one. They were all empty, and there was no sign of the drivers. He turned and shrugged.

"No-one here."

A movement in John's peripheral vision caught his attention, and he turned his head to see a man appearing from behind a wall, zipping up his pants. John looked at Mansur and jerked his head in the man's direction. Mansur nodded and walked over as a thin cat with half a tail scampered across his path and hid behind the taxis.

A twitch from an upper floor window caught John's eye, and he looked up to see an elderly woman watching them before she stepped back out of sight, pulling the shutters closed behind her.

After a brief discussion, Mansur returned.

"He said Ferhad would be here soon. That's his car there, the third one."

They turned to look. It was small, about the size of a Corolla, and there wasn't a body panel that wasn't dented or scraped. Thick layers of dust hinted at its heavy mileage, and the tires seemed to be lacking tread.

"It will be a tight squeeze."

"Yeah, well, beggars can't be choosers," John replied.

"This guy said he can take us," Mansur nodded toward the man who was now smoking and leaning on the hood of the first car in the row.

John looked at Steve, "What do you think?"

Steve looked back at the taxi and shrugged.

"I think we should stick with Hemin's guy. He said we could trust him."

"I agree." John turned to Mansur. "We'll wait."

52

The phone buzzed, and Adriana opened her eyes. She reached for the phone on the bedside table and looked at the screen. *All okay. In Syria. Heading to Idlib. See you soon.*

She heard Maadhavi stirring beside her, and she looked over and smiled.

"They're okay. They're in Syria and heading to Idlib."

"That's good." Maadhavi rubbed her eyes and sat up. "What time is it?"

Adriana peered at the screen. "Just after six-thirty."

They had talked for a while once the men left before finally dropping off to a fitful sleep. Adriana kept waking and checking the phone for messages and in between, had been troubled by disturbing dreams. Maadhavi must have been going through the same thing as she had tossed and turned beside her.

"I'm going to close my eyes again for another half-hour."

"Okay." Adriana put the phone back on the bedside table. She doubted she would get back to sleep, she was too wound up. Instead, she tried imagining where John was but had nothing to compare it to. She'd never been to Syria and thankfully, never to a conflict zone. She believed if anyone could pull this off, it would be John, but it didn't stop her worrying. She wouldn't relax until she knew he was safely back on the Turkish side of the border.

Her life had changed so much since that day in Bangkok when she first met him. Yes, there had been danger, but her life seemed fuller, and she felt more alive as if she had been living life in black and white before she met him. He was a unique man, loving and caring, yet with a steel core. He had his moments, times when he would withdraw into himself, nights when he would wake up covered in sweat, troubled by memories from the past, but she loved him more than anything else in the world.

Her eyelids slowly drooped shut, and she drifted off into a dreamless sleep.

She woke about an hour later, feeling a little more rested. Maadhavi was already awake.

"Did you manage to sleep some more?"

"Yes." Maadhavi yawned. "Still tired, though."

"It will be a long day." Adriana sat up in the bed and swung her legs over the side. "Why don't we have a nice breakfast and see what the town has to offer? I don't think I can stay here the whole day. I need to keep my mind busy."

"Yes, good idea. If I sit in the room, I'll spend the entire day worrying." Maadhavi rolled off the bed and stood. "Is there anything to see here?"

"Well, it's an ancient town. The Romans were here, as was Alexander the Great, and Noah's Ark is supposed to have ended up in the mountains near here, but I don't know if much remains of the town. There was a terrible siege four or five years ago, and much of the town was destroyed."

"Really? Why?"

"The people here are mainly Kurds, and there was conflict between them and the Turkish government."

"Oh, no."

"Yes, mankind never seems to be able to live in peace."

"No," Maadhavi sighed. "Well, I'll have a shower and knock on your door in say thirty minutes?"

"Perfect."

Adriana sat back on the bed as the door closed behind Maadhavi. She knew Maadhavi was worried, and the best thing to do was to keep her mind occupied. Adriana needed it, too. The confident and relaxed front she was showing Maadhavi was just that... a front. She too needed to keep her mind busy, or her thoughts would take her on a rapid downward spiral. She had learned this, waiting for John to come back from India. Worrying helped neither of them. She had to keep busy.

53

Mia had been awake for half an hour, listening to the sounds of the fighters stirring and chatting among themselves. She kept her eyes closed, pretending to sleep. After a while, she felt Naeem get up, and she pulled Malak closer.

The men's voices slowly reduced, and she opened one eye, raising her head slowly to look around the room. The men had all left. Opening both eyes, she sat up. Some of the other women were awake but showed no signs of getting up. Her stomach growled as it did every morning. It had been weeks since her stomach had been full. Perhaps the men would bring back food, but she didn't hold much hope. Most of what she had, she gave to Malak, anyway.

Mia looked over at Nour, who lay on her back, her eyes open, face expressionless, staring at the ceiling. Mia couldn't imagine what the poor girl had gone through... what any of the women had gone through. She suppressed a shudder and slowly got to her feet as if she was going to the toilet. Stepping over the bodies, she made her way to the door and down the stairs to the first floor. Entering the room, she gagged at the overwhelming smell of stale urine and feces, pulling her *hijab* across her face to cover her mouth and nose. Moving away from the door and to the side, so anyone passing would not see her, she squatted, facing away from the door. She arranged her *abaya* for modesty as if she was going to the toilet, then reached underneath and retrieved the phone.

Powering it on, she checked the battery indicator; ten percent. She breathed a sigh of relief. It should last if she was careful. The phone searched for a signal, then vibrated in her hand—a message. Opening it, she read the words on the screen, and her heart leapt. She couldn't believe it. She read it again—Uncle Steve. She checked the date on the message, and her stomach did a little dance. Tonight, he would be here tonight! She permitted herself to smile, an expression that almost felt unnatural. Pressing reply, she typed a message, then pressed send. Oh, she was so excited, she had forgotten to tell him where to find her. She gazed at the wall in front of her. She needed to think of somewhere. He couldn't come to the house, it was too risky. But where?

The streets were unrecognizable from each other, just rubble-strewn paths between shells of buildings. How would he find her? Even more important, how would she and Malak get out? She would have to find a way and quickly. Looking down at the phone again, she remembered something they had passed the night they arrived—the garden opposite the stadium. That was the best landmark. She started typing again.

Her fingers froze in mid-message as she heard a scuff, and a stone kicked behind her. Keeping the phone out of sight, she turned her head and looked over her shoulder, and her heart froze. Standing in the doorway, leaning against the frame, was Abu Mujahid.

54

They waited for almost thirty minutes. They could hear sounds of activity as the village awoke, but there were few signs of people, and those they saw were mainly elderly.

"Have you noticed there aren't any young people around?" John asked as a dog approached cautiously and sniffed the air.

"Yeah." Steve shaded his eyes against the sun, now just above the level of the buildings. "Maybe it's too early. You know how youngsters like to sleep in."

"Ha." John grinned as he watched the dog cock its leg and pee on the rear wheel of a taxi.

"They've all left."

John and Steve turned to look over at Mansur, who was leaning against the car.

"The baker told me. The young people have either joined the fighting or crossed the border into Turkey." He nodded toward the buildings, "The old people, they cannot run, they cannot fight." He shrugged. "So, they stay." He suddenly straightened, and John followed the direction of his gaze.

"Is that him?"

"Maybe."

They watched an older man cross the square. He eyed them warily and spoke to the other taxi driver. He nodded, still frowning, and walked over.

Mansur stepped forward, his arms open wide to his sides, a big smile on his face. He spoke in Arabic, but John recognized the words Ferhad and Hemin. His face relaxed, and he shook hands with Mansur. Mansur appeared to make introductions. John heard his name and Steve's, then Ferhad stepped forward and shook their hands and waved toward his taxi.

Mansur turned to John. "He said Hemin called him. Told him everything. He just wasn't sure it was us."

"Oh. Is that good or bad?"

"Good. He will help us. He'll take us as far as Manbij but can't take us any further. It's not safe for him."

John frowned briefly, then nodded. "Okay. Hemin warned us. We'll worry about the rest of the way when we get there. Tell him okay."

"How much do you want to pay?"

"I'll leave that up to you, Mansur." John moved, so Mansur was between him and Ferhad, then reached into his pocket and pulled out a handful of U.S. dollars. He lowered his voice in case Ferhad could understand English. "Take this. The price doesn't matter, but don't let him know that."

Mansur nodded and went back to Ferhad while John walked around to the other side of the car, opened the rear door, and looked over the roof at Steve.

"Keep your bag with you. Don't put it in the trunk."

"You don't trust him?"

"I don't know, but best to be safe."

Both men levered themselves into the rear of the car while Mansur paid Ferhad, and they both climbed into the front. John's knees were wedged into the back of the driver's seat, and Steve wasn't much better off. John slipped the bag off his knees and jammed it into the space between them, and Steve placed his on top.

"What kind of car is this, Mansur?" Steve grumbled. "I've seen bigger go-karts."

Mansur chuckled. "It's a Saipa. Made in Iran. Very cheap."

"Not surprised. Made out of a bloody soup can." Steve turned to John. "How far do we have to go?"

"About four hundred and fifty kilometers."

"Great."

The car started on the fourth attempt, Ferhad revving it until it settled into a noisy idle. He looked across at Mansur.

"Yalla."

Ferhad grinned, and with a wave of his arm out the open window toward the other driver, he pulled out of the square.

John wound down his window and allowed the crisp morning air to flow over him while Mansur conversed with Ferhad.

"There's some money on the backseat," John said in English. He shook his head at Steve, who was looking at him with a puzzled look on his face. He leaned over and said in a low voice, "Just checking to see if he speaks English."

Steve grinned. "I'd say that's a no."

John smiled back and tapped Mansur on the arm.

"Ask him how long it will take?"

Mansur spoke for a while, then turned to look back. "He says it will take around nine to ten hours. It will depend on the checkpoints."

"Are there many checkpoints?"

"He said yes, but not to worry. He drives this way a lot. He said he is Kurdish, and the road until Manbij is controlled by the Kurds."

"That's a relief," John muttered to Steve.

"What do we do when we get to Manbij? We still don't know how to get to Idlib or where she is."

"Check the phone again, maybe she's seen your message."

Steve shifted his weight to one side and retrieved the phone from his pocket and peered at the screen.

"Still nothing. Shit!" He banged his fist on his leg and stared out the side window.

"Hey, Steve, we'll work something out. We've got this far. Just keep checking the phone."

Steve kept looking out the window but nodded. John looked back at the road ahead. He hoped he was right.

55

From the village of Zuhajrijja, a dirt road headed west toward the town of Al-Malikiyah through fields, stretching off to both sides as far as the eye could see, acres and acres of brown and green patchwork. There were few people to be seen, and those they did see were, as in Zuhajrijja, mostly elderly.

After around fifteen kilometers, Ferhad muttered something to Mansur.

Mansur nodded and turned in his seat.

"We are approaching the town of Al-Malikiyah, and there is a checkpoint coming. Should be okay, it's just a local militia, but he said hold your passports and press cards up so they can see them." He turned his head even more. "Mr. Steve, no photos."

Steve exchanged a nervous glance with John, and both men removed their passports and press cards.

John took a series of deep breaths in an effort to keep his increasing heart rate under control as Ferhad slowed and joined onto the end of a line of slow-moving traffic, dusty pickups and battered sedans like theirs. John peered through the windshield toward the checkpoint. Large concrete blocks with Arabic script spray-painted across them blocked the road. He could see a white pickup with a man standing in the rear. In front of him, resting on a bipod on the roof was a machine gun, pointed in their direction. At the end of a long aerial, a yellow flag with a red star in the middle fluttered in the wind. John swallowed and tugged on his bulletproof vest, making sure it was secure. The cars edged forward, and as they got closer, John saw three men with shotguns, leather jackets, and bandoliers of ammunition strung around their bodies. Two approached the car in front, one on each side while the third stood in front, his shotgun aimed at the driver, only moving out of the way when the other men gave the vehicle the all-clear to move on.

John heard Steve exhale loudly and glanced across.

"It'll be okay, Steve. Don't worry."

Ferhad edged forward and pulled up at the checkpoint. He called out a greeting to the man on his left while on the passenger side, the other man approached and looked inside at Mansur. He saw Mansur's Omani passport and spoke to him in Arabic. Mansur replied, and John recognized the name of Adriana's paper. The man nodded, stepped to the side, and stared at John, then glanced at the passport and press card he was holding up. He nodded and took a step back, waiting for his partner to finish talking to Ferhad.

There was a buzzing sound from somewhere in the car, but John ignored it, his sole focus on what was happening outside.

John tuned into Ferhad's conversation. Was he helping them or betraying them? He couldn't follow what they were saying but observed the body language, trying to get a feel for what was going on. Ferhad was laughing, and the man on his side seemed relaxed, his left hand on the roof of the car, the shotgun in his right pointing at the ground. His beard hid the lower part of his face, but his eyes looked happy. He slapped Ferhad on the shoulder and stepped back, nodding at the man in front of the car who stepped aside. Ferhad waved out the window and pulled away slowly.

Nothing was said for five-hundred meters until Steve exclaimed, "Fuck me! I need to change my underwear."

John realized he had been holding his breath and exhaled, the tension flowing out of him with his breath.

Mansur was saying something to Ferhad, and Ferhad burst into laughter. Mansur turned to look at Steve,

"I told him about your underwear."

"Thanks, mate. You're a true friend."

"He said, don't worry, these people all know him."

"Hmmm, I hope so."

John heard buzzing again, and he fished his phone out of his pocket and looked at the screen. Nothing. Frowning, he turned to Steve,

"Did your phone buzz?"

"I don't know, mate. I didn't notice."

"Check it. I heard buzzing."

Steve retrieved his phone and looked at the screen. He grinned.

"It's Mia. She's okay."

56

"There's another message." Steve excitedly scrolled down. "She says she'll wait for us in front of the park opposite the stadium tonight." He puffed out air in relief and looked at John. It was the happiest John had seen him since he first arrived in Dubai.

"See, Steve, I told you things would work out." John leaned forward. "Mansur, ask him if he knows where the stadium is in Idlib. We have to go there."

Mansur spoke to Ferhad, asked a few questions, then turned back to John.

"He does. The *Al-Baladi* Stadium. He said everyone knows it. Before the war, they used to play football there."

Ferhad continued talking with Mansur, interjecting with a question now and then before Mansur turned in his seat to look at John. His face was troubled.

"What?"

"He says Hemin told him why we are here. He thinks it's... how do you say... noble? But he says we won't be able to get there. It's impossible."

"Why not?"

"That area is controlled by *Hay'at Tahrir al-Shams*. The enemy. There's heavy fighting around there between the government and them. He says we can't cross over. He says even if we could, they will probably kill us."

"Well, we sort of knew that, anyway."

Mansur nodded, his eyes moving from John to Steve and back again.

"So, what do we do?"

John glanced at Steve, whose face was set in a worried frown.

"Ask him how far it is from Manbij to Idlib."

Mansur asked, then replied, "Around one hundred and fifty kilometers."

"Hmmm, okay, let me think about it. There will be a way. There always is." John looked at his watch and settled back in his seat. "We have a lot of time yet before we need to worry about it."

"How can you be so relaxed?" Steve asked.

John looked over and studied Steve's worried face.

"I'm not relaxed at all, but if I sit here worrying, I won't come up with a solution. At least we are in the country and heading in the right direction. Two days ago, we couldn't have imagined this." He gestured around the car. "So, let's just keep moving forward and take it one step at a time."

"Mr. John is right." Mansur agreed. *"Inshallah,* we will find a way."

Steve nodded reluctantly. "So, what do I tell her?"

John thought for a moment. "Tell her to hang on. There's no point in her waiting for us at the stadium when we don't know yet when and how we'll get there. Say we are on our way and will let her know later when and where to meet."

"Okay." Steve started typing a message into his phone.

"Mansur?"

Mansur turned in his seat. "Yes."

"Ask him if he can take us any closer than Manbij?"

Mansur and Ferhad spoke for a while, Ferhad shaking his head and looking more and more uncomfortable.

Mansur turned back to face them.

"He says okay, he can maybe take us to Arima. It's another fifteen kilometers, but he said it would be risky. More checkpoints, maybe fighting."

"Okay." John stared at the back of Mansur's seat, thinking of what to do next. "Tell him okay and ask him if he can wait for us, maybe a day or so. We'll double his fare. What do you think, Mansur?"

"I don't think he'll mind. From what he's told me, he doesn't have much business."

John nodded and waited for Mansur to translate.

"He says he will wait for one day. If we are not back by then, he will leave."

"Good, thanks." John turned his head to look out the window as Ferhad guided the car along the road that bypassed the town. From a distance, the town looked unremarkable, the outskirts dusty and rubbish-strewn.

"We'll have to put the bags in the back to make room for them," John spoke aloud, as he thought.

Steve looked away from his window. "But what about the checkpoints? She won't have any papers."

"I was thinking about that. Let's remember where the checkpoints are. On the way back, we'll stop before each one, and she'll have to climb into the trunk until we are through the checkpoint." He turned to look at Steve and grimaced. "I know it sounds horrible, but I think it's the safest way. We just have to hope they don't check the trunk." He shrugged. "If as our friend here says, they all know him, we should be able to get through safely."

"I hope so."

So do I. John went back to gazing out the window.

57

Hemin switched off the engine and climbed out of his pickup. He could hear children playing, and his face lit up in a smile. Stepping through the front gate, he called out, "Dilnaz, Parwen."

He heard a squeal of delight, and two little girls came piling out the front door. He squatted down with his arms open, and they ran into his arms. He gave them both a squeeze, setting them off into a round of giggles, then looked up to see his wife, Rosna, standing in the doorway, drying her hands on a dishcloth. Hemin ruffled the two girls' hair and stood. He winked at Rosna as the girls ran back inside.

"How did it go?" Rosna asked.

"Good." Hemin smiled. "Easy."

His phone buzzed, and he reached behind him to pull it out of his rear pocket. He glanced at the screen and raised a finger.

"I'll be in in a minute."

He waited for Rosna to turn around and head back inside, then tapped at the screen.

"Yes, boss."

"Did they get across okay?"

"Yes. It all went smoothly."

"Good."

Hemin waited for Mehmet to continue. He walked over to the gate and leaned his elbows on the top. The street was still quiet, the low rays of the morning sun throwing long shadows across the road.

The men should be well on their way by now. He heard the girls behind him and turned to see them run out the front door again, giggling and laughing. They wrapped their arms around his legs and clung tight as their mother came out and tried to shoo them away. Hemin smiled and pried their arms loose, waving them back inside. If the men had found Ferhad, he would look after them. Hemin hoped they succeeded. No-one deserved to have a family member stuck in a war zone.

He heard Mehmet clear his throat. "Did they say where they were going?"

Hemin frowned. "Yes. Idlib."

"Idlib? Are you sure?"

"Yes." Hemin ran his fingers through his hair. He was uneasy. He had done a lot of work for Mehmet in the past, lucrative work, most of it on the wrong side of the law. He had to. He had no formal education; his family had been poor, and he had grown up the hard way. There was little work now, trade between the two countries affected badly by the war, and he needed to make ends meet. He had two daughters to look after, and if that meant working for people like Mehmet, that's what he had to do, but he didn't necessarily like or trust the man.

"And there were just the three of them?"

"Yes."

"Good."

"Boss?" The phone line had already gone dead.

Hemin stared at the phone screen. What was Mehmet up to?

58

Mia knelt in the dirt, the stones digging into her kneecaps, but she daren't move. She kept her head down, her *hijab* pulled forward to hide her face, just an anonymous black-clad figure crouched in the street.

She tried to understand the raised voices around her, but they spoke too fast. There were four or five voices; she thought one was Naeem's but wasn't sure.

Despite everything she had gone through since she had arrived in Syria, she had never felt as low as she did now. From the joy of hearing that Uncle Steve was about to save her to groveling in the street as the fighters stood around her, arguing. There was no hope now. She had managed to send the last message, but Abu Mujahid spotted the phone as she tried to slip it back inside the folds of her *abaya*.

Her ribs ached from where he had kicked her, and the sweet taste of blood was on her tongue. She probed her teeth with her tongue and winced as pain shot through her head from a loose incisor. The right side of her face throbbed, and she could barely see out of her right eye as it closed up. A tear trickled down her left cheek, and she sniffed. The argument grew louder, two voices, in particular, screaming at each other in rapid-fire Arabic. She heard a click, then felt something cold and hard press against the back of her head. This was it... the end. She took a deep breath as panic welled within her. Maybe it was better this way. The suffering would end... but Malak.... her life had barely started. Mia's lip quivered, and she closed her left eye, took another deep breath, and retreated inward. The shouting grew fainter. Her lips began to move in silent prayer.

Bismillah ar-raḥmān ar-raḥīm, in the name of God, the Merciful, the Compassionate. If you really do exist, now is the time to prove it. You can take me, I am ready, all I ask is that you look after Malak, my beautiful angel. Please protect her, keep her safe from harm, so she can lead a full, joyful life away from all this suffering.

59

Exiting Al-Malikiyah was trouble-free, passing through the checkpoint on the west of the town easier than coming in. The guards were more interested in who was coming in than going out.

The road continued west, following the line of the Turkish border through more fields and patches of stony, uncultivable desert before joining the M4 near the town of Qamishli.

Until then, the only signs of war had been the checkpoints, but as they headed further west, there were more signs of military activity. Along one stretch of road, a convoy of armored vehicles was parked, the soldiers sitting beside their vehicles, brewing coffee, and watching idly as they passed. John noticed the red, white, and blue of the Russian flag flying on some of the vehicles. In the opposite direction, pickups and sedans passed, laden high with personal belongings, furniture, bags as people fled the fighting in the west, heading for a more peaceful area closer to the Turkish border.

At one point, an almighty roar filled the air as two fighter planes screamed past overhead so low, the vibration from their engines rocked the car. It was unclear whose air force they belonged to, and when Mansur questioned Ferhad, he shrugged, explaining it was hard to keep track of who was flying overhead, Turkey, Syria, Russia, or even America.

Ferhad explained that for people like him, the people in power were all the same, all interested in control and lining their pockets. No-one had the best interests of the populace in mind.

They made slow but steady progress, the road mostly straight and uninteresting. John struggled to keep awake as kilometer after kilometer of sand and dust passed by on each side. Occasionally, they had to detour where the road had been bombed, and large craters blocked their passage. They stopped several times to stretch their legs, pee, and remove layers of clothing, the temperature rising as the sun climbed across the sky. John shared a packet of biscuits while Ferhad smoked and chatted with Mansur. The time passed slowly in an unending blur of sandy brown and grey.

Approaching Ain Issa in the middle of the afternoon, Ferhad warned of another checkpoint, and they made themselves ready. Despite checkpoints so far being mainly a formality, John's heartbeat increased again. He took a series of slow, deep breaths to bring it back under control—five seconds in, five seconds out, six breaths a minute. He emptied his mind of what might happen and focused on his breathing. It worked, and as they joined the queue for the checkpoint, he felt calmer than he had all morning. He glanced across at Steve, who didn't seem to be doing so well, his face creased in a nervous frown. Mansur, however, seemed outwardly relaxed.

As before, they edged slowly forward, and John took the time to observe the checkpoint. A large armored truck faced them on the right-hand side of the road, a yellow flag, with what looked to be a map of Eastern Syria in white in the middle, flew from an aerial on the vehicle. John reached forward and tapped Mansur on the shoulder.

"Ask him who these people are. The flag is different from the other checkpoints."

Mansur translated, then replied, "They are the Syrian Democratic Force. Their headquarters are in this town. He said, don't worry. They are also Kurdish."

"Okay, should be alright then." John leaned back in his seat and looked at Steve. "Bloody confusing here."

Three men in camouflage clothing lounged on the top of the armored vehicle, automatic weapons cradled on their laps. Ostensibly, they looked relaxed, but their eyes scanned every vehicle as it approached.

John switched his attention to the left side of the road, where a dusty Humvee was parked at right angles to the road. Mounted on top and pointed in their direction was a large machine gun behind an armored shield. A man with a red and white checked shemagh wrapped around his face sat behind it, his finger inside the trigger guard.

John gulped and brought his attention back to his breathing—five seconds in, five seconds out.

Ferhad drove slowly forward and stopped, calling out a greeting to the men approaching him on the driver's side. There were two men on his side and three men on the passenger side, all armed with versions of the Kalashnikov, faces hidden behind *shemaghs* or balaclavas.

One of the soldiers barked a series of terse questions at Ferhad while the other men looked inside the car, weapons at the ready. They were tense, jumpy, not relaxed like the checkpoints they had been through so far.

The man questioning Ferhad raised his voice, and Ferhad shook his head, gesticulating with his hands.

"Mansur, what's happening?" John asked from the corner of his mouth, his eyes still on the men on his side, a smile fixed on his face.

Before Mansur could answer, the man on John's side stepped forward and pointed his weapon at John's face, shouting something in Arabic. John's heart skipped a beat. Another man stepped forward and pulled open the door, gripped John's vest by the shoulder and pulled him out of the vehicle. John stumbled, trying to regain his footing, his hands held high in the air. Bile rose in his throat as his system went into panic mode. What the fuck was happening? He was pushed to his knees, while the other soldier kept his weapon trained on John's head. From the corner of his eye, he could see the same thing happening to Mansur, and a moment later, Ferhad and Steve were pushed to the ground beside him. Their backpacks were thrown to the ground, and the men stood back, weapons trained on them. John could hear Steve breathing fast and heavy. Ferhad remonstrated in rapid Arabic, only to receive a shouted response from the leader of the guards. He sank back into silence.

John's mind went into overdrive. *Had they been betrayed? Was it Mehmet or even Hemin? Was his life going to end here, in the dirt on the side of the road in Syria?*

He turned his head slowly to look at Steve and caught his eye. He tried to look confident and gave him a nod of encouragement, but he daren't ask Mansur anything after they shouted at Ferhad.

John noticed a movement in his peripheral vision and slowly turned his head to look at the armored truck. The men on top were alert now, their weapons raised, but from behind the vehicle, a man approached. He was tall and like the rest of the men, dressed in camouflage clothing, his only weapon, a handgun in a holster on his waist. His face was unmasked, and his close-cropped beard was flecked with grey. He carried himself with confidence, and John assumed he was their officer. Two of the men stepped to one side, giving him room as he stood in front of them and studied them.

John guessed his age to be in his late forties, although his weather-beaten skin and dark-circled eyes could have been misleading. He studied them one by one, then issued a quiet command. A soldier slung his weapon over his shoulder and knelt down in front of their backpacks. John felt a bead of sweat on his temples, and again, he attempted to bring his attention back to his breathing, but it wasn't working. The soldier unzipped Steve's bag and looked through the camera equipment, pulling out each lens and examining it before putting it back. He pulled out the camera, thumbed it on, and scrolled through the photos Steve had taken earlier that morning in Zuhajrijja. He then checked all the side pockets before zipping the bag up again. Moving to John's bag, he went through it, pulling out the notebook, and John cursed, wishing he had at least written something suitable inside to make it look more genuine. The man leafed through the blank pages, then tossed the book back inside. He pulled out the laptop, turned it over, examining it, opened it up, closed it again, then put it back. He checked all the side pockets, then zipped the bag back up before standing up and nodding to his commander.

Another soldier passed over the passports, the press cards, and the plastic folder of letters and permits. In the stress of being dragged out of the car, John hadn't even realized he had left them behind on the seat. The commander looked through them, holding them up and checking the photos against their faces. He leafed through the passports, examining their visas, and John held his breath, hoping that Ramesh's forgery was good enough to pass this inspection.

He handed the documents back to the soldier and stood, staring at them one by one. His eyes stopped on John and seemed to hold his gaze for longer than necessary. John's heart stopped, and he waited for the command that would send bullets tearing through them. The commander said something and turned away to walk back to the armored truck. A soldier shouted something in Arabic—the only word John understood was *Yalla.*

Ferhad and Mansur got to their feet, and John looked nervously at Steve.

"It's okay, we can go," Mansur explained, turning to face them.

John let out an enormous sigh of relief and got to his feet. He reached down for his backpack as Steve did the same.

The soldier handed the documents to Mansur, and they all climbed into the car as the soldiers turned their attention to the vehicle behind them. Ferhad started the engine, slipped the car in gear, and pulled away. John scanned his body, releasing all the tension, body part by body part. He could hear Steve muttering under his breath, repeating the same word over and over again. It sounded like "fuck, fuck, fuck." John glanced toward the armored vehicle as they eased past and saw the officer talking to a man in a different uniform. He was watching them, his eyes locking with John's as they passed. John wasn't sure but thought he saw the red white and blue of the Russian flag on a badge on the man's shoulder.

Payback

60

Out of sight of the checkpoint, Ferhad pulled over, switched off the engine, and climbed out of the car. He walked to the front and rested his butt on the hood, removing a crumpled pack of cigarettes from the breast pocket of his shirt.

John looked across at Steve, shrugged, and they both opened their doors and climbed out, followed by Mansur.

Ferhad cupped the flame of his lighter in his hands and lit a cigarette, then offered the packet to the others before stuffing it back into his pocket.

He took a long drag and blew the smoke up into the air, watching as it was snatched away by the breeze.

John twisted his body, then bent forward, stretching out his back. It was good to get out of the little car, and the stretching helped to burn off the excess adrenaline pumping through his veins. Steve watched him, then, catching his eye, gave a shake of his head.

"Fuck me, I almost shat myself."

"Me too." John nodded. "For a moment, I thought it was all going to end there."

"Look at my hand." Steve held up his hand, and John could see it shaking. "What a shit hole. Imagine dealing with this every day?"

John stood with his hands on his hips, looking back down the road in the direction of the checkpoint. A car moved toward them, the driver raising a hand, and giving a thumbs-up, and John nodded back. He had been behind them in the queue and seen what they had gone through.

"Yeah, we take so much in our lives for granted."

"I hope we don't have many more of these to go through before we get to Idlib," Steve commented. "I don't think my heart can take it."

"I'll find out." John walked to the front of the car and nodded at Ferhad.

"Is he okay?" John asked Mansur.

"Yes." Mansur smiled. "He's just angry. He says they didn't need to treat you like this. You aren't dangerous to them." He paused, listening to Ferhad, then translated. "He says he is sorry you are experiencing this in his country."

John nodded, his eyes on Ferhad's face. The man looked genuinely upset.

"Why did they pull us out of the car? I thought he said they all knew him?"

Mansur asked, and Ferhad threw his cigarette butt on the ground and trod it into the dirt with his toe.

Looking up, he spoke to Mansur. Mansur listened then turned to John.

"He says this is a new commander, and he's probably trying to impress his bosses. He asked if you saw the Russian officer?"

"I did."

"He says they need to show the Russians how good they are; otherwise, their funding will be cut off."

"So, it was just a random stop for us?"

"He thinks so, yes."

John nodded thoughtfully. "Good." He exhaled, feeling a little more relaxed. "Ask him how many more checkpoints before we get to Arima."

John watched the two men conversing, Mansur asking another question now and then, then he turned back to John.

"He says there should only be three more, one on the way in and out of Manbij and another just before Arima." Mansur paused as Ferhad said something else. "He says there may be others, but there were only three the last time he came through this way."

"When was that?"

"About four weeks ago."

"Okay, thanks, Mansur."

Ferhad looked at them all questioningly as if waiting for more questions, and when none came, he asked, *"Yalla?"*

John reached out and gave him a reassuring pat on the shoulder.

"Yalla. Let's go."

61

The highway skirted the edge of Ain Issa as it headed west. There were signs of hard-fought battles everywhere—bomb craters, destroyed buildings, and burned-out tanks and armored vehicles. Ferhad explained, through Mansur, it had once been controlled by the Islamic State and had even been attacked by Turkish backed forces just a few months previously. He waved his hand to the right side of the road and explained Turkey still controlled a lot of land to the North.

John looked over at Steve. "That would explain why they were so jumpy at the checkpoint."

On the western edge of town, makeshift tents filled the fields on both sides of the road, some just blue and white plastic sheets draped over boxes or abandoned cars. Children played in the dirt between the shelters while their parents sat on the ground, staring listlessly into space. There was garbage everywhere, and a sense of hopelessness hung heavy in the air.

"Where are these people from, Mansur?"

Mansur asked, then turned and looked over his shoulder. "He says they are from all over but a lot from towns to the west. There has been heavy fighting in recent weeks. It is not safe for these people to go home."

"What will happen to them?"

"He doesn't know. Some will go to Turkey, but most will stay here. It's been like this for years now."

"Poor bastards," Steve muttered as they gazed at the mass of humanity whose lives had been destroyed by greed and politics.

The road continued northwest through a landscape of sun-scorched earth and untended fields, and not for the first time, John considered the futility of it all. Millions of lives being destroyed, for what? There was nothing out there but dirt. What was the point?

About an hour and a half out of Ain Issa, the highway took a sharp turn and they slowed to join a long queue of traffic filing into single lanes to cross the Euphrates, the bridge reduced to one span by bombing and sabotage. Soldiers stood at each end of the bridge, fingers on triggers, eyes scanning the slow-moving vehicles as they crossed. John's breath caught, but the soldiers were more interested in keeping the traffic flowing than stopping individual vehicles. Once on the other side, everyone in the car relaxed as they headed the final fifty kilometers to Arima.

The sun was beginning its descent, its rays coming almost directly through the windshield. Military traffic had noticeably increased in the last few kilometers, convoys of armored vehicles, and armored patrols, flying either the yellow flag of the Syrian Democratic Force or the red, white, and blue flag of the Russian forces. They paid little attention to the small yellow taxi cruising along the highway.

On the outskirts of Manbij, they passed through another

two checkpoints with little trouble, the soldiers content with the documentation Ramesh had forged.

The heat inside the car and the monotonous landscape were having a soporific effect, and John was on the verge of drifting off when he was brought alert by the sound of Ferhad saying something to Mansur.

"He says we are about thirty minutes away from Arima."

"Good." John turned to Steve. "So far, so good. Hopefully, not long now."

"Yeah, mate." Steve pulled out his phone and looked at the screen. "No message from her yet. I'll try calling again." He dialed and waited, then shook his head. "It's just ringing. No answer."

"Okay." John frowned. "Send another message that we will be in Arima soon." He looked out the window as the fields slipped by.

Until she was in the car, John couldn't relax. Despite his reassurances to Steve that all would turn out alright, the experiences at the checkpoints and seeing the refugees in the tents made him realize nothing was guaranteed or easy. John allowed his mind to wander to thoughts of Adriana.

Once they were back in safety, he would make sure he treasured every moment of his time with her. It had been too easy to think his life was empty and boring, but back in Lisbon, they had a comfortable home and a peaceful life. They knew where their meals were coming from, and with John's wealth, they never had to want for anything. Despite all he had been through, his life was a breeze compared to the people living in Syria. People who had lost their homes, their livelihoods, and their loved ones. People who didn't know if they would survive the day.

John pulled out his phone to send a message to Adriana

and saw a message on the screen. *Good luck and come back soon. I love you.*

Despite his nerves, he smiled. He would make sure they got back safely. He typed a reply and slipped the phone back into his pocket—time to think about the next part of the journey.

62

Twelve hours after leaving the Turkish-Syrian border, they rolled into the little town of Arima on the western edge of Kurdish controlled territory. They were tired, thirsty, and more than eager to free themselves from the cramped confines of the little Iranian made taxi.

It was a town much like the others they had passed through—dusty and battered, overgrown with weeds in parts, strewn with garbage and rubble in others. None of the buildings had glass in their windows, and many of the walls bore the scars of urban warfare. There was little sign of civilian life, the people in the streets made up of soldiers on patrol or groups of listless young men hanging around on corners, idly watching the traffic pass. Ferhad pulled into a small square and switched off the engine. He spoke to Mansur for a while, then climbed out of the car. The others climbed out and stretched, shaking the cramp out of their legs, and twisting their spines and necks.

"Am I glad to get out of that car," Steve grumbled.

John gave a half-smile, then asked Mansur, "What did he say? Where's he going?"

"He said to wait for him. He will ask around and see if anyone can take us closer to Idlib. He said he's not comfortable doing it himself."

John nodded and looked around. He noticed people staring at them, averting their eyes when he looked their way. He looked down and realized they were all still wearing their ballistic vests with Press written on them.

"We seem to be attracting a lot of attention. Do you think it's our vests?"

"Could be." Steve looked around. "I feel safer with it on, though."

"Yeah, me too. Let's see if we can get something to eat. I'm starving."

"There's a food stall over there." Mansur pointed across the square. "You wait by the car. I'll get something for us."

John and Steve leaned against the car and watched as Mansur crossed the square and approached one of the few businesses that didn't have shutters pulled down. A small group of men hung around outside, smoking or squatting in the dirt, and Mansur pushed through them and spoke to the stall owner, the men listening in for a while but soon losing interest.

"Realistically, Steve, we won't get there tonight."

"No," Steve sighed.

"It will be dark soon. I think we need to find somewhere to sleep for the night and continue on in the morning." John turned to face Steve. "I don't want to be here any longer than necessary, but we'll be rested and better able to deal with anything that comes our way."

"Yeah." Steve crossed his arms, looked down at the ground, and kicked a stone out of the way.

"Hey, Steve, we'll get there. Think of where we've come today. We'll bring her back, but let's stay focused. One day at a time. We're much closer than we were yesterday."

"Yeah, you're right, mate." Steve unfolded his arms, squared his shoulders, and looked up. "Thanks, mate. Really. I couldn't have done this alone."

"Yes, you could. It just would have been harder." John grinned. "But you would have had more room in the car."

"Huh. Yeah, maybe I should have done it myself. I hope the next guy has a bigger vehicle."

Mansur came back with food, and they stood beside the car, using the trunk lid as a table, feasting on flatbread, hummus, and boiled eggs.

Ferhad returned after thirty minutes, accompanied by a fair young man with a clean-shaven chin and pale blue eyes. He spoke to Mansur for a few minutes, and Mansur translated.

"This man can take us to Saraqib, just fifteen kilometers south of Idlib, but he says it's dangerous. He wants extra for the danger, and he won't go at night. He can take us in the morning."

"Tell him okay. Work out a price you think is reasonable. Tell him we'll leave at seven."

Mansur spoke for a while, the conversation going back and forth between him, Ferhad, and the new driver. After a couple of minutes, Mansur reached out, and the man shook his hand.

"All done. He'll meet us here at seven. I told him half now and half when we get there."

"Good." John turned to Steve, "Send her a message. Tell her we will be in Saraqib by ten. It will give her some confidence that we're getting closer."

"Good idea." Steve pulled out his phone and started typing.

John looked at Mansur. "Do you think you can find us somewhere to spend the night?"

"Yeah, Mansur." Steve looked up from his phone. "See if you can book us into the Ritz."

63

Mia shifted her weight from one buttock to the other. The concrete floor was cold and hard, and her head throbbed with pain. She had no idea of the time but guessed, based on the falling light, the whole day had passed since she was caught with the phone. When the gun barrel was pressed to her head, she thought it was all over, but then it was taken away, and she was hit on the side of her head, and everything went dark. She was alive, but what was the point? Everything had gone wrong. Where was Malak? Were the women looking after her? What about Uncle Steve? Where was he? What would he do when he couldn't reach her? She rocked back and forth, a heavy lump in her chest. Why? Why? When she was so close to getting out of there and providing a new life for Malak, why did it all have to go wrong?

A pellet of anger began to smolder in the pit of her belly. The more she thought about her situation, the more the fire grew, her frustration transmuting into anger and hatred—anger at Abu Mujahid, anger at Naeem who had dragged her to this horrible place, anger at the world, anger at religion. It was all wrong. And where was Naeem? She thought she'd heard his voice earlier in the street but couldn't be sure. Where was he now? Couldn't even defend his wife and daughter. Man of god? Holy warrior? Huh! She shook her head.

She had to do something herself, at least try. She couldn't sit around, feeling sorry for herself, and put it all down to Allah's will. It wasn't Allah's will that Malak was born into an environment like this. Malak didn't have a choice. The fault was with her parents, and Mia had to do everything she could to make sure Malak didn't suffer because of her poor decisions. She clenched her jaw and straightened up against the wall she was leaning against.

"Hey." She heard a noise by the door. "Hello."

The guard appeared in the doorway. He was the young fighter who had been on guard duty in the building with the Yazidi women. He watched her, his face expressionless. He was young and thin, perhaps in his mid-teens, his beard just thin wisps of hair on his chin. The Kalashnikov in his hands looked too big for him, almost comical.

Mia dug deep into her memory, piecing together all the words she knew in Arabic.

"Shuu ismak? What is your name?"

He didn't answer.

"My name is Mia."

He glanced over his shoulder, then back at her.

"Karam," he mumbled.

"Karam?" Mia nodded slowly. "Where are you from?"

Again, he looked over his shoulder and nervously shifted his weight from one foot to the other.

"Raqqa."

"You are Syrian?"

"Yes."

"I am from Australia. Do you know where that is?"

Karam shook his head. He turned, so he was sideways in the doorway, a position where he could see outside at the same time.

"It's a long way from here, on the other side of the world."

He said nothing but continued to listen.

"It's a beautiful country. People are free and happy there. I want to go back."

Karam frowned and shifted the weapon in his arms.

Mia thought she should try another tack.

"Why are you fighting, Karam? With these people? They are not your people. They are from somewhere else."

Karam looked out the door, not answering. Mia wondered if she had pushed too far. The answer when it came was almost inaudible, and Mia had to strain to hear.

"They killed my mother, my sister."

"Who?"

He looked back at her.

"They bombed our house. These men found me, dug me out. They said the best way for me to get my revenge was to join them."

"I'm sorry, Karam, that's horrible." Mia thought quickly. "But... how do you know who bombed your house?"

Karam stiffened, and he stood straighter.

"It could have been anyone. This war is confusing," Mia pushed.

"No. These men, my... brothers." Karam shook his head, anger mixing with confusion on his face. "They are doing the work of God."

"Karam, killing people, taking women from their homes... it's not God's work."

"Be quiet!"

"The Yazidi women in the other house, what if they had done the same to your mother, your sister?"

"They are *kufaar*!" He spat the last word out.

"They are just like you and me, Karam. The world is full of people who have different ways, eat different food, wear different clothes. We should not hate them because of that."

Karam shifted the position of his weapon, his face contorted in confusion.

"I used to believe in the Caliphate. It could have been a wonderful world, all of us living according to Allah. But there has been too much killing, too much destruction. These men are filling your head with hatred." Mia paused. "Karam, I'm truly sorry about your family. It is a terrible thing, but doing the same thing to someone else will not bring them back. These men, they just want another fighter, they don't care about you or your family, they don't even care about Syria."

"No, no, no." Karam continued shaking his head. His fingers tightened their grip on the Kalashnikov.

"Yes, Karam. Abu Mujahid, he is from Egypt. Do you think it matters to him what happens here? Do you see how he treats the women? He... these men are using you."

"They are my brothers!"

"Karam, they don't care. You are just another gun to them. Why do you think they only put you on guard duty? You are nothing to them."

"No!" Karam turned to face her, his eyes filled with anguish. He raised his weapon and pointed the barrel at her chest. "You are wrong!"

64

It didn't take long for Mansur and Ferhad to find somewhere for them to stay, the promise of easy cash opening doors easily in a town with little business remaining.

It was in what would have been the living room on the ground floor of a two-story building. There was no furniture, just rugs on the floor, and boards over the window, keeping the worst of the night chill out. A single kerosene heater in the corner warmed the room, the temperature dropping significantly once the sun had gone down.

They had removed their vests but kept their jackets on and stretched out on the rugs, drinking hot sweet tea from a large samovar.

Mansur had persuaded the owner, for an extra fee, to run the generator for a while, and they used the time to recharge the phone batteries. John was checking the battery status when Steve's phone buzzed.

"You've got a message, Steve. Maybe it's Mia."

Steve sat up and held out his hand. "Toss it here."

John unplugged it and tossed it across the room, Steve

catching it deftly with one hand. He unlocked it and stared at the screen, a smile growing on his face.

"It's her. She will meet us tomorrow morning at ten." Steve looked up, an enormous grin on his face. "She's shared a location where we can find her." Steve exhaled loudly. "Fuckin' ace."

"Hang on, Steve." John frowned, not keen to ruin Steve's mood. "Check the location first. I don't want to sound negative, but it won't be so easy to get into Idlib. It's in Al Qaeda territory."

Steve's smile faded a little, and he looked down at the screen. He tapped on the link and waited for the location to open in the phone's web browser. Narrowing his eyes, he squinted at the screen, then his smile grew again.

"Look, it's not Idlib, it's the countryside just north of Saraqib." He handed the phone to John, who looked at the map. The location was in a patch of what looked like open farmland west of the M5 highway and north of Saraqib. John zoomed in and saw a narrow access road leading off the highway into the fields. He nodded and handed the phone back.

"That makes things a lot easier. Tell her we'll see her there."

"Yes. It's happening, guys." Steve grinned and gave Mansur a friendly punch in the shoulder.

John smiled. He hoped so.

65

The drive toward Saraqib was uneventful for the most part. There were numerous checkpoints on the ring road around Aleppo, but their forged documents passed the test each time. At one point, John joked to Steve that Ramesh deserved a bonus when they got back.

Signs of conflict were everywhere—military patrols, damaged buildings, and in places, the highway was heavily cratered. At one point, a pair of military helicopters flew beside them for several kilometers before heading south away from the highway.

John was on edge; he couldn't relax. There was something niggling away in his subconscious, but he couldn't grasp it. He hadn't slept well, the room cold in the middle of the night, the chill seeping up through the rugs. At one point, after finally drifting off, he had woken in a panic, his heart racing, and it had taken a moment to remember where he was. After that, he hadn't been able to sleep for hours, the faces of the men who haunted his past appearing every time he closed his eyes. He hadn't had nightmares for a long time, but guessed stress was triggering the repressed memories.

Eventually, he gave up, splashed water on his face, and went outside to sit on the front step of the building to watch the town slowly awaken. Steve joined him soon after, having had a similarly troubled sleep. They sat in silence as the street became visible in the dawn, listening to the birds chattering in the trees and watching rodents scampering along the gutter.

The driver, a taciturn man who went by the name of Samir, arrived dead on seven in a battered old Toyota pickup with a twin cab. They piled in and set off, Mansur trying in vain to engage Samir in conversation before giving up and concentrating on the passing scenery.

Once the M4 became the M5 on the southern side of Aleppo, progress slowed considerably, the road heavily damaged and constant checkpoints manned by Russian military police and Syrian Arab Army soldiers, meaning they had to constantly stop and start.

It was around nine-thirty when Steve tapped on Mansur's shoulder.

"Tell him to take the next right turn. It's a minor road about five-hundred meters ahead."

Mansur translated, and Samir started shaking his head. He said something to Mansur, and the conversation went back and forth until Mansur raised his hands in frustration and turned to face the back.

"He says he won't. It's too dangerous for him. He will drop us at the turn, but he said to go along that road will take him into H.T.S. territory."

"Fuck," Steve cursed. "Tell him we'll pay him extra."

"I did." Mansur shrugged. "He won't do it."

"The little fucker..."

"It's okay, Steve." John raised a placatory hand to Steve. "Let's not have a fight. Mansur, tell him to drop us but to wait for us. Tell him we'll double what we've paid him if he waits for us to come back. We won't be long."

Mansur translated, Samir nodded, then Mansur gave a thumbs-up to the back as Samir spotted the turn and pulled over.

Steve double-checked his phone and pointed up the road. "It's about two kilometers that way."

"Okay, let's go."

They climbed out and looked around. Fields stretched out in all directions, unplowed and overgrown. Off to the west, twin plumes of black smoke reached up into the sky, and they could hear the distant thump of explosions. A couple of lorries rumbled by, the drivers waving out the window as they passed, but apart from them, there was no-one around.

"Let's go."

Mansur leaned in the window and said something to Samir, then straightened, and looked at John and Steve.

"He said, he'll wait for two hours."

"Good." John shouldered his backpack. He felt uneasy, something wasn't right. He shook the thought off. He was tired and stressed. He shouldn't be negative. Everything would be okay.

"Ready? Lead the way, Steve."

Steve set off up the narrow single-lane road, John and Mansur following in single file behind. They had gone only around a hundred meters when they heard an engine start. They turned to look behind them.

"Motherfucker!" Steve cursed as they watched Samir drive off. "Fuck!" He turned to look at Mansur. "Great translator, you are."

Mansur shrugged and looked down at the ground.

"Hey, Steve, it's not Mansur's fault."

Steve exhaled. "Yeah, sorry, mate. I guess I'm a bit on edge."

"It's okay. I'm sorry, too. He promised."

"What do we do now?"

John frowned and looked up the road.

"We keep going. Let's get Mia first. One step at a time."

They walked up the road for another ten minutes as it separated two large fields, the fields uncultivated, bare dirt in patches, overgrown with weeds in others. Steve kept checking his phone, and as they approached a building on the left side of the road, he said, "This looks like the place."

John studied the building. It would have been a farmhouse at one time but by the looks of it, long abandoned. A large concrete area separated it from the road, the building itself missing most of the roof, the skeleton of rafters and broken tiles all that remained. Bullet holes pockmarked the walls, and one corner had collapsed completely.

"Wait."

Steve stopped and turned to look at him.

"What? This is the place she sent."

John ignored him and stared at the building.

"Just wait."

Steve shrugged and turned back to look at the building. The three men stood staring at the deserted structure, looking for any sign of movement. John had a prickling feeling in the back of his neck, a sign that had stood him in good stead before. Something was wrong, but he couldn't figure out what.

"I don't like it."

"Why? She said she would meet us here." Steve looked

at his watch. "It's ten. She said she would meet us now." Steve looked up. "Maybe she's inside hiding?"

John made a face, his eyes still on the building.

"What is it?"

"I don't know, just a feeling."

"Look, mate, I respect your intuition, but look at the place. There's no sign of anyone. She herself told us to come here."

"Yeah..."

"Mate, we didn't come all this way to stop now."

John nodded slowly, then turned to Mansur.

"Mansur, you hang back, stay out of sight. Keep an eye on things."

"Sure." Mansur stepped off the side of the road and moved toward a patch of long grass.

"Let's go, Steve."

Steve turned and walked quickly toward the building, John following slowly behind him. He understood Steve's eagerness to find his niece, but John wanted to be careful.

Steve stepped onto the concrete parking area and approached the building. The windows had long been blown out, and the front door was flat on the ground outside, leaving a black hole leading into the house. Steve stood in front and called out.

"Mia? It's Uncle Steve."

There was no reply. John caught up and stood beside him, his forehead creased in a frown. He turned around and scanned the fields on the opposite side of the road while Steve called out again.

"Mia?"

Still no response. Steve pulled out his phone and dialed her number. It took a moment to connect, then they heard a phone ringing from inside the building.

"She's inside."

John turned back to see Steve rushing forward toward the building. John opened his mouth to say something when a figure appeared in the doorway. A bearded man in camouflage fatigues held a ringing cell phone in the air, his mouth open in a sinister grin, exposing a row of yellowed teeth.

"Iqboth 'alayhom!" he shouted. "Seize them!"

John sensed someone behind him, but before he could turn, someone grabbed him by the arms, and he tried to break free. He heard sounds of struggle nearby and shouts in Arabic. He pulled his arms harder, the grip loosening on his arms, and he stumbled forward, losing his balance. The last thing he felt was a sharp blow to the back of his head.

66

John groaned and blinked his eyes open, but it was still dark. He felt something against his face. His head appeared to be covered. What the...? He struggled to remember what happened... the man with the phone, the blow to the head. Fuck! John should have trusted his gut. He should have thought it had been too easy, but he had wanted so much for Steve to succeed. Shit! How did they find them? Where was he? Where were the others? He tried to move his arms, to sit up, but his arms were bound behind his back.

His head throbbed, and there was the coppery taste of blood in his mouth. He tried moving his legs, but they were bound together at the ankle. He stopped moving and tuned into his surroundings. The floor was hard and cold, probably concrete. He could see a faint light through the fabric of his headcovering, not bright enough to be outside, so he must be in a room. Slowing his breathing, he strained to hear any sounds that could help identify his surroundings —Arabic spoken in low tones outside the room, the distant thump of artillery on the frontline, a vehicle crawling slowly past, then stopping, a dog barking in the distance.

He heard a rustle of fabric and then a cough.

"Who's there? Steve?"

"John, are you okay?"

"Steve... I'm okay. You?"

"Yeah. Sorry, mate, I should have listened to you. Bastards."

"Did Mansur get away?"

"I'm here too, Mr. John."

"Shit! What happened? I blacked out when someone hit me on the head. Where are we? Can you see?"

"The bastards have put hoods on us. Can't see a fucking thing," Steve growled.

"I can't see either. They caught me in the field, put us in a pickup, drove for about thirty minutes, then brought us into this building. We came up one flight of steps. That's all I know," Mansur explained. "They don't know I can speak Arabic. I heard them arguing. They can't decide what to do with us."

"He had Mia's phone," said Steve.

"Yes. They were arguing about her, too. But..." Mansur's voice trailed off.

"What?"

"I don't know. They left the room, and I couldn't hear anymore."

"Fuck," Steve cursed. "What do we do now?"

John couldn't answer. He had no idea.

They heard footsteps outside, and John tensed, listening for clues as to what was happening. A door crashed open, then a shout in Arabic. He heard footsteps in the room, and a pair of hands grabbed his arm, dragging him backward until he was propped against a wall. The hood was pulled off his head, and he blinked rapidly as his eyes adjusted to the light. He sensed Steve and Mansur beside him. As his vision cleared, he saw three men standing in front of them, each with their weapon held ready, the barrels pointed at their chests. Checked *shemaghs* covered their faces, leaving only their eyes visible. They stared, not saying anything, waiting.

John heard more footsteps, and another figure appeared in the doorway. He stepped closer, and John recognized him from the farmhouse.

67

The man stood in front of them, looking at each one in turn with dark hooded eyes set deep in his face. He was thin, his cheekbones pronounced over a grey-flecked beard that reached to the middle of his chest. He stood with his hands on his hips, his lip curled in a sneer. He locked eyes with John, and John forced himself to maintain eye contact before the man looked away. He tilted his head to one side, then stepped forward and kicked Steve's feet with his boot. When he spoke, it was in thickly accented English.

"You are... Uncle Steve?"

Steve said nothing, staring back in defiance.

"I have your girl."

"Motherfucker."

"Ha," the man scoffed. "She is mine now."

"You bastard, rag head son of a bitch, I'll...."

One of the fighters stepped forward, reversed his Kalashnikov, and drove the butt into Steve's stomach.

Steve gasped, doubled over, then flopped to one side, the air knocked out of him.

The man switched his attention to John.

"Who are you?"

John ignored the question. He raised his chin and looked him square in the eyes.

"What do you want?"

The man grinned. He turned and said something to the fighters, who laughed. Turning back, he squatted down in front of John until his eyes were at the same level. John's nose wrinkled at the smell of stale sweat and unwashed clothing.

"What do *I* want?" he asked. "What can you give me?" he sniggered. "You are tied up. You have nothing. You are mine now. But I will make you famous." He looked at Mansur. "All of you. Your families will see you on the internet."

He stood up and barked a command in Arabic. A fighter stepped forward and dragged the backpacks into the center of the room. He went through the bags, tossing the contents into a pile in the middle of the floor. He handed the biscuits and medicines John had carried for Mia to the other men. The plastic folder of letters and permissions was handed to the leader who scanned through it, then tossed it on the pile. John's laptop was also passed to him, and after looking at it briefly, dropped it on the floor and stamped on it with his boot. The fighter went through Steve's bag, removing the cameras and lenses, placing them to one side. Everything else was thrown onto the pile forming at the leader's feet. Once the bags were empty, the fighter upended them and shook them out, ensuring nothing remained, then tossed the empty bags behind him. He then stood and approached John. Crouching down in front of him, he went through his pockets, removing his phone, passport, and press card, and money, handing it all back to his leader. He did the same with the other men, then stood and stepped behind his leader.

The leader passed the phones back to him, said something in Arabic, and the fighter ripped the backs off the phones, popped out the SIM cards, and threw everything separately onto the pile. While he did this, the leader opened the passports, looking up to match the faces with the passport photos.

"Steven Jacob Jones. Australian. John Hayes. English," he read out loud, spitting out the word English with derision. "Mansur Wahibi. Oman." He looked up and stared at Mansur. He said something in Arabic, and Mansur refused to answer, but John could see his eyes blazing. The man shook his head, cleared his throat, and spat on the floor at Mansur's feet. He then stuffed the passports into the thigh pocket of his camouflage pants, turned on his heel, muttered something to the guards, then walked out the door. The men stayed still, weapons still trained on the men until the sound of a vehicle leaving carried through the window. They then stepped forward and rummaged through the pile, selecting pieces of clothing, and picking up the phones and reassembling them before sliding them into their own pockets. One stepped forward, knelt beside John, and pushed him over to his side. John could feel his fingers near his bound wrists. What was happening? Were they going to let him go? But then he felt the strap of his G-Shock being loosened and slipped off his wrist. The fighter stood up with a grin and held the watch in the air in front of his colleagues. The other men commented, and they each stepped forward and removed Steve's and Mansur's watches, slipping them into their pockets before turning and walking out the door, pulling it shut behind them.

68

"Have you heard from Steve yet?"

Maadhavi shook her head. "Not since this morning's message. You?"

"No." Adriana looked at her watch, four p.m. She frowned and walked to the hotel room window and stared out the window at the Tigris flowing past. On the other side of the river was Syria. *Where are you, John?* She turned around and leaned against the windowsill and crossed her arms.

"I hate the waiting."

"Me, too. Why do you think we haven't heard? Steve's message said they were meeting Mia at ten this morning." A note of worry was creeping into Maadhavi's voice. It was understandable. It was the not knowing that was always worse.

Adriana had been there before, but she'd learned the hard way, you had to keep busy and stay positive. Otherwise, negative thoughts would drag you in a downward spiral that was almost impossible to get out of.

"It could be anything. No signal, flat battery. There's no

point in worrying just yet. They're not likely to make it back here until tonight or tomorrow. I'm sure one of us will get a message soon."

"I hope you're right."

Adriana smiled. "Hey, don't worry. I'll send a message to John, too. I'm sure one of them will reply as soon as they get a signal." She walked over to the bedside table, picked up her phone, typed out a message, and hit send.

"Come, let's go down to the restaurant and see what they have for afternoon tea. We need to do something to pass the time, and we've already seen what there is to see in the town. Might as well eat some good food."

69

The room was growing dark when they heard footsteps and voices outside again. The door swung open with a bang, and two of the fighters dragged a black-clad figure through the doorway and threw it on the floor. One gave the body a kick with his boot, but the figure didn't move or make a sound. He said something to the other fighter, and they laughed before leaving the room, pulling the door closed behind them. John peered through the darkness at the black shape lying at his feet. Who was it? It wasn't moving, but he could see the faint up and down movement of the fabric as the body breathed. Whoever it was, they were alive.

John turned to look at Mansur and nodded. Mansur understood, cleared his throat, and spoke in Arabic. There was no response. He spoke again—nothing. He looked back at John and shrugged as well as he could with his hands bound behind his back.

John looked at the body again.

"Hey. I know you can hear us."

There was no response. John tried again.

"Hey."

The body moved and groaned.

"Who are you?"

The voice was soft and feminine. Before John could reply, he heard Steve.

"Mia?"

The body stopped moving.

"Mia, is that you?"

"Unc... Uncle... Steve?"

"Mia!" Steve shuffled along the floor until he was next to the body. "Mia, it's me, it's me..." His voice broke.

The body moved and tried to sit up. They heard a groan, then the body was still. "Uncle Steve... I'm so sorry..."

"Hey, hey, it's okay." Steve looked to John for help. Using his feet, John dragged himself closer.

"Mia, my name is John. I am Steve's friend. I'm going to help you."

Mia didn't say anything.

"We'll remove your hood, so you can see each other. Okay?"

"Okay."

"Steve, I'm going to turn my back, so my hands are facing her. Guide me so I can grip the hood, and I'll pull it off."

Steve nodded, his face filled with emotion. John shuffled around until his back was to Mia, then pushed himself closer until he felt his fingertips touching the rough hessian cloth of the hood.

"Is that it?"

"Yes."

"Okay, Mia, I'll pull it off now." John gripped the cloth with his fingertips, then shuffled away from her.

"Keep going," Steve encouraged, "keep going, keep..."

Steve's voice trailed off, and John turned to see what had happened. Tears streamed from Steve's eyes as he looked down at the young lady lying on the floor. She was pale as if she hadn't seen the sun for a long time, her hair lank and greasy, and her face was thin and hard. A single tear trickled from a swollen eye and tracked a path down over the livid black and green bruise on the side of her face.

"Oh, Mia, what have they done to you?"

"Uncle Steve," Mia's voice came out as a whisper. "You are here."

"I'm here, Mia. I'm here."

John exchanged glances with Mansur. They had found her, or rather, she had found them, but what was the point? It didn't mean anything if they didn't get out of there. He shuffled his butt away from Steve toward Mansur, giving the pair what little privacy they could in the confined space.

"We have to get out of here, Mansur," John muttered. "Otherwise, they'll kill us."

"They won't do it until tomorrow."

John looked at Mansur with surprise. "How do you know?"

Mansur sighed. "They will want an audience. It will be a public execution. So, they will wait until daylight."

"Fuck."

"Yes."

"I'm sorry, Mansur. I should never have asked you to come."

"Don't be sorry. It's not up to you." Mansur smiled at John. "The time and place of my death is already written. Maybe it is tomorrow, maybe it isn't."

John sighed. "I wish I had your faith, Mansur, but I'm not going to sit here and wait. We have to try something."

"John, I never said we shouldn't try, but the end result is not up to us."

"Hmmm, okay." John struggled his hands against the rope binding his wrist together. "How tight are your hands bound?"

"Tight. I've tried already."

"Mine, too." John thought for a bit. "Do you think if we backed up to each other, we could untie them?"

"We can try."

Both men adjusted their positions until their backs were to each other.

"I'll try yours first," John said. His fingers probed the knot on the rope holding Mansur's wrists together. The rope was hard, possibly nylon, and the knot was tight. John couldn't get his fingertips to loosen the knot, and after several minutes' struggle, he had to admit defeat. "I can't do it."

"I will try yours."

John felt Mansur's fingers exploring his restraints, but after a minute or two, he gave up as well.

"It's too tight, John. The rope is very hard. It needs to be cut."

"Shit." John looked over at John and Mia. Mia was sitting up, leaning her head against Steve's shoulder as they carried on a quiet conversation.

"Maybe there is something in here we can use?" John swung his feet to the side and rolled onto his knees. He looked around the room as Mansur did the same. "You look that side, I'll search this side."

John maneuvered himself across the floor on his knees, peering into the darkness, looking for anything that could be used as a sharp edge. He lost balance twice and fell to his side, and by the time he had checked his side of the room, he was out of breath, and his knees were bruised.

"Nothing."

"Same here," Mansur replied from the other side of the room.

"Shit," John cursed under his breath. What the fuck did they do now?

70

Adriana chewed her lip as she waited for the phone to connect. Maadhavi stood in front of her, waiting nervously, her hands clasped together in front of her chest.

When they hadn't received a reply to their text messages by seven, they had both tried calling John's and Steve's phones. Maadhavi tried first, but all she got was a recorded message in another language. Adriana got the same result.

Adriana was struggling to keep herself together, but she had to put on a confident front for Maadhavi and had decided to ask for help.

The phone connected, and she heard the ringing tone in her ear.

"It's ringing." She smiled at Maadhavi.

"Hello?"

"Craig, it's Adriana."

"Adriana, hi, what's happening? Where are you?"

"Craig, I'm putting the phone on speaker. Maadhavi is here with me." Adriana tapped the screen and then held the phone out between them.

"Hello, Craig."

"Hi, Maadhavi. Is everything okay?"

"We..." Maadhavi's voice broke.

Adriana took over. "Craig, we haven't heard from John and Steve all day. They haven't replied to our messages, and their phones aren't ringing."

"Okay, okay, let's take a step back. Tell me from the beginning. Where are they?"

Adriana took a deep breath and realized the hand holding the phone was shaking.

"They messaged this morning, saying they were heading to a location near Saraqib. They were going to pick up Mia, then head back here."

"Okay, well... there could be any reason why you can't get hold of them. The signal can be terrible. Their phone batteries might have died. Sometimes, there is no electricity, and you can't charge the phone."

"Yes, okay."

"You are in Cizre, right?"

"Yes."

"It's a long way from Saraqib to the border there. It will take a full day of driving, maybe more. There are checkpoints everywhere. The road is terrible in places. What time were they meeting her?"

"Ten o'clock."

"Hmmm, okay... Assume she could have been late. If they left at eleven... it's now seven-thirty. Look, they won't reach you tonight. They probably won't travel in the dark. It's too risky. They must be resting up somewhere and will continue on in the morning."

"Okay, Craig. It's just..."

"I know. Waiting is horrible."

Adriana heard him sigh.

"Let me make some calls. I have contacts in the aid agencies. I even know a few officials. I'll see if there are any reports of anything happening, but I don't want to say too much to them. I don't want to alert anyone."

"Thank you, Craig." Adriana smiled at Maadhavi. "I'm sure it will all be okay, but please, if you hear anything, let us know."

"I will. There was nothing on the wire about anything north of Saraqib today. There was shelling west of the city and a few minor skirmishes, but nothing where they were. It looks like the ceasefire will happen, so I'm sure they'll be okay."

"Thank you, Craig, we appreciate it. If we hear from them, we'll let you know."

"I know it's hard, but get some rest. For all we know, they will be back with you by this time tomorrow."

"I hope so."

"I'll be in touch soon. Goodnight."

"Goodnight, and thanks, Craig."

Adriana ended the call and looked at Maadhavi. She smiled.

"It will be okay."

"I hope so," she gulped.

Adriana stepped forward and pulled her into a hug.

"Hey, as Craig said, by this time tomorrow, they will be back with us."

Maadhavi said nothing, just rested her cheek on Adriana's shoulder as Adriana stared at their reflection in the darkened window.

She hoped Craig was right.

71

They couldn't sleep, so they talked. No-one wanted to think about the next day, so they talked of happier things—childhood, love, funny events that had happened to them. They hadn't eaten since the morning, so when their stomachs growled, they moved on to food, deciding on the first thing they would eat if they got out of there. Steve craved a cold beer while Mansur described Warda's mutton biryani so well, their mouths were watering. Mia's desire was simpler. She just wanted to sit at a table with a tablecloth, clean cutlery, and plates, and to eat enough to fill her stomach. It had been so long since she had eaten a proper meal, she had forgotten what it felt like.

John listened quietly. He was hungry, and the thought of a well-made Botanist and tonic, crossed his mind, but mostly he thought of Adriana. He wondered what she was doing. How worried she must be. Closing his eyes, he pictured her standing before him, her hair falling on the sun-kissed skin of her shoulders, the sparkle in her hazel colored eyes as she smiled. He wished he could contact her, reassure her, tell her not to worry, tell her he loved her. He could feel the emotion welling up inside him, and he willed himself to think positive.

He remembered his conversation with Mansur. Maybe he was right. Maybe the time and date of his death was already written. Maybe it wouldn't be tomorrow. The thought gave him a little hope. He visualized Adriana again, slowed his breathing, feeling his body relax. *Adriana, I love you. Don't worry. Everything will be fine.* If there was a metaphysical world, perhaps she would get his message.

Anyway, he felt calmer and somehow perhaps a little confident for the first time. It was ridiculous, given that he was tied up on the floor of a house in a war-torn country, but tomorrow was another day. Anything could happen. He turned his attention outward again and tuned into the conversation between Steve and his niece.

"I'm sorry, Uncle Steve."

"It's okay."

"No, it's not okay. Because of me, you are here, your friends are here."

"Hey, hey, I'm glad you reached out to me." Steve paused. "You know, the day I found out you had crossed into Syria was the worst day of my life." John heard Steve's voice break. "I thought I would never see you again. So, whatever happens tomorrow, at least I got to see you once more."

Mia said nothing.

John cleared his throat. "Where's Naeem?"

"I don't know."

"Does he know where you are? What happened to you?" John heard Mia sigh.

"I don't know. I... thought I heard his voice at one stage, but..."

"If he does know, is he likely to help you?"

"I... I don't know anymore. He's different. I mean, he loves..." Mia's voice trailed off.

John waited.

"He loves... Malak."

John heard a sniff, and when she spoke again, her voice was quiet, just above a whisper.

"She didn't deserve to be born into a place like this. I made a mistake... I've ruined so many lives...."

72

John watched the room take shape as a fresh day began, the black turning to grey as the sun peeked above the horizon.

He had slept little but didn't feel tired. His fingers were numb, and his buttocks sore from sitting in one position, but his mind was on the day ahead. What was going to happen? He looked over at Mansur lying on his side, his chest rising up and down as he slept. He said he wasn't worried, but could that be true? He was sleeping soundly enough.

John glanced over at Steve, leaning against the wall, the slight figure of Mia leaning against him. She slept soundly, a look of peace on her face. As if feeling John's gaze, Steve's eyes blinked open, and he turned his head to look at him, held his gaze for a moment, then nodded. Turning away, he looked toward the window where long rays of sun began to stream through, highlighting the dust motes dancing in the air. John followed the direction of his gaze, and they sat staring at the light. The constant shelling of the previous day was absent, and they could hear the chirping of birds.

Mansur stirred and with difficulty, maneuvered himself into a sitting position. He smiled at John and Steve, then closed his eyes, and his lips moved silently.

John watched him, wishing he believed in something, something that gave him the inner peace Mansur seemed to possess, but he couldn't bring himself to surrender to the unknown. He had to be alert, ready for any possibility they could free themselves. He wouldn't give up just yet.

In the distance they heard vehicles, the sound getting nearer as they waited. The vehicles stopped outside the building, and they heard voices and the slamming of doors.

The three men exchanged glances. It was time.

"Mia, Mia." Steve nudged her with his shoulder. "Wake up, my darling."

She blinked, her eyes meeting John's, then Mansur's. Mansur smiled. She turned her head to look up at Steve. John saw his throat move as he swallowed before forcing a smile.

John looked toward the door and concentrated on his breathing as his heart rate increased. He slowed his breathing down. Deep inhalation, he heard footsteps on the steps, full exhalation. If he was about to die, he wouldn't let them see that he was scared. He straightened up, raising his chin. Again, deep inhalation, the door crashed open, full exhalation, fighters stepped into the room, faces hidden behind *shemaghs*, their weapons on slings over their shoulders. John watched them as if in slow motion as they approached each of them, then a hood was pulled over his head and hands gripped his arms and pulled him to his feet.

"Yalla, yalla!"

John's feet dragged across the floor as he was half-carried and pulled out of the room. He felt his feet drop from step to step as they carried him downstairs, the light behind the hood increasing as they reached the street. He heard footsteps behind him and the grunts and thuds of the others being dragged out.

He heard shouts in Arabic, what sounded like commands, and his feet dragged through the rubble as his captors pulled him across the road. He struggled to make sense of the sounds outside, to get an idea of what was happening, and heard more vehicles approaching. His captors stopped. The other vehicles stopped, and he heard raised voices, shouting, arguing.

"Mansur?" He felt the grip on his arms tighten, and he was pulled upright. "Mansur, what are they saying?"

John heard what sounded like a curse in Arabic, and the grip on his arms loosened. He fell forward, turning his head just in time to avoid smashing his face as he landed with a thud on the ground, the impact driving the air out of his lungs. He gasped for breath, sucking air in, then realized his hood had shifted. There was a gap, and he could see boots and sports shoes facing each other. The voices were still raised, angry Arabic filling the air. One set of boots stood toe to toe with another before the pair on the right stepped abruptly back as if the person wearing them had been pushed away. The shouting continued for another minute, then John saw boots and shoes moving away. He heard vehicle engines starting, then the sound of vehicles, one, two, maybe three, moving away.

What was going on? Through the gap in his hood, he saw a pair of scuffed and torn sports shoes approaching. They stopped in front of him and shifted position as the wearer squatted down. He felt fingers on his hood and blinked violently as the hood was removed, and his eyes struggled to cope with the influx of light. When his eyes adjusted, he was staring into the face of a young bearded man.

73

A knife sawed at the rope binding John's wrists together, and he winced as the restraints broke free, and the blood flowed back into his hands. He wriggled his fingers, rolled onto his back, and sat up as his ankle restraints were cut. The young man—boy—moved toward Mansur and released him before removing his hood. Mansur sat blinking against the light, shaking his arms out, then grinned at John.

"Today's not the day."

John looked over his shoulder and saw Mia already released and another man cutting away Steve's restraints.

What just happened?

The second man finished with Steve and walked over to Mia and helped her to her feet. She threw her arms around him, and he stood, looking uncomfortable, his hands by his side, a commando knife in one hand, Steve's black hood in the other.

Steve got to his feet and looked at the man in Mia's arms.

"I never thought the day would come when I would say I'm happy to see you."

Mia stepped back, holding the man at arm's length, "Where's Malak?"

"She's here."

"Where?" Mia looked around frantically.

He jerked his head toward a Mitsubishi pickup parked behind them. "She's in the pickup."

Mia spun around and ran to the vehicle, pulled the door open, and reached inside. She stood and turned to face them, a small child in her arms. She kissed the child on the forehead over and over again as Steve approached her.

Mia looked up, her eyes moist. "Uncle Steve, this is Malak." She kissed her on the forehead again. "My little angel."

Steve reached out and touched the girl's face with his fingertips. "Malak." His face beamed, and he turned to John and Mansur. "This is my grandniece. Isn't she beautiful?"

John still couldn't understand what had just happened and wasn't about to relax, but he didn't want to ruin Steve's moment.

"She sure is, Steve."

Steve turned back to look at Mia and her daughter. John caught Mansur's eye before stepping closer to the older of the two men.

"Are you Naeem?"

The man regarded John with suspicious eyes, then nodded. John held out his hand.

"I'm John." He gestured toward Mansur. "This is Mansur. We're friends of Steve." Naeem shook John's hand and nodded at Mansur.

"What happened here, Naeem? Who were those men, and why did they let us go?"

Naeem adjusted the position of the AKM on the sling around his shoulder and looked down at the ground.

"My brothers," he mumbled.

"Your brothers?" John frowned and glanced at Mansur. Mansur understood and moved away to talk to the boy. "How did they get Mia's phone?"

Naeem jerked his head up, "My phone. They took it from her in the other place."

"Why did they capture us?"

Naeem sighed and looked over at Mia and Steve.

"It's complicated. You are... *kufaar*. Do you know what that means?"

"Non-believers, yes, but why did they let us go?"

"Because I told them to."

"Because you told them to." John frowned. That didn't make sense. "And how did you find us?"

"He told me." Naeem nodded toward the young boy talking to Mansur. "He followed them here when they brought Mahfuza here."

"Mia?" John saw his face twitch.

"Yes."

"Okay, good." John looked away and for the first time, took in his surroundings. They were in what at one time would have been a residential street but now was a vehicle-wide track between piles of rubble and coils of rebar. On each side stood partially destroyed buildings, the one they had been in one of the few still standing.

"Where are we?"

"Idlib."

John conjured up an image of the map he had poured over before coming. Idlib was around fifteen kilometers inside the territory held by *Hay'at Tahrir al-Sham*. They needed to get out of there.

"So, what do we do now?"

Naeem gestured toward the pickup. "You come with me."

"Where?"

"We need to go south. I know a place to cross."

John nodded and called out, "Steve, Mia, we have to go." He glanced over at Mansur, who nodded. He patted the young boy on the shoulder, said something to him in Arabic, and the boy turned and walked toward the Mitsubishi.

Naeem walked toward the rear of the pickup and reached in, pulled out a large piece of cloth, and tossed it to the boy, saying something in Arabic. The boy vaulted into the back, then climbed onto the cab roof. He shook out the cloth and tied it to the aerial. John recognized the white flag with the green insignia from his internet research. The flag of *Hayat Tahrir Al-Shams*.

"Steve, you and Mia get in the front with Naeem. Mansur and I will sit in the back."

John climbed in and reached a hand down to help Mansur. The boy sat in the rear with them and unslung his weapon, holding it across his lap. John studied him as he sat down with his back to the cab. He looked maybe sixteen or seventeen, his beard barely taking hold, but his eyes were that of a man much older, hard and empty. John reached forward and held out his hand.

"*Shukraan*. Thank you." The boy hesitated, then shook John's hand. John pointed at himself. "John."

The boy nodded and pointed to himself. "Karam," he replied then looked at John's chest. He mimed ripping something off, and John looked down, puzzled.

"Shit." He ripped the Velcro press badge off his ballistic vest and stuffed it into the thigh pocket of his cargos. Mansur did the same, then they ripped them off the back of each other's vests. The boy had been watching them, and once they were done, he looked away as the vehicle started up and moved off.

John tilted his head toward Mansur and lowered his voice. "What did the boy say?"

"He said the girl was being held prisoner. He didn't know why, something to do with a phone. Then they brought her here. He overheard them, saying they would execute us. So, he went to find the other guy. Naeem?"

John nodded.

"They came here and told the men to let us go."

"And they just let us go because Naeem and a boy told them to? It doesn't make sense."

"No, he said there was another man, an *Emir*."

"What's an *Emir*?"

"A... general."

John frowned as the vehicle jolted and jumped over a pile of stones.

"The *Emir* and his men came with them in another vehicle."

"I thought I heard three vehicles leaving,"

"Yes." Mansur reached out and grabbed the side of the truck to steady himself as they rocked back and forth. "He told the other men they had to release us."

"Why would he do that?"

"I don't know." Mansur grunted as the pickup crashed over another pile of debris. "But we are free, that's all that matters."

"Yes." Mansur was right, but it still didn't make sense.

"Why did this boy help us?"

"He said he's tired. He doesn't want to fight anymore. He wants to go home."

"Where's he from?"

"Raqqa, Central Syria. His family was killed in an air raid."

"Shit. He must be only fifteen, sixteen?"

"Sixteen."

John shook his head and looked back at the troubled young boy with the automatic weapon in his slender hands.

The pickup turned left onto a wider road that had been cleared of debris, and the ride smoothened out. Now the going was easier, John could hear raised voices in the cab. He turned to look through the rear window just as the vehicle pulled to a stop. The passenger door opened, and Steve stepped out.

"What's the matter?"

Steve leaned his hands on the side of the tray.

"She says she won't leave without the others."

"The others?"

"She says there are others."

74

Craig stood on his tiny balcony and looked down on the street below, already bustling with traders. He loved living in this part of Istanbul. Many of his colleagues stayed across the river in Cihangur with the other expats, but he preferred to be here in Balat, right in the heart of things. He knocked back the last half of his espresso and rested the glass on the handrail. He had worked the phones late into the night and early this morning without any luck.

No-one had seen or heard of any incidents involving three journalists from a Portuguese newspaper. He had tried everyone—Sophie at Médicins Sans Frontières, Trevor at the U.N., Yusuf at The Red Crescent—nothing. Despite promising him a bottle of expensive single malt, even Sergei, his contact in the *Voennaya Politsiya*, the Russian Military Police, had drawn a blank. As a last resort, he had phoned his government contact in Damascus, a contact he rarely used unless it was extremely important, but no-one had heard anything. Apart from shelling southwest of Saraqib and a couple of Turkish drones spotted above the M5, it had been a quiet twenty-four hours. His thoughts were disturbed by the sound of his phone buzzing, and he stepped back inside to pick it up off his desk.

"Adriana, any news?"

"No." He heard the worry in her voice. "I was hoping you had heard something."

Craig grimaced. "I... sorry, Adriana. I've worked my contacts, but no-one has seen them."

The silence on the other end was deafening.

"Adriana, don't worry yet. Just keep trying their phones. As I said, it could just be a network problem. Whenever I'm there, I always have problems." He heard her sigh, and he closed his eyes, feeling her pain. "Look, I'll keep trying, too. If I hear anything, I'll be straight on the phone to you."

"Thank you, Craig. I'm sorry to trouble you, I... I just don't know what to do."

"It's no trouble at all. Stay positive, Adriana, everything will turn out alright."

"I hope so." He heard her sigh again. "Thank you, Craig."

"Don't mention it. I'll be in touch as soon as I can."

He ended the call and tossed the phone back onto the desk. He picked up a packet of cigarettes and his lighter and went back out onto the balcony. He tapped out a cigarette, flicked open the zippo, shielding the flame with his hands, and lit up. He took a long drag and blew the smoke into the air. Leaning his forearms onto the handrail, he stared down at the street below. There must be something he could do, someone he could call. He took another drag and flicked the ash off the end, watching the particles float out over the street. An idea was forming, but he didn't like it. He thought over the possible connotations as he finished his cigarette and then reached a decision. Flicking the butt onto the floor of his balcony, he grabbed his espresso glass and walked back inside, putting the glass and cigarette pack down on the desk and picked up the phone. Scrolling through the phone book, he selected a number and dialed.

"Alo."

"Mehmet, it's Craig."

75

"How many are there?"

"Seven."

"Shit," John muttered almost to himself. He glanced at Steve and John, then looked back at Mia who sat half out of the pickup cab holding Malak in her arms. Steve and Mansur stood beside him while Karam perched on the edge of the rear tray, monitoring the street. "And you say they are slaves?"

"Yes, they've been kidnapped from their villages and raped repeatedly. Some are only teenagers. One girl, Shayma, has been bought and sold five times. She's fourteen!"

"They are not our problem," Naeem grumbled from inside the cab.

"I told you I'm not leaving without them!" Mia snapped.

"Mahfuza, we cannot go back there. We have to leave."

"No." Mia shook her head. "I'm not going anywhere. And my name is Mia." She looked up at John and Steve. "Don't listen to him. He thinks it's their right to take women as slaves. He says the Koran allows it." She looked over at Mansur. "Is that right?"

Mansur shook his head.

She turned back to face Steve.

"Uncle Steve, if you had seen these poor girls, you wouldn't hesitate."

"Mia, it won't be safe." Steve sighed. "We have to get out of here. I've put John and Mansur in enough danger already."

Mia looked at John. "Please. We can't leave them. Mansur?"

John exhaled loudly and looked up the street. A vehicle approached from the other direction, weaving its way through the rubble. Mia reached up and arranged her *hijab* to cover her face as the vehicle got closer, another pickup with bearded, armed men sitting in the back. Naeem raised a hand and waved to the driver as it approached. The driver waved back, and the pickup continued by, the fighters in the rear staring at them as they passed. John waited until they were further up the street, then turned to Mansur and Steve.

"What do you think?"

"I don't like it, mate. We came here to get Mia and Malak. We've got them. The sensible thing is to leave as soon as possible."

"Mansur?"

"Mr. Steve is right. The sensible thing to do is to leave. But..." Mansur hesitated and looked down at Mia and her child.

"But what?"

"What these men are doing is wrong. These are mothers, daughters, someone's sister."

John nodded. Mansur was right. They should at least try. He looked at Steve.

"Imagine it was Maadhavi."

"I know, I know." Steve rubbed his head in frustration. "You're right, you're both right." He kicked the tire of the pickup. "But how do we do it?" He bent over so he could see inside the cab. "Naeem?"

"I'm not doing it."

"Now listen to me, you little shit," Steve growled. "I've been tolerant so far because you got us free, but..." He held up his hand, the tips of his thumb and forefinger an inch apart. "I'm this close to ripping your fucking throat out. If you want to redeem yourself, you get off your arse, come out here, and tell us how we can do this."

Naeem didn't move.

John bent down to look inside, and he could see the knuckles of Naeem's right hand turn white as he gripped the butt of his AKM. He turned to Steve and tried to catch his eye, but Steve ignored him, glaring at Naeem. After a moment, there was a click, the driver's door swung open, and Naeem got out. John and Mansur exchanged glances, then stepped back to give him space as he walked around the front of the vehicle. Naeem refused to make eye contact with Steve and stood sullenly, looking at the ground.

"Describe the building, Naeem," John asked.

"It's... a three-story building, abandoned," he mumbled.

"Speak up," Steve snapped.

John raised a calming hand.

"Go on."

"They are on the second floor."

"Any guards?"

Naeem shook his head. "Just one." He glanced toward Karam. "It used to be him."

"And are the men there now? During the day?"

Naeem shrugged. "I don't know. Maybe."

Steve grabbed Naeem by the shoulders and pushed him up against the side of the car, his face just inches from Naeem's.

"Why do I get the feeling you aren't being very helpful?"

They heard a click and looked up to see Karam standing up, his AK 47 cocked and pointed at them both. Mansur spoke softly in Arabic, and Karam relaxed a little, the barrel dropping toward the ground, but he stayed standing, watching.

Naeem stared back at Steve. "Because it's a stupid idea. We can't just go in there and take those women. They belong to my brothers. We will get killed."

"Are you afraid?"

"I'm not afraid of anything." Naeem stuck his chin out. "Allah is with me."

John stepped forward as Steve glared at Naeem from inches away.

"Hey, hey, calm down, guys. This is not helping anyone." He looked up and down the street. "You are just going to attract attention."

Steve relaxed his grip and stepped back. John caught his eye, and with a jerk of his head, indicated he should move away. Steve stepped back further, still glaring at Naeem, his eyes hard, flexing his hands. John stepped between them and fixed Naeem in his gaze.

"Naeem, Mia says she won't leave without them..."

"I won't," Mia piped up from the front seat.

"See?" John nodded at Naeem. "Now, if you want her and your daughter to get out of here safely, I suggest you help us. Understand?"

Naeem nodded reluctantly and straightened his jacket.

"The sooner we get out of here, the better." John waited until Naeem nodded again. "Now, tell me how many men are there? Will they be in the building?"

Naeem sighed. "There are normally eight of us, including me and Karam. They might be there, I don't know. We have a couple of days' rest from the front, there's a ceasefire, so they could be there or out getting food." He shrugged. "I really don't know. There will be at least one there. A guard."

John pursed his lips and studied Naeem's face.

"Aren't you supposed to be with them?"

"Yes..."

"And?"

"I don't get on with my commander, Abu Mujahid."

"The guy who captured us?"

"Yes."

"So, something I'm puzzled about, Naeem. Why did they let us go?"

Naeem looked down at the ground and scuffed the ground with his boot.

"I told them to."

"You told them to? You and,"—John nodded toward the boy standing in the tray and gave him a reassuring smile—"Karam here?"

"That's right." Naeem's tone was defensive.

"And they just said okay?"

"Yeah." Naeem looked away, crossing his arms across his chest. John looked across at Mansur, who gave a subtle shake of his head.

They knew he was lying. But why? What was really going on?

"Okay, so you will take us to this house, we'll check it

out, and if we can get the women out safely, we will. But first, we will take a look. Okay?"

"Okay," Naeem mumbled.

"Is that okay with you, Mia?"

"Yes, thank you."

"Steve, Mansur?"

"Yup."

John looked at Mansur, who nodded in return.

"Mansur, tell Karam what we are doing."

Mansur started translating, the young boy looking down at his weapon as he listened. Mansur stopped speaking, and the boy nodded. John saw him glance in his direction, then back at Mansur. He said something, and when Mansur replied, he nodded again, lowering himself down, so he was sitting in the back of the pickup again.

"He'll help us if we help him go home."

"Raqqa?"

"Yes."

"Shit." John pinched the bridge of his nose. "This is neverending." He looked over at Karam, who was watching him from the back of the pickup. He nodded at him and smiled. "Poor kid. Okay, one thing at a time." He looked at Steve. "You okay?"

"Yeah, mate. Let's do it."

John turned back to Naeem, who was still leaning against the vehicle, a sullen look on his face.

"Let's go, Naeem."

John climbed back into the rear of the pickup and placed a hand on Karam's shoulder.

"Shukraan, Karam."

The boy nodded and looked away shyly.

John sat down beside Mansur as Naeem started the pickup.

"One thing's for sure, we will need another vehicle. We won't fit another seven women in the back here."

"Don't worry, John, it will be okay." He smiled. "We have a saying, *la tehmel ham Allah yehellha.* God will provide."

"We will find out soon enough, Mansur."

76

Naeem slowed to a stop beside a row of damaged buildings and parked. He climbed out and came around to the rear of the vehicle.

"We can't go any closer in this. It's too dangerous."

"Where is it?"

"I'll show you."

John vaulted out of the pickup and looked around. The street reminded him of pictures he had seen of European cities during World War II—partially destroyed buildings on each side, separated by gaps where other buildings had once stood, piles of rubble and garbage filled the gaps and lined the road. There were few people around, and those who were, hurried with their heads down, avoiding eye contact.

"This way." Naeem walked off while Steve and Mansur climbed out of the car and followed, leaving Karam to watch over Mia and Malak. About two hundred meters up the road, there was a road heading left. Naeem stopped just beside the junction, keeping close to the wall of the building on the corner and waited for John, Steve, and Mansur to catch up.

"Down this street on the left. There are three buildings, then a gap. It's the building after the gap."

John nodded, stepped forward to the edge of the building, and peered around the corner. He counted and found the building. The angle was wrong, though. He needed to see it from the other side of the street. He ducked his head back and thought for a moment.

"Give me your jacket." He pointed at Naeem's camouflage jacket.

"Why?"

"Just give it to me."

Naeem unfastened his jacket, unslung his AKM, passed it to John, then shrugged off the jacket. John passed the weapon back and took the jacket. He slipped it on, covering his vest, then stepped into the junction and crossed the road, turning his face away from the street. He hoped anyone looking in his direction would just see another fighter walking down the road. Reaching the opposite corner, he crouched down as if relacing his boot. He had an unobstructed view of the building now. It stood alone, the buildings on each side destroyed in earlier air raids, but it was partially damaged, exposed rafters showing in the roof, and the walls peppered with bullet holes. No glass remained in the windows, and the corner of the upper floor had a gaping hole in it. John spotted movement as a figure stepped out of the doorway into the street, wearing a mixture of camouflage and what looked like an AK47 on a sling, hanging off his shoulder. He seemed relaxed as he put a cigarette in his mouth and lit it from a lighter cupped in his hands. John stood up and crossed back the way he had come before the man looked in his direction.

"There's a guard, but he looks relaxed. I couldn't see anyone else, but I don't know if there are more inside. There're no vehicles outside."

"Then maybe they aren't there," said Naeem. "Usually, the pickup is outside, and if they were there, they wouldn't keep a guard. The guard is to stop the... women escaping."

John stared at Naeem, a retort on the tip of his tongue. What would drive a man brought up in modern civilization to think keeping women as slaves was okay? That it was God's reward? He bit his tongue and returned his thoughts to freeing the women.

He was sure they could handle one guard, but they desperately needed another vehicle before they rescued the women. There was no way everyone would fit in the single pickup they had, but so far, the only vehicles he had seen were rusted shells or filled with H.T.S. fighters armed to the teeth.

"Naeem, where can we get another vehicle? Where did you get this one?"

"I took it."

"You took it?"

"Yes. This morning before we rescued you."

"Took it from where?"

"One of the locals." Naeem shrugged. "He was driving past. I needed a car, so I took it off him."

"They must love you in these parts," said Steve, shaking his head.

"If I hadn't done it, you would be dead by now," Naeem shot back.

John gestured to Steve not to respond and looked back at Naeem. "I need you to get another one and quickly. Bring it back here."

Naeem frowned, hesitating.

"Now, Naeem!"

He nodded, adjusted the strap of his AKM, so it hung in front of him, and set off down the street.

"Do you trust him?" Steve asked as they watched him walk off.

"No."

"Maybe Mansur should go with him?"

John considered the idea, then shook his head.

"No, we need an Arabic speaker with us just in case anyone comes."

"Mia?"

John shook his head. "No. No-one will speak to her. They'll only want to speak to another man." He exhaled loudly. "We have to trust him. Let's go back to the car."

"Okay."

"I still don't buy his story about how he freed us," John mused as they weaved their way through the rubble.

"Neither do I. Little shit. I want to strangle the bastard."

"Steve, we need him, so stay calm." John put a placatory hand on Steve's arm.

"But let's be careful."

77

It was a tense thirty minutes before Naeem returned. Two other vehicles had passed, but the H.T.S. flag flying from the aerial and the sight of Karam standing on the back, cradling his AK47, had prevented anyone from stopping.

Naeem pulled up behind them in a small Hyundai Truck. John walked around it and nodded his approval. The goods tray had tall sides, and anyone sitting down in the rear would be hidden from sight.

"Perfect, Naeem." He beckoned to Steve and Mansur to join him. "Call Karam."

He waited until they were all standing by the truck, Naeem still sitting in the driver's seat.

"Mansur, please translate for Karam." Mansur nodded, and John continued. "The guard won't have seen this vehicle before. Steve, you and I will approach the building from the rear on foot. Naeem, you and Mansur drive up in the truck. Stop just short of the building, so he can't see you clearly... maybe call out for directions or pretend the truck has broken down... you decide. Anyway, wave the guard over, distract him, we'll approach him from behind, and grab him. Then we go in, get the women, put them in the truck, and get out of there." John looked at each of their faces, "What do you think?"

"Sounds okay." Steve looked back toward the pickup. "What about Mia and the baby? I don't want to leave them alone here on the street."

"No."

"And the women might not want to come with us," added Mansur. "They don't know who we are. They will be suspicious."

"Yeah," John sighed. "You're right." He closed his eyes and visualized the street, pictured what they were planning to do. Opening them again, he asked, "Can Karam drive?"

Mansur asked, and the boy shook his head.

"What about Mia? Naeem?"

"Yes, she can."

"Great. Naeem, wait here. Steve, come with me, you too, Mansur, bring Karam."

The four of them walked forward, and John crouched down beside the open door of the cab. Looking inside, he saw Mia staring out the windshield, a distant look in her eyes while Malak dozed on the seat beside her.

"Mia?"

She jumped as if surprised she wasn't alone, blinking rapidly as she tuned back into the present.

"Mia, we're going to rescue your friends. We are leaving Karam here to protect you. Naeem says you can drive?"

"Yes."

"Good, I want you to wait in the vehicle. Karam will wait on the corner over there." John pointed up the street. "When he sees us grab the guard, he will signal you. I want you to bring the pickup down to the building. Can you do that?"

Mia nodded, her eyes flicking toward Karam, who was listening to Mansur's translation.

"Then I'll need you to come inside the building and tell the women to come with us. They'll need to see someone they can trust. Okay?"

"Yes."

John stood up, stepping back as Steve leaned over and looked in.

"Are you okay?"

Mia nodded at Steve and John.

"Don't worry, I can do it."

"I know you can." Steve smiled and winked. "See you soon."

"Wait."

The two men paused and looked back in.

"What is it?"

Mia leaned forward and flipped open the glove compartment. "Look what I found." Lying in the glove compartment was a handgun.

Steve reached and took it out. He stood, making sure his body blocked Naeem's line of sight and showed it to John.

"A Glock 17." He pressed the magazine release button, checked the magazine, and popped it back in again. "Fully loaded, too."

"Give it to Mansur. He's in the car with Naeem." John looked at the tall Bedouin. "Mansur, keep this with you in case Naeem tries anything stupid."

Mansur took the weapon and slid it into his waistband, pulling his jacket over the top.

"Karam understands what he has to do?"

"Yes."

"Good. Okay, guys, let's do it."

78

It took John and Steve a good twenty minutes to get in position. Fortunately, this part of town had been shelled heavily at one time and was now mostly abandoned. However, it took them time to work their way around behind the building and approach it from the rear. By the time they were pressed up against the back wall, they were covered in dust, and their hands and knees were scraped from tumbles and falls in the piles of rubble. John crouched down and moved slowly along the side of the building until he could see the corner where they had left the others and could just see Karam's head. He raised his hand and gave him a thumbs-up signal. John saw Karam nod, then his head disappeared behind the wall. John slowly turned and keeping low, moved carefully back to the rear of the building.

"Okay?" Steve whispered.

"Yup." John looked back to the front of the building. "Let's go around the other side. When Naeem stops, the guard might see us. We'll be better hidden on the other side."

Steve nodded, turned around, and headed toward the far side of the building. They made their way carefully through the piles of broken concrete and bricks. A pile of bricks dislodged and slid to the ground. John winced and held his breath. They both waited, crouched low to the ground, in case someone had heard them, but all they could hear was the truck approaching on the road. John crept forward until he was at the corner of the building, waited until he heard the vehicle stop, then peered around the corner. Naeem had stopped the truck just short of the building, and fortunately, the angle of the sun prevented a clear view into the cab through the windshield. John heard a noise and saw the guard step out of the doorway onto what remained of the pavement. He held an AK47 in his left hand, but it was pointed at the ground, and his trigger finger was outside the guard. He seemed relaxed, the battered Hyundai mini-truck not appearing to be a threat. An arm waved out of the vehicle window, followed by a shout in Arabic. The guard stepped into the road and slowly walked over to the vehicle.

"Here we go," John muttered to Steve and stood. He stepped around the corner, bent down, and picked up a brick, then walked quickly and quietly after the guard.

The guard approached the vehicle, and just as he neared, a cloud went across the sun. The reflection on the window disappeared, affording him a clear view inside. He stopped and raised his weapon.

"Naeem?"

John sprinted forward, raising the brick. The guard must have heard him. He turned... but was too late. John brought the brick down on the side of his head, knocking him to the ground. The guard groaned but was still conscious. John kicked the AK out of his reach and followed it up with a kick to the guard's stomach, knocking the wind out of him. He laid in the dirt, gasping for breath as blood ran from a split in the side of his head.

"That's going to hurt in the morning," Steve said as he joined John beside the truck.

"Quick, let's secure him and get him out of sight." He looked over at Mansur and Naeem, who had climbed out of the truck. "Check the building. There might be others. Mansur, take the AK." John bent down and flipped the guard onto his stomach and knelt between his shoulder blades as Naeem and Mansur set off at a run toward the building.

"Steve, find something to tie him up." John pressed the guards face into the dirt with his right hand and turned slightly, so he could monitor the street. He heard an engine and saw the pickup rounding the corner at the end of the road as Steve came back with some rope he had found in the rear of the truck. John bound the guard's wrists, then removed a Glock from the holster on his belt before going through his pockets. He found a cell phone, which he pocketed and a pocketknife which he used to cut the excess end off the rope, then threw it to Steve.

"Tie his feet together."

Using the knife, John tore off a section of the guard's shirt and tied it around his mouth as a gag, then stood, slipping the knife into his pocket.

Mia pulled up behind the truck, and both she and Karam climbed out and ran toward them.

"Mia, wait until they've checked the building, then go tell the women we have to leave straight away." As he said that, he saw Karam look past him and turned to see Naeem in the doorway, giving the thumbs-up.

"Mia, all clear. Go!"

Mia ran across the road as John bent down and grabbed the guard's arm.

"Steve, give me a hand. We'll hide him in the building." Steve grabbed the other arm, and they dragged the fighter across the street and through the doorway past Naeem. "Over there." John nodded toward a gap under the stairs. They dragged him over and dumped him face down in a dark corner. John turned and saw a look of discomfort on Naeem's face.

"You know him?"

Naeem nodded. "Abdul."

"It was him or us." John grabbed Naeem by the arm. "Come on, bring the truck in front, and let's get out of here."

Naeem nodded and stepped out the door.

"Steve, watch Naeem and bring the pickup over. I'm going to check upstairs."

John jogged up the stairs and stopped on the first floor. He waved a fly away from his face and peered through the doorway leading into the first-floor room. He ducked his head back as the stench of stale urine and feces hit him. Grimacing, he heard voices above and continued on up the stairs. As he reached the second-floor landing, Mansur, who was standing in the doorway, turned and looked at him, an expression of great sadness on his face. John glanced past him.

"Shit."

79

It took them another fifteen minutes to get the women out of the building. At first, they were scared to leave, but once Mia explained her Uncle and his friends were rescuing them, they had finally agreed.

John stood beside the doorway, watching the women as they filed from the building and climbed into the back of the truck.

"Bastards," he muttered under his breath. Mansur, standing beside him, didn't comment, but the look on his face said everything. As the last girl walked out, Mia came over and put a hand on John's arm.

"Thank you."

"It's okay. You were right not to leave without them."

Mia gave his arm a squeeze and smiled at Mansur.

"*Shukraan* Mansur."

"*Afwan, habibi*. Don't mention it."

John looked across to where Steve was fastening the tailgate of the truck.

"Mia, tell Steve he can ride with you in the pickup.

Mansur, Karam, and I will ride in the truck. We'll leave in a minute. There's one more thing I have to do."

"Okay." Mia turned and crossed the road.

John looked at Mansur. "Come with me."

John walked back inside and approached the guard who had turned himself over on to his back and was glaring at them from under the stairs.

"Mansur, ask him where the others are."

Mansur crouched down and pulled the gag out of the guard's mouth. He said something in Arabic. The guard looked at him, then cleared his throat and spat at Mansur. Mansur wiped the phlegm from his face and wiped his hand on the guard's shirt. He looked up at John, and John nodded. Mansur raised the AK47, reversed it, and slammed the butt into the guard's nose. The guard cried out as his nose split, and blood poured down his face.

"Ask him again."

Mansur spoke, and the fighter raised his head, looked straight at John, then at Mansur. He thrust his chin out, lip curled in a sneer, and shouted, *"Allahu Akbar!"*

Mansur shook his head, raised his weapon, and rammed the butt into the man's face again, knocking him sideways. He reached forward, stuffed the gag back in his mouth, and stood. Looking down at the man, he took a step back and slammed the toe of his boot into the man's groin, once, twice, a third time, then turned and headed for the door. As he passed John, he said, "He'll be praying for Allah now."

80

Mansur shifted into a lower gear as the truck dropped down into a partially filled bomb crater where the road had once been, the truck rocking from side to side on the uneven surface. John turned to look back through the rear window of the cab. Karam stood in the rear corner, leaning against the tailgate, his AK 47 cradled in his arms, while at his feet, out of sight from the casual observer, sat the women The boy saw John looking at him and nodded before going back to scanning the road ahead with worried eyes, his forehead creased with a permanent frown. John turned back and stared out the windshield. Ahead, the pickup climbed out of the crater, a puff of black smoke coming out of the exhaust as Naeem changed gear.

"Why are people so cruel to each other, Mansur, in the name of God?"

Mansur glanced over at him, gave a half-smile before concentrating on the road again. He gunned the engine as the truck exited the crater, then changed into a higher gear once they were on the relatively smooth surface of the road again.

"If these people truly knew God, they would never do these things, John. They misunderstand, misinterpret, or are brainwashed by people who twist the teachings to gain power."

"I'll never understand it, Mansur. Why can't we all just get along?" He shook his head. "These poor women... I can't imagine the horror they have been through. The girls, Nour, Shayma. Did you see them? They're just kids, for fuck's sake."

Mansur exhaled. "I know."

"Evil fucking bastards."

"Their time will come, my friend."

"Hopefully, soon." John looked ahead to the pickup, "I don't trust this Naeem, either."

"No," Mansur agreed, eyes on the road.

Ahead, the pickup turned left, and Mansur slowed for the turn. They had entered a part of the town that was relatively unscathed. Many buildings seemed to be abandoned, but there were still businesses open, selling food, cigarettes, and glass bottles filled with diesel and petrol. There were more people, too—groups of men gathered around smoking or just talking, watching the vehicles pass, many of them armed and wearing a mishmash of military uniforms. Some nodded at Naeem, the H.T.S. flag doing its job.

"I'll be glad when we're out of town. Way too many people around."

Mansur nodded and swung the wheel to avoid a large pothole.

"Checkpoint ahead," he muttered as they rounded a bend and saw the pickup slowing. John leaned forward, removed the Glock from his waistband, and wedged it under his thigh. He glanced down at the AK 47 lying on the seat between them. Hopefully, they wouldn't need it. When questioned earlier, Naeem had been confident he could talk his way through the checkpoints, and they had no other option but to trust him.

"Here we go," John muttered as they pulled up behind the now stationary Mitsubishi. Concrete blocks forming a chicane partially blocked the road, and behind it was another Japanese pickup with what looked like an anti-aircraft gun in the rear bed.

John took a deep breath, his fingers moving toward the Glock as they watched a bearded fighter approach the driver's side of the Mitsubishi. Apart from him, John counted three other men, two standing on the road and one seated behind the anti-aircraft gun.

"If it all goes wrong, Mansur, you take out the two on the ground, I'll aim for the guy on the pickup."

Mansur nodded, reached for the AK, pulled back the charging handle, released it, and laid the weapon on his lap.

They watched the man glance up at the flag, then lean down to question Naeem.

"Can you hear what he's saying?"

"No," Mansur replied.

John took another deep breath, his heart racing. Pulling the Glock out from under his thigh, he kept it below the window, ready.

The fighter took a piece of paper from Naeem and examined it before handing it back. He then straightened and looked back at the truck. John held his breath, then saw the fighter turn and call out something to the men behind him. He banged on the roof of the pickup, and this time, John heard him call out, *"Yalla, Yalla."*

The pickup moved off, and Mansur put the truck in gear,

moving the vehicle forward. As they passed the fighter, he smiled out the window.

"*Ya'teek al ayfa.* May God give you strength."

"*Teslam.*" The man raised a hand in thanks, then they were through the checkpoint and following the pickup down the road.

John exhaled loudly and grinned at Mansur.

"That's a good start."

81

They drove in a northeast direction, heading toward Route 60, which led to the town of Binnish. On the outskirts of Idlib, just after the Alhal market, they came upon another checkpoint. Mansur and John repeated the procedure, weapons held ready as they waited for Naeem to talk his way through. Once again, they saw him pass a piece of paper to the checkpoint guard.

"What do you think that paper is?"

Mansur shrugged. "I don't know. Maybe a special pass for these *Hay'at Tahrir al-Sham* men."

"Well, as long as it works," John replied as the guard waved them on.

He nodded at the guard on his side as they drove past, then something, he didn't know what, made him lean forward, so he could see the man in the wing mirror. The man was staring after their vehicle, and John frowned as he watched him lift a radio to his mouth and say something. It could be nothing, his nerves had been on edge all morning, but he felt uneasy. He leaned back in his seat.

"I can't wait to get back into Kurdish territory. I don't trust any of these guys."

"No, but it will not be any easier there. We don't have our passes and passports anymore, or any money."

"I know." John exhaled loudly. "One thing at a time. Let's cross the frontline first."

About three kilometers out of Idlib, the pickup in front slowed and turned off the main road onto a dirt farm track. Mansur downshifted and followed as the track led east through uncultivated fields. They bumped and ground along the track, the rough surface hard going for the heavily laden mini-truck. They struggled to keep the pickup in sight, but fortunately, there seemed to be only one way out of there.

John heard a shout from behind and twisted in his seat to look through the rear window. Karam was gesticulating at him, then looking behind, clearly worried. John turned back and looked in the wing mirror. In the distance, he could see a white pickup following them, and judging by the dust cloud it was throwing up, it was approaching at speed.

"Shit. Mansur, someone is following us. Step on it."

Mansur glanced in his wing mirror, then downshifted with a crunch, and slammed his foot on the accelerator. The truck slowly picked up speed, slamming from hole to ridge, the impacts on the rough road throwing them around inside the cab. John hung onto the grab handle on his side and looked behind him into the rear of the truck. He could hear shrieks and cries as the women bounced around. Karam had wedged himself in the corner, legs spread wide, holding onto the rail with both hands.

Mansur flashed the headlights, hoping the pickup in front would see them as he swung the steering wheel from side to side to avoid the worst of the bumps.

"They're catching us," John said, his eyes on the reflected image in the wing mirror.

"I can't go any faster."

"Fuck." John thought fast. The speed the pickup was approaching meant their intention wasn't benign. He glanced back in front and saw the brake lights of the pickup go on as they noticed Mansur flashing the headlights behind them. The pickup pulled to a stop, and the doors opened. John switched hands on the grab handle and thrust his right arm out the window, gesturing at them to get down. Naeem and Steve looked puzzled, then they seemed to realize. John saw Naeem reach inside the pickup and pull out his AKM, and Steve removed the Glock from his waistband.

"Go round them, Mansur, get the truck on the other side."

Mansur braked heavily, and they heard screams from behind as the women were thrown forward. He slammed the truck into a lower gear, then swung the wheel over, swerving into the field. The truck tipped precariously and struggled for traction as Mansur wrestled with the wheel. They crashed over a shallow ditch into the field, then he swung the wheel back again, and they lurched up onto the road on the other side of the pickup.

"Stop here," John shouted as the truck skidded to a halt. He tossed the Glock to Mansur, grabbed the AK47 from the seat, opened the door, and jumped out. "Wait for Mia, then take the truck farther up the road. We'll try to hold them off."

Mansur nodded, revved the engine, and put the truck in gear, but kept his foot on the clutch.

John shouted at Karam to join him as he ran toward the pickup. The young boy vaulted out of the back of the truck and ran after John. The following pick up was only about five-hundred meters away as John rounded the pickup door and grabbed hold of Mia.

"Get in the truck," he screamed as he dragged her out. Mia struggled to hold on to Malak, a look of confusion on her face. "Go, now!"

She looked behind her, saw the approaching vehicle, and realization dawned. She sprinted for the truck, passed Malak inside to Mansur, and climbed in. The truck revved and moved off down the road as John turned his attention to the approaching vehicle.

Naeem and Steve were standing on either side of the pickup, weapons held ready.

"Who is it, Naeem?"

"I don't know." He tightened his grip on his AKM,

"Fuck. Steve get off the road into that long grass. Naeem, try to talk us out of it." John looked around for Karam. "Karam over there." John pointed to the left side of the road. The boy understood and ran off the road and dropped onto his stomach in the dirt, flattening himself into the shallow ditch.

"Naeem, come to this side." John moved around to the front of the pickup and dropped to the ground where he was out of sight but could still see the vehicle approaching from underneath the chassis. Naeem moved around to the driver's door and stood, his AKM held across his chest.

The vehicle slowed as it got nearer, and John rolled over and peered around the side of the Mitsubishi. He could see the H.T.S. flag flying from its aerial and three men standing in the tray facing toward them. As the vehicle stopped, the men raised their weapons and pointed them at Naeem.

Naeem cursed in Arabic.

"Who is it?"

"Abu Mujahid."

"Shit," John muttered and slid back over to where he could see Steve. "Steve," he hissed. "Stay down, this could get messy."

He moved back to the middle and peered underneath the vehicle. He heard the driver's door open, but from his viewpoint, looking under the chassis, he could only see the boots and lower legs of the driver. He slowly got to his feet and popped his head just above the hood of the vehicle and looked through the cab of the pickup. Abu Mujahid stood behind the door, his left hand holding the door frame, his right balled into a fist, and raised in the air as he shouted in Arabic. Naeem replied, but his answer didn't satisfy Abu Mujahid, and the two argued back and forth, Abu Mujahid gesticulating wildly from his position behind the door.

John crouched back down and looked at the weapon in his hand. He'd never held an AK47 before, let alone fired one. Did it have a safety? There was nothing on the left, but on the right-hand side, above the trigger, was a lever. That must be it. He clicked it down, and remembering what Mansur had done, pulled back on the charging handle. Raising the stock to his shoulder, he turned his head to look over the hood again. The discussion didn't seem to be going well, Abu Mujahid sounding increasingly angry and Naeem sounding more and more desperate.

John glanced across to Steve, who had his head down and remained out of sight of the men in the pickup. He looked across to the other side where Karam was practically invisible, his slim frame pressed flat to the bottom of the ditch. So far, Abu Mujahid's men only knew about Naeem. That was in their favor. Hopefully, they thought everyone else had gone ahead with the truck. John tuned back into the shouting. He raised his head again. Not being able to understand the language, he needed to watch the body language. Abu Mujahid looked furious, his eyes wide, and now, both hands were waving in the air. Naeem shouted back, and whatever he said, it was the last straw. Abu Mujahid turned his head slightly and said something to his men. It was so quick, if John hadn't been watching for that very sign, he would have missed it. As one, the three men on the back of the pickup raised their weapons and shouted, *"Allahu Akbar!"*

82

All hell broke loose as three AKs opened fire simultaneously. Glass and pieces of metal flew into the air, and John dropped to the ground in a panic. A rapid and continuous klunk, klunk, klunk filled the air, accompanied by the sound of breaking glass and tortured metal. Stray bullets flew overhead and kicked up fountains of dirt in the road beyond John. He flattened himself to the ground, and despite himself, clenched his eyes shut and covered his head with his arms. Fuck, fuck, fuck! He pulled his elbows into his sides, curling himself into a ball, trying to make himself as small as possible. His entire body tensed, anticipating the moment a bullet would carve its way through his flesh. The firing seemed to go on forever. When it stopped, his ears were ringing, and the air was thick with the smell of smoke, dust, and burned metal. Someone shouted *Allahu Akbar,* which was then repeated, and he forced himself to open his eyes.

He had dropped the AK, and he reached for it, pulling it close to him. As he peered under the pickup, he could see fluids dripping from the damaged engine. One of the rear tires was flat, and there was no sign of Naeem. He seemed to have vanished. All John could see ahead were the boots of Abu Mujahid, where he stood behind the driver's door. The boots moved sideways as he stepped out from behind the door and walked toward the Mitsubishi.

John took a deep breath, his heart in his mouth. Bringing the weapon to his shoulder, he realized the curved magazine sticking out from underneath the AK prevented him from getting a good angle of fire. Shit. He thought fast, rolled onto his side, and pulled the stock to his shoulder. He took another deep breath, counted to three, then pulled the trigger. The sound underneath the vehicle was deafening, and ears ringing, John looked to see if he had found his target as the men in the pickup opened fire again. John had missed. Abu Mujahid had thrown himself to the side of the road and was crawling rapidly on his belly for cover in the field.

John heard a high-pitched cry of *Allahu Akbar,* and another weapon opened up to his left. He glanced across to see Karam standing in the ditch, his AK held in front of him, firing wildly at Abu Mujahid's men. The sight spurred John into action, and he pushed himself to his feet, moved to his right, and aimed around the fender of the pickup. The men on the pickup were now directing all their fire in Karam's direction. John raised the barrel toward the cab and pulled the trigger. He knew what to expect now and was able to control the movement of the barrel. Two bullets hit the fighter on the right in the chest, the third going wide. John stood straighter, more confident now, and aimed at the remaining two. He fired twice more, both rounds going through the windshield. He raised the barrel slightly and fired again, this time finding his target, the top of a fighter's head exploding in a shower of crimson fragments. The remaining fighter ducked down, and John began to move forward when he heard a bang and then the ping of a bullet embedding itself in the vehicle wing in front of him. Instinctively, he threw himself flat, and wriggled backward in the dirt. He had forgotten about Abu Mujahid. Where the fuck was Steve?

Another couple of bullets whacked into the engine block of the Mitsubishi, and John scrambled backward, then rolled across to the far side of the vehicle, putting as much of the vehicle between him and Abu Mujahid as possible.

More fire came from the pickup, but it wasn't aimed at him. John turned his head to look for Karam. He was flat in the ditch again. John slid over and peered around the side of the pickup. The remaining fighter wasn't even bothering to aim, staying hidden and holding his AK at arm's length above the cab, firing wildly in John's general direction.

There was a shout from John's right, followed by an answer from the pickup. John looked out again, and a hail of bullets rained into the dirt to his left. He rolled back in front of the vehicle as another round of fire hit the dirt to his right. Shit. He pulled his legs into his chest, pressing himself up against the front bumper. He was hyperventilating, fighting to gain control of his breathing as his hands and legs trembled with adrenaline. He was pinned down and couldn't go left or right.

Then he noticed the engine noise and looked up to see the Hyundai mini-truck speeding toward him. The windshield starred as it drew fire from the H.T.S. pickup, but it kept on coming. John stared in horror, the truck showing no signs of stopping. The driver's door opened, and John saw a figure leap out. The sight spurred John into action, and he leaped to the side, rolling off the road into the field as the truck plowed into the Mitsubishi, forcing it backward toward the pickup. John rolled over twice, wincing as stones dug into his sides. He oriented himself, raised the AK, held his breath, and squeezed off a burst of three shots. He missed, but the fighter ducked down behind the cab of the pickup as the truck and Mitsubishi came to a stop. John cursed and crawled forward to where he had last seen Karam.

"Karam," he hissed, but the boy didn't move. John crawled closer and saw a sticky crimson patch staining the back of the boy's jacket. John was overcome with rage, adrenaline coursing through his body, and he roared. Pushing himself to his feet, he sprinted toward the pickup, his vision narrowed to a single point as he fired round after round at the cab. Dirt fountained up around his feet, but he didn't see or hear anything, just a pounding in his head. He fired continuously into the cab until he heard a click. He pulled the trigger again, but the magazine was empty. Rounding the cab, he flung the empty AK47 at the fighter as he picked himself up off the bottom of the tray where he had been sheltering. John's AK bounced off him and landed in the dirt, and the fighter grinned and raised his weapon, pointing the barrel at John's head. John heard a bang and flinched but saw a look of surprise on the fighter's head as a hole appeared in his forehead and the back of his head exploded behind him. John spun around to see Mansur kneeling beside Karam, the Glock held in a two-handed grip pointed in his direction. John breathed out, realized his legs were shaking, and collapsed against the side of the pickup. Shit. There was a constant ringing in his ears, and his heart was pounding away. He took a deep breath, trying to calm his nerves, but they couldn't relax yet, there was still Abu Mujahid.

"Mansur," John called out. Mansur looked up and John

held up one finger and pointed toward the place where John had last seen the H.T.S. commander. "There's one more."

Mansur nodded and ran at a crouch to the side of the mangled remains of the Mitsubishi.

John ducked down and moved around the back of the fighter's pickup. He picked up the AK, then remembered it was empty. "Shit," he cursed and dropped it on the ground. He needed another weapon. He was about to reach into the pickup tray when he heard a shot and a man crying out in pain. John peered around the side, then heard a familiar voice.

"I've got him."

83

John straightened up and looked out from behind the pickup to see Steve standing in the field, pointing the Glock at a figure lying on the ground.

"Are you okay?"

"Yeah, mate. He won't be going anywhere quickly."

John walked around the pickup. A movement inside the cab caught his eye, and he looked inside to see another fighter slumped against the seat. His chest rose and fell rapidly as he struggled for breath, a wound in his chest bubbling pink froth as he breathed, a hole in his lung. John reached inside and pulled the fighter's AK from his reach. The fighter's lips moved silently as he struggled to say something. John looked down at him and searched inside himself for any feeling of sympathy or compassion. He couldn't find any. Grabbing the fighter's combat jacket by the shoulder, he pulled him closer, the fighter slipping down onto the seat. John lifted the hem of the jacket and found a firearm in a holster at his waist, removed it, and tucked it into the waistband of his cargo pants. Picking up the AK, he turned away from the vehicle, leaving the man to bleed out.

On unsteady legs, John walked over to Mansur, who sat in the dirt, holding Karam's body in his arms. He looked up as John approached and shook his head. Tears ran down from his eyes, and with one hand, he reached up and gently closed the boy's eyes. For the first time in many years, the child was finally at peace. The sight rekindled John's anger, and he turned around and walked around the wrecked Mitsubishi and across the road to Steve. Lying at his feet in the dirt, his face screwed up in pain, Abu Mujahid's breathing was rapid and shallow, low moans escaping from his mouth.

"I shot the bastard in the knee."

John looked down at Abu Mujahid's leg. Where his knee should have been, was a bloody mass, the lower part of the leg sticking out at a strange angle.

"Good."

"It seemed the least I could do."

John stepped closer, and with the toe of his boot, gave the damaged knee a nudge.

Abu Mujahid screamed in pain.

John did it again, a little harder

He screamed again, then seemed to pass out, his face white, his forehead a sheen of sweat.

Steve raised an eyebrow at John. "Are you okay, mate?"

John nodded. "Take his weapons, and let's go."

"What do we do about him?"

"Leave the fucker."

John turned, then hesitated.

"On second thought." He reached behind him and removed the Glock from his waistband before crouching down beside Abu Mujahid. With his left hand, he slapped him in the face.

"Hey." He slapped him again, and Abu Mujahid stirred,

blinking his eyes open. He looked lost for a moment, then his eyes widened in recognition. John nodded. "I wanted you to be awake for this." He stuck the barrel of the Glock into Abu Mujahid's groin. Abu Mujahid's eyes widened, his chin trembling, and he tried to wriggle out of the way. John kept the barrel pressed into his groin.

"Allahu Akbar," he said and pulled the trigger.

84

John reversed his grip on the Glock, stood up, and handed it to Steve, who was watching him with a frown.

"Let's go."

He turned and walked back to Mansur. He had laid the boy's body on the ground and was kneeling beside him, his hands raised in prayer, his eyes closed, and his lips moving silently. John knelt beside him and placed a hand on the boy's arm.

"Oh, fuck," Steve muttered as he walked over and stood beside them. They waited until Mansur had finished and opened his eyes. He looked at the two of them, but said nothing, his eyes still moist.

"He was a brave little bugger," Steve said, and Mansur nodded.

John placed a comforting hand on Mansur's arm.

"We have to go, my friend."

"I know."

John stood and scuffed at the ground with his toe.

"The ground is hard as rock. We can't bury him." He

sighed, his hands on his hips, and turned to look at the vehicles. "And we can't take him with us. What do we do?"

"Bring some rocks." Mansur stood. "We'll cover him with them."

John and Steve gathered rocks and stones from the side of the road while Mansur gently laid Karam out straight in the shallow ditch. He arranged his arms, so his hands were crossed on his chest, then the three of them covered him with the rocks. Finished, they stood and looked down at the pile of stones that were now the only thing that remained of the lion-hearted boy.

"Wait," John said. He walked over to the pickup and retrieved his discarded AK. Walking back, he wedged it barrel first into the pile of stones. Stepping back, he said, "If there is such a thing as heaven, little warrior, I hope you find it."

"Amen." Steve placed a hand on John's shoulder. "Let's go, mate."

"Yeah," John sighed and looked at Mansur. "Where are the women?"

"I left them about a kilometer up the road."

"Let's go get them." He slapped Mansur on the back. "I'm glad you came back, my friend. You saved my life. *Shukraan jazilan.*"

"*Afwan, habibi.* Don't mention it. You would have done the same for me."

They heard a voice calling from the cab of the Mitsubishi, and the three of them exchanged puzzled glances. Walking over, they peered in through the window and saw Naeem trapped in the crumpled footwell, wedged between the dashboard and the seats.

"Naeem, there you are." Steve turned to John and muttered, "I wondered where the little shit had gone."

"I can't move."

John looked closer and saw the edge of the accelerator pedal wedged into Naeem's thigh.

"Steve, give me a hand."

"Do I have to?" Steve muttered but came forward to help John wrench the buckled door open.

John reached down, grabbed Naeem by the shoulders, and tried to pull him free. Naeem groaned in pain but didn't move.

"Steve, go around the other side and see if you can move him from that side."

Steve walked around the back of the pickup, grumbling to himself, and pulled the door open on the other side. He looked down at Naeem's legs and winced.

"He's wedged in pretty tight, mate. It's not going to be easy."

John frowned and straightened. He looked up at the sky. They needed to get out of there. Judging by the sun, it was already after midday, and who knew what attention their gunfight would have attracted.

"Can we lever the dashboard back?"

"Hmmm." Steve puffed his cheeks and scratched his head. Leaning over, he grabbed Naeem's lower leg. "Naeem, I will count to three, and on three, I'm going to try to pull your leg free. Okay?"

Naeem nodded and closed his eyes, gritting his teeth in anticipation of the pain.

"Ready?"

"Yup."

"One..." Steve tugged hard on Naeem's leg. Naeem screamed as Steve straightened and winked at John. "His leg's free now."

John shook his head, grabbed Naeem under the shoulders, and dragged him free from the vehicle, laying him on the road. Naeem laid panting as John looked at the wound in his leg. He suppressed a wince as he glimpsed the white of bone inside the wound.

"It's a nasty gash, Naeem, but you'll live." John removed the pocketknife he had found earlier and cut two strips of cloth from Naeem's jacket. He balled one up and pressed it on the wound, passing the other to Mansur, who tied it around Naeem's leg, securing it in place.

"Can you walk?"

"I think so," Naeem grimaced.

John stood and pulled Naeem to his feet, supporting him as Naeem tested his weight on the leg and gasped in pain.

"Are you okay?"

Naeem's face contorted, but he nodded.

"Right, let's go."

85

All three vehicles were too damaged to continue, so the four men walked up the road to where Mansur had hidden the women.

They were well-armed now, having stripped the bodies of weapons and ammunition, Naeem showing them how to reload the AKs.

They spread out across the track, Steve and Mansur on each side, John in the middle, supporting Naeem with his right arm, the AK hanging from his left.

Naeem winced with each step, but they made reasonable progress, eager to put as much distance between them and the wrecked vehicles as possible.

"Do you think the gunfire will have attracted any attention?" John asked Naeem.

"I doubt it," Naeem muttered between steps. "Not out here." He took another step, and John heard a sharp intake of breath as he put weight on his wounded leg. "But..." Naeem pointed at the sky with the index finger of his right hand. "We never know who is watching up there."

John was puzzled. "What do you mean?"

Naeem took another breath. "Drones. Turkish, Russian, Syrian, American."

John looked up at the sky. It was clear and blue, barely a cloud in sight, nothing moved. Would he be able to see a drone, anyway? Best not to think about it.

They walked for ten minutes before John saw a cluster of trees in a field ahead and to their left. Mansur went ahead while Steve hung back, alternately scanning the road behind and the surrounding fields.

As John and Naeem neared the trees, Mia ran out and grabbed hold of Naeem's arm.

"What happened? Are you okay?"

"Yeah," Naeem said through gritted teeth. "It's just my leg."

The women sitting beneath the trees watched silently as John and Mia lowered him to the ground with his back against a tree.

"Will he be okay?" Mia asked.

"Yup." John didn't see any point in having Mia worry about Naeem's wound. "He'll need stitches, but nothing antibiotics and painkillers won't put right," he reassured her.

Mia nodded and crouched down beside him, resting a hand on his arm as Naeem sat with his eyes closed, his forehead wrinkled in pain.

John looked around at the women gathered beneath the trees. Mansur was talking to them in Arabic, and judging by the way they were listening avidly, John guessed he was explaining what had happened.

One woman held Malak in her arms, the little girl still dozing. She seemed to spend a lot of time sleeping. John didn't know much about kids but assumed they would be a lot more active. Hopefully, they could get her to a doctor soon and get her checked over. He saw Steve step over and whisper something in Mansur's ear. Mansur raised an eyebrow, nodded, then spoke to the women in Arabic. After a moment, the women turned to look at John. Some nodded, a couple gave him a thumbs-up. Puzzled, John turned to Steve.

"What did you say?"

"I just told Mansur to tell them what you did to that Mujahid dude." He glanced over at the women. "They seem to approve."

John looked away. In the aftermath of the gunfight, with adrenaline running high and the sight of Karam lying dead in the field, it had seemed the right thing to do, but he didn't want to think about it now. There was no place for guilt or regrets.

"Where's Karam?"

John turned back to look at Mia. She saw his expression, and her hand went to her mouth. Shaking her head, she repeated, "No, no, no."

John didn't know what to say that would comfort her, eventually settling for, "He fought 'til the end, Mia."

"Yeah, he was a brave little bugger," Steve added.

Mia sat back on her haunches, her shoulders slumped, and stared out into the field with dull, empty eyes.

John and Steve exchanged a glance. They would never forget the boy, but they still had a long way to go until they were safe. John squatted down beside Naeem.

"Naeem, how far do we have to go from here?"

Naeem opened his eyes. "About two kilometers that way." He nodded toward the road. "Then there is a path leading across the field. About another kilometer or so, and it will come out near the M5 highway. The highway is in government territory."

"So, maybe forty-five minutes on foot."

Naeem nodded. "Maybe. These women... I don't know, it might take longer. But we shouldn't go now. Wait until dark. It will be safer."

"Okay." John looked around at the women, then up at the sky. "What time is sunset?"

"Around seven."

"What time is it now?" John frowned. "The bastards took my watch."

Naeem turned his wrist and slid his sleeve up to show his watch. "One-fifteen."

John exhaled and shook his head. "Six hours. Damnit." He stood. "Okay, let's hope no-one comes this way."

"They won't. That's why I picked it."

John nodded slowly, staring down at the young man leaning against the tree. He was a strange fellow. John despised everything he stood for and couldn't figure out what was going on in Naeem's head. Why was he helping them? What was his motivation? He had just seen all his so-called brothers killed, was betraying everything he believed in, and was leaving the land he had given up everything for. Was it really all for his daughter? Would John do the same? He thought of Adriana, how worried she must be. She hadn't heard from him since yesterday morning. Yes, he would give up everything to make sure she was safe. He'd done it before. He shrugged. Maybe he was overthinking it.

"Get some rest." John turned and looked for Mansur and Steve. He needed to explain what they would do next.

86

Hemin stood on the riverbank, watching the murky waters of the Tigris flow past. On the opposite bank, just over a hundred meters away, was Syria.

It had been three days since he had ferried the men across. He had seen a lot of things in his time, but the bravery of the three friends, venturing into a war-torn country, where they knew no-one, couldn't speak the language, and not knowing whether they could come back alive, all to save a girl and her daughter, was to be admired, and he couldn't get them out of his mind. Where were they now? Had they succeeded?

The call from Mehmet three days ago had been niggling away in the back of his mind. He hoped Mehmet wasn't up to his usual tricks. Hemin really wanted the three men to succeed. They had said they would call him when they were on the way back, but until now, he hadn't heard a thing. He stupidly hadn't taken their number, so he had no way of checking on them or even warning them Mehmet had called.

He bent down and picked up a flat rock, hefted it in his hand, then sent it skipping across the surface of the slow-moving river. It bounced three, four times before sinking to the bottom, the movement startling a white egret into flight from its perch on the opposite bank. He watched as it sped across the river, just above the surface as it flapped its wings to gain height. Reaching the opposite bank, it slowed and gracefully landed on a rock on the Turkish side of the river. Why couldn't human beings live like that? In harmony with each other, the freedom to move around whenever and wherever they want.

He gazed back over the river to the fields, stretching away from the riverbanks. The other side looked just like where he was standing yet had seen so much death and destruction. It was all so unnecessary. He reached into his pocket and pulled out his phone. He would call Ferhad. Maybe he would have news.

The afternoon dragged as they waited for darkness to fall. The countryside had remained quiet, the distant shelling and gunfire from previous days absent.

Fortunately, they were shaded from the harsh sun by the trees, which hopefully also shielded them from any drones patrolling the skies. The women had talked in low tones or dozed while Naeem drifted in and out of consciousness. He wasn't looking good. The pain must have been immense, and John suspected the wound was getting infected and would need antibiotics soon.

John, Steve, and Mansur had taken turns keeping watch, but John had not been able to rest. Whenever John sat down and tried to relax, his body started trembling, and if he closed his eyes, memories of the gunfight kept flashing before his eyes, so he gave up. He would get through it, he knew that. He'd been under intense stress before, and the trauma would eventually fade, as long as he kept himself busy. The main thing was to get Mia, Malak, and the women to safety. Otherwise, it would all have been for nothing.

John stood and walked over to where Mansur leaned against a tree, eyes on the road, his AK47 cradled in his arms.

"Kaif halek, habibi?" John asked. "How are you, my friend?"

"I'm good, John." Mansur smiled briefly before his face returned to the sad expression he had when John approached. "I keep thinking about the boy. He should have been in school, not living like this."

"Yeah," John sighed. "I know. It's all so bloody pointless." He turned to look back at the women. "But his death was not a waste. These women will now have a chance at freedom."

"Yes."

John turned to gaze out across the fields. "It looks so peaceful out there."

"Nature is beautiful, my friend. It's us who ruin it."

"Yup." John smiled. "I still remember that morning vividly, when you took me out to see the sunrise in the dunes. That experience will stay with me forever."

"You have to come back, John. You and Adriana."

"I'd like that."

Mansur shifted his position, adjusting his shoulder against the tree and adjusting the weight of the AK in his arms.

"I plan to spend more time with Warda and the girls. Recently, some days I've not seen the girls before they go to bed." He shook his head. "Not anymore. Life can change in the blink of an eye." He turned to face John. "Don't you forget that, John. We have to value every moment we have with the ones we love."

"I won't forget." John smiled. "Why don't you get some rest? I'll stand watch for a while."

Mansur shook his head. "I can't."

"No, neither can I."

"John, there's something bothering me about Naeem."

"You, too?"

"Yes." Mansur looked over John's shoulder to where Naeem was dozing. He reached into his pocket and pulled out a folded pile of paper. "Look at this."

"What is it?" John unfolded it. "It's in Arabic."

"It's some kind of special pass. I took it from the glove box of the pickup when we left. See, that is the official stamp of *Hay'at Tahrir Al Sham,* and this is his name." Mansur pointed at a line of script. "It says here that he is to be allowed free passage through any checkpoint, as are the people with him."

John frowned. "Maybe all these guys have one?"

"Maybe." Mansur shrugged. "But I don't think like this. It's signed by a senior commander. Remember Karam mentioned an *Emir* had come when they rescued us? It doesn't make sense. We are the enemy to them. We are *kufaar,* unbelievers. Even me."

John handed the paper back and turned to look at Naeem.

"I don't trust him either, but maybe we're overthinking it? He's got us this far."

"I don't know, but it doesn't feel right."

"No," John exhaled loudly. "To be honest, though, there's not much he can do right now with that injury." John looked toward the sun, which was noticeably lower in the sky. "Anyway, it will be dark soon. The sooner we are out of here, the better."

88

Steve bent down, cleared a patch of ground, and sat down beside Mia.

"How's she doing?"

Mia didn't look up, just continued gazing at her daughter asleep in her arms.

"The same. She's still warm."

Steve reached out and felt the child's forehead with the back of his hand.

"Yeah, she still has a temperature." He sighed. "It won't be long now. Don't worry, we'll get her to a doctor, get her some nutritious food, and she will be fine."

Mia nodded.

"Are you okay?"

"I keep thinking of Karam. He was just a kid."

"I know. Brave but just a kid. A sad waste of life." Steve looked away, his gaze going out past the edge of the trees, across the fields. "Remember that time we went out to Ballarat for the weekend." He looked back at Mia. "We panned for gold in the river, do you remember?"

Mia looked up at Steve, then past him at the fields beyond. "I remember."

"You were so excited when you saw those tiny flecks of gold in the bottom of the pan."

Mia nodded, a distant look in her eyes.

Steve looked down at the ground, picked up a pebble, and played with it between his fingers.

"That was the last trip we did together before you left."

"It seems so long ago."

"It does." Steve looked up, "Why, Mia? Why did you come here? We were heartbroken."

Mia turned to look at Steve.

"I'm sorry, Uncle Steve. I never meant to hurt anyone." She shrugged. "I thought I loved him." She looked away again. "No, I did love him. He was so nice to me. No boy had ever been nice to me before. I just... I got swept away."

Steve nodded and looked over at Naeem.

"I wanted to kill him... I think I still do."

"Yeah," she sighed. "I know. It wasn't all his fault, though. He was naïve, too. He was brainwashed, sold a dream, but it was nothing like they said it would be."

"But he still believes."

"Yes." Mia glanced over at Naeem, remembering their discussion about the Yazidi women. "He does. I thought maybe now, with Malak, he would go back to how he was before." She shook her head. "But he's too far gone."

"Do you still love him?"

Mia sighed heavily.

"I've searched my heart for any trace of the love I once had, but it's gone." She looked down at Malak, her face softening briefly, but when she looked up, her eyes were hard. "He gave me the most beautiful thing in my life, but he also destroyed my life. I've tried hard to find forgiveness, but I feel nothing for him now."

89

Craig was just about to file his report on the overcrowding crisis at the refugee camps in Northern Syria when the phone vibrated on his desk. He clicked send on the laptop, then reached for the phone, glancing at the screen as he picked it up.

"Sergei, any news?"

"You owe me a bottle of Glenlivet."

"Tell me more."

"Your friends were spotted going through a checkpoint at Ain Issa."

"Fantastic." Craig breathed a sigh of relief. Finally, some news. "When was this?"

"Three days ago."

"Three days? Shit. Nothing more recent?"

"No, my friend. That was all I heard. They were in a taxi heading west on the M4."

Craig sighed and rubbed his face. He'd hoped to share some good news with Adriana but was back to square one.

"Okay, thank you, Sergei. I appreciate the update."

"You are welcome, my Scottish friend. When are you coming to this side again?"

Craig screwed up his face as he tried to remember his schedule. "Next week, I think, Wednesday or Thursday. I'll let you know."

"Good. Bring the whisky. We'll have a drink."

"I will. Thank you, Sergei."

Craig ended the call and stared down at his desk. Where the hell were they now?

He looked at the phone screen again. He'd better call Adriana. Some news was better than none at all.

90

They set out as soon as the sun dropped below the horizon, John leading the way with Naeem, Mansur in the middle of the column of women, and Steve taking up the rear.

Naeem had weakened over the afternoon, and John was supporting more and more of his weight as they crossed the field and rejoined the dirt road. John waited until everyone was on the road, then led them, walking southeast. The temperature had dropped considerably, and a cool breeze blew across the fields. The sky had clouded over as the afternoon wore on, and now the sun had set, the darkness was almost complete, the moon and stars conspicuously absent. Fortunately, the road was clear, and despite the darkness, they could follow it, the only sound coming from the scuffing of feet on loose pebbles and Naeem's labored breathing. It was slow going though and it was over thirty minutes before John could see what looked to be the path Naeem had mentioned.

"Naeem," he whispered, "Is this it?"

Naeem panted heavily and peered into the darkness. "I

think so, I... don't know."

"You don't know?"

"It's dark, I... I've only been here once before."

The rest of the group caught up, and Steve moved to the front.

"What's the matter?"

"He thinks this is it, but he's not sure."

"He thinks?" John could see Steve shaking his head. "For fuck's sake, Naeem."

"It's dark."

"Yeah, and you're a fucking idiot," Steve muttered.

"Steve, we don't have any other option. We have to try it."

"Yeah, well, I hope the little shit is right," Steve grumbled and moved back to the rear of the group.

John stepped off the road, and slowly, Naeem leaning heavily on his shoulder, made his way along the track as the others followed behind.

The further away from the road, the grass and uncultivated wheat grew higher, closing in around them until they were walking through a tunnel of grass. Crickets chirped, and now and then, there was a rustle from the undergrowth as a nocturnal creature scuttled away to safety.

Naeem's breathing grew heavier as they progressed, John taking more and more of his weight.

"Stop," he whispered, and John halted, the woman behind him bumping into him in the darkness.

"What's the matter?"

"I just need to get my breath."

John lowered him to the ground, Naeem groaning as he stretched his leg out.

Mansur came forward, and John whispered to him to tell the others they would take a short break. While Mansur worked his way back down the group, whispering instructions, John did a quick mental calculation. They had been walking for ten minutes since they left the road. The highway must be near, if they had taken the right path, but it was hard to tell in the dark. Their pace had been much slower than John had expected, Naeem slowing them down considerably. He reached down and tapped Naeem on the shoulder.

"Come on, we have to get moving." He grabbed Naeem's arm and pulled him to his feet, Naeem groaning with the effort. "Let's go." John turned and whispered to the woman sitting behind him, "*Yalla, yalla.* Let's go." The woman whispered to the woman next to her, and so on, and slowly, the group got to their feet.

John frowned as someone spoke, their voice carrying easily in the quiet country air. He waited until they were all on their feet, then set off along the path. The cloud cover had cleared a little, allowing a small amount of moonlight to filter through, and he could just see the path ahead as it curved away out of sight in the grass. Hopefully, not far to go now. He rounded the bend and stumbled as Naeem tripped and put all his weight on John. John gritted his teeth, regained his footing, and pulled Naeem upright.

"Come on, Naeem, get it together," he hissed.

Suddenly the world lit up as a powerful spotlight blinded John. Instinctively, he raised his arm to shield his eyes, and voices screamed at him in a language he didn't understand. More lights came on around him, more shouted voices, mingling with the screams of the women. The lights disoriented him, and he let go of Naeem. The next thing he knew, hands were forcing him to the ground, and he was flat on his stomach in the dirt.

91

John slumped against the back of the chair with a peculiar sense of déjà vu.

He had been forced to the ground, his hands secured behind his back with flexi-cuffs, a hood pulled over his head, then had been drag-carried for about five minutes before being dumped on the floor of a vehicle. He had no idea where he was or what had happened to the others, everything blurring into a mess of screams and shouts. He had tried to tune into the conversations around him, but it was a language he hadn't heard before, not Arabic, and he didn't think it was the Kurdish he'd heard being spoken in northeastern Syria.

The vehicle had bumped and jolted for another ten minutes before joining a smoother surface. He lost track of time until the vehicle stopped, and they dragged him out, up some steps, then dumped him in the chair. No-one spoke, and he sat for a long time with only his thoughts for company. He wouldn't allow himself to admit the fear lurking inside, forcing himself to be positive. He had been in this position before, and the universe had conspired to get him out of it. He had to believe it would happen again. There was no point in sitting in the chair, feeling sorry for himself.

He heard a door opening and a light being switched on. Someone walked behind him and pulled the hood off his head. He blinked rapidly, his eyes trying to adjust to the light. Another more powerful light turned on, and someone behind it adjusted it, so it was pointing at his face. Despite the situation, he felt slightly amused. What a cliché.

He saw a figure move out from behind the lamp, but that's all it remained—a silhouette. He angled his face away, the light too bright for his eyes.

The figure spoke, but again it was in the language he didn't understand. The figure spoke again, this time a little louder.

"I don't know what you are saying."

The figure said something else, and this time, the man behind him answered, then walked out from behind John. John got a glimpse of a military uniform, then the man left the room. The other man watched him for a while before he left as well.

What was going on? Who were these people?

About ten minutes later, the door opened again, and a man walked in. John wasn't sure if it was one of the men from before or a different one, the light in his eyes too bright. The man stood unmoving, and when he spoke, it was in accented English.

"What is your name?"

John hesitated. Did he tell the truth? Did he refuse to answer? He had no idea what the others were saying, assuming they had been captured too, so it was easiest to go with the truth.

"My name is John Hayes. I am an English citizen."

"Why are you here, John Hayes?"

Again, he hesitated. Should he tell the whole story? The interrogation seemed a little more sophisticated than the one he had undergone with Abu Mujahid. Were they Syrian government? Then why weren't they speaking Arabic? Was the dialect different in Syria? Not that it would help, he only knew a few words, anyway. He suddenly realized he was exhausted. The strain of the last few days had taken its toll, and he couldn't be bothered fighting anymore. His head dropped down, and he stared at the floor.

"I came here to help my friend. His niece wanted to leave Syria, to go back home. We came to save her."

The man said nothing for a while, and John wondered if he had understood.

"Can I have some water?" John's mouth was dry, and he was hungry, very hungry. He hadn't eaten since they left Arima. When had that been? Two? Three days ago?

"What is your friend's name?"

"Steve. Steve Jones. He is an Australian citizen. Is he here?"

"What is the name of the... niece?"

"Can I have some water, please?"

"Answer the question."

"Mia. She has a daughter, Malak."

"Malak?"

"Yes."

The man turned and knocked on the door. The door opened, and he said something, and the door closed again. The man stood watching silently until the door opened again, and another man entered. He walked toward John, and as he passed the light, John could see he was in uniform. His hair was cropped short, and he held a plastic bottle of water in his hand. He stood in front of John, unscrewed the cap, and held the bottle to John's mouth.

John gulped the water down until the bottle was empty. The man turned, and as he did, John glimpsed a flag on the man's shoulder.

"You are Turkish?"

His interrogator said nothing as the soldier with the bottle left the room, and the door clicked shut behind him.

"Are you Turkish?"

"I ask the questions."

John began to feel a little hope. He would rather deal with an official force who, hopefully, would be bound by some rules rather than a rag-tag bunch of fundamentalists.

"I think you are the Turkish Army."

Again, the man didn't answer, so John continued.

"I am a British citizen. My friend is an Australian citizen. Another friend is with us. He is from Oman. Our governments won't be happy if you mistreat us."

John saw the man change position. He moved slightly, a little away from the light but not enough to make out any detail.

"John Hayes, Englishman. No-one knows you are here."

"Yes, they do. Our wives know. They will inform our governments."

"Ah, so your governments don't know you are here." John could hear the amusement in the man's voice, and he cursed himself for his slip-up.

"What is the name of your friend from Oman?"

"Mansur Wahibi."

"How did you come here?"

"Look, you have to let us go. We only came to save Mia and her daughter."

"How did you come here?" The man's tone was firmer.

"We came by taxi from Zuhajrijja."

"And how did you get to Zuhajrijja?"

John sighed. "We crossed the border near Cizre. At night. We caught a taxi from there to Arima."

"And this niece, what was her name?"

"Mia."

"Mia, Mia. That's right, and her daughter?"

"Malak."

"Malak. Where did you find them?"

"In Idlib."

"Idlib? Hmmm."

John saw the man take two paces to his right, turn and pace back as if he was thinking.

"I don't believe you."

John shook his head. "It's the truth."

"You are lying."

"No."

"I think, John Hayes, Englishman," he said Englishman slowly, almost as if it was distasteful, "that you are a spy."

John shook his head.

"You have come to spy on us. I think you are... what do they call you? MI6. Yes, that's what you are."

John shook his head. "Do I really look like a spy to you?"

But the man had walked out of the room.

92

It was a long time before anyone returned.

John's arms were cramping. He tried to change position a few times, but nothing helped, the sides of the chair digging into his arms, and eventually, they went numb, anyway. The light stayed on. He closed his eyes but could still feel it on his face, burning into his eyelids.

He thought of Adriana, how worried she must be. He should never have agreed to come. He had been selfish, partly agreeing to help Steve because he craved adventure, but it wasn't worth it. He should never have put Adriana through this. He should have stayed in Lisbon. He knew deep down, though, he could never have done that to his friend. Steve had saved his life, and he owed him. He could never have spent the rest of his life, knowing he had chosen comfort over his debt to his friend. Where were Steve and Mansur now? Where were Mia and Malak? Had they got away?

His thoughts were interrupted by the door opening and a man stepping inside. He still couldn't see who it was, but when he spoke, he recognized his voice.

"Why was Mia here in Syria?"

John frowned. Did that mean they had also captured her? "She... came with her... boyfriend."

"Why did he come here?"

"He..." John sighed, no point in hiding it now. John didn't really care if Naeem got into trouble. He was the reason they were all there. "He joined the *jihad*."

"He joined the *jihad*." The man repeated slowly. "What is his name?"

"Naeem. I don't know his full name."

"Describe him to me."

The question confused John. If they had captured him, they would know who he was unless he was refusing to answer questions. Anyway, it wasn't John's problem.

"He's about five-eleven, thin, brown hair, beard. He has a wound in his left thigh."

The man turned and left the room.

"Turn the fucking light off!" John shouted after him.

93

John jerked awake. Despite his discomfort and the light burning a hole in his face, he had somehow drifted off. The sound of the door opening had woken him, and again, the man stood in the shadows.

"You are lying, John Hayes, Englishman."

John closed his eyes and counted to ten. He was struggling to remain calm.

"You have no proof, John Hayes, if that's what your name is. You have no identification, no passport, no papers. You expect me to believe you traveled across Syria like that?"

John shook his head, his eyes still closed.

"Well."

"Oh, fuck off." John gave up. The stress and strain of the last few days got the better of him. He would either end up dead or in a prison camp. What was the penalty for spying? Death? Fuck him. "It's all fucking true. Do you think I'd want to come to this fucking shithole if I didn't have a good reason? For fuck's sake! Go ahead, fucking kill each other in the name of God. The joke's on you. There is no fucking

God. It's all in your imagination. Allah? Bullshit! There's nothing out there. No Allah, no God, no Jesus, no Buddha. Fuck it, there's no fucking Jedi! It's all a load of bullshit. We get born, we all fucking hate each other, then we die and rot in the ground. If you don't believe me, that's your problem. Just fuck off and leave me alone!"

John took a deep breath and exhaled. He felt better. A smile grew on his face. "Fuck you all." The smile grew wider, and he began to laugh. He laughed louder and louder, his body shaking. He threw his head back and laughed to the ceiling. He laughed and laughed, feeling the release of tension, a heaviness leaving this body until finally, the laughter stopped. He lowered his head, catching his breath, and looked toward the shadowy figure standing near the door. He hadn't moved.

John closed his eyes, and his chin dropped to his chest. He was exhausted. All he wanted to do was sleep. A noise caught his attention, and he lifted his head and opened his eyes to see the man walking out the door. John watched the door close behind him and closed his eyes again. A moment later, John heard the door open, someone walked in and turned off the light before walking out.

94

Hours passed, John didn't know how long. He drifted in and out of consciousness, his fitful sleep plagued with the faces of Abu Mujahid and the young boy, Karam.

He had lost all feeling in his arms and his buttocks. His mouth was dry, and he had long ago given up trying to control his bladder, feeling great relief as he urinated where he sat.

In one dream, he saw the face of Charlotte smiling at him and woke up weeping, tears running down his face. Why had his life been like this? When he was young, he had so many dreams for the future, so much hope, yet nothing had turned out the way he had imagined. There had been moments of happiness, of love, but they had been canceled out by great sorrow, loss, and hatred. What was the point? How did people like Mansur seem so calm and content? Why did he have to suffer so much?

John drifted back into sleep and was woken sometime later by someone walking into the room. By the time he remembered where he was, the person had already moved behind him, pulled a hood over his head, and exited the room.

Fuck. Finally? An execution in some godforsaken hellhole that no-one in the rest of the world really cared about? An image of Karam flashed before his eyes—the young boy standing in the field, firing his AK47, his mouth open in a defiant yell, while John cowered behind the pickup. John lifted his chin. If he was going to die, he would die like the young boy—brave and defiant to the end.

He heard the door open and footsteps approaching. Arms grabbed him from both sides and lifted him to his feet. He gasped as the blood rushed back to his arms and legs, his limbs tingling and spasming. He forced himself to stand straight and held his head high. Pushed forward, he stumbled, the hands catching him and guiding him out the door. He was marched along, half-carried down some steps, then lifted into a vehicle and dumped on his side onto a hard-ridged metal floor. Doors were closed, then he heard the rumble of an engine, and the vehicle moved off.

John tried to focus on the sensations, the direction of travel, how many turns, and in what direction, but the journey went on too long, and he gave up. Again, he drifted in and out of consciousness, waking now and then as the vehicle jolted and bumped over rough surfaces. Sometime later, he sensed the vehicle slowing, then stop. He heard shouting outside, then the vehicle moved off again. Eventually, John had no idea when, the hood and sleep deprivation robbing him of all sense of space and time, the vehicle stopped. He heard doors slam, then there was silence. He drifted off again.

After a while, he heard the doors opening, and someone grabbed his feet and pulled him backward. He felt them hang out into space, then someone grabbed him by the arms and eased him out, his feet touching the ground. He struggled to stand upright, again the blood rushing to his legs, his limbs tingling with pins and needles. He remembered Karam and straightened, pushed his shoulders back, and held his head up high.

The hands under each arm turned him around and marched him for what felt like a couple hundred meters, up some steps, and into a building. Then the hands pushed him to a kneeling position on the ground. This was it... the end. Despite the hood, John closed his eyes, the act giving him some peace, and took a deep breath. His heart was racing, and he fought to bring it under control—deep breath in, deep breath out, five seconds in, five seconds out.

He thought back over his life. Would he have done anything differently? No, he had no regrets. He had done what he had done, and he still felt it was right. He had loved and lost but had lived a full life. Everyone he had killed had deserved it. There was nothing gratuitous. He had done what had needed to be done.

He heard footsteps, then from behind, he felt fingers tugging at his hood. It was removed from his head, and once more, he blinked rapidly, his eyes trying to adjust to the increase in light. Before he could see, he heard a voice he had heard somewhere before.

"Welcome to Turkey."

95

John struggled to focus. Where had he heard that voice before?

Mehmet.

The smuggler was standing in front of him, a smile spread across his corpulent face. John struggled to process.

"What? How?"

"It's okay, you are safe now." He nodded to someone behind John, and John felt fingers on his wrist and something cutting away at his flexicuffs. He shook his hands out and glanced over his shoulder. A Turkish soldier stood behind him. He nodded and slipped a hand under John's arm, helping him to his feet and guiding him to a chair.

"You are safe now, John," Mehmet repeated.

"Where are the others?"

As if on cue, the door opened, and two hooded figures were escorted in. Mehmet nodded at their escorts, and they removed the hoods and cut the flexicuffs from the prisoners' wrists. John jumped to his feet and strode across the room, grabbing both Steve and Mansur in a hug as the two blinked against the light.

"I thought I wasn't going to see you guys again."

"Where are we?" Steve asked, looking over John's shoulder and recognizing Mehmet for the first time.

"Turkey. We are safe," John reassured him.

"Where's Mia, Malak?" he asked frantically.

"They are okay." Mehmet smiled and raised his hands. "The doctor is seeing to the child."

"I want to see them."

Mehmet nodded to the soldiers, and one of them stepped back and opened the door.

"He will take you."

Steve nodded and followed him out.

John held Mansur at arm's length.

"Are you okay, my friend?"

Mansur smiled. "I am now."

"Good." John let go and turned to face Mehmet. "How the hell did you get us out of there? And where are we now?"

"You are on a Turkish military base, just across the border in Hatay province. Your friend Craig called me. I called in a few favors."

"Thank you, Mehmet." John exhaled loudly, feeling the constant tension of the last few days leaving his body. "There were others. Are they here, too?"

"No. I'm sorry." Mehmet shook his head. "But they are safe. They have been sent to a camp near Manbij. They will be looked after, food, medicine, shelter."

"The women?"

"Yes."

John glanced at Mansur and frowned. Turning back to Mehmet, he asked, "And Naeem?"

"Who?"

"Naeem. Mia's husband. Australian. He was wounded in the leg."

Mehmet shook his head. "There was no-one else."

"There was. He was with us when we were caught."

Mehmet shook his head again. He looked at Mansur, and back at John, clearly puzzled.

"There was no-one else. I asked them to release everyone. They did. The only reason the Yazidi women aren't here is it's too political, but..." He shrugged. "There was no Naeem."

John studied his face. He didn't seem to be lying, and why would he? What would he stand to gain? John turned to look at Mansur, and Mansur shrugged.

"We are safe, that's what's important."

John nodded slowly. "Yeah."

"Come, you must be hungry. The Turkish Army is providing food for you. I hear their Mess is quite good."

John's stomach growled as if it had heard Mehmet, but John had something more important to do.

"Mehmet, first, I need a phone. I have to make a call."

"Adriana?" Mehmet smiled. "She knows." He removed a phone from his pocket and passed it over. "Craig has kept her informed. She and... Maadhavi? They are on their way here."

John breathed a huge sigh of relief and took the phone from Mehmet's hand. He dialed from memory and held the phone to his ear. He waited impatiently as the phone connected, then rang. A moment later, he heard the most beautiful sound in the world.

"Hello, John?"

96

John stood by the window, looking out over the classical gardens of the villa. Below on a patch of lawn, between a row of immaculately manicured hedgerows, Adriana, Maadhavi, and Mia sat, Malak running around them.

In the two weeks since they had been rescued from Syria, the young child had blossomed. The army doctor had given her a dose of antibiotics and deworming medicine, then gave her the all-clear, saying all she needed was regular food and a healthy environment. She had filled out, had color in her cheeks, and instead of sleeping all day, it was hard to get her to sit down.

Mia looked much healthier, too, and the bruising on her face had all but disappeared. She had abandoned the black *abaya* and was now dressed in western clothing, although she still covered her hair with a *hijab*. John had even seen her smile, an expression that transformed her face, the years dropping away, becoming a young lady again. But now and then, when she thought she was unobserved, a deep sorrow crossed her face, and John knew from experience, she would be troubled by her past for a long time to come.

The disappearance of Naeem remained a mystery, but Mia said she no longer cared. Puzzled, yes, but she had closed her heart to him a long time ago.

Mehmet had graciously given them the use of a villa he owned in Istanbul's Bebek district for as long as they needed while they waited for their replacement documentation to come through. John's, Steve's, and Mansur's passports were replaced quickly, and Mansur had already departed for Oman, eager to be back with Warda and his daughters. The departure had been a sad one, but they made promises to meet again, the bonds formed in the shared stress of Syria would not be severed easily.

John and Adriana agreed to stay on with Steve and Maadhavi while they waited for Mia and Malak to get a passport, Mia's having been lost in Syria a long time ago. At first, the Australian government had refused, claiming she was a foreign combatant and would be refused entry back into the country. But after a series of articles written jointly by Craig and Adriana about how Mia and her uncle had rescued a group of Yazidi women from slavery, the government reluctantly bowed to public pressure and instructed the Australian Ambassador to Turkey to issue them with the documentation they needed.

Adriana followed up her reports with interviews conducted over video link with the women in Jadidet al-Hamar IDP camp, southwest of Manbij, the heartbreaking stories garnering worldwide attention. The last she had heard was a deal was being brokered to return the women to their homes in Eastern Syria and Iraq.

John watched her now as she tossed her head back in laughter, her thick mane of hair catching the light as it flicked back over her shoulders. He could hear the joy in her voice as she played with Malak.

John was proud of her and loved her more than anything else in the world. There was no way he would forget it, and now more than ever, he would value every moment he spent with her.

John looked up and across the rooftops of the city. The faces of all the people who had helped them flashed before his eyes—Ramesh, Craig, Hemin, Ferhad, and finally, the brave young Karam. There were good people in the world, and as long as he remembered that and did his best to be a good person, too, he could live with himself. Focusing on negativity was not a way to live a full and happy life.

Mehmet had been the biggest surprise and proof that a kernel of good lurked inside everyone, no matter how they filled their days. John's initial impression of the man, who made his living smuggling people and weapons, had not been good and John had been convinced the man would double cross them.

His instincts weren't often wrong, so in a quiet moment, while they waited for Adriana and Maadhavi to join them at the army base in Hatay, John had probed Mehmet on the motivation for his good deed.

Mehmet had remained silent for a while as if searching for the right words, and when he answered, he looked almost embarrassed.

"When I met you in the hotel, my aim was to make as much money as I could from your situation." His mustache twitched, and he looked away as if ashamed. "It's what I do, what I have always done." He shrugged, then looked back at John.

"I lied to you. I have children, a boy and a girl. My daughter, Zehra,"—he smiled—"she is six. She means everything to me. When I left you that night after our meeting and went home, she was already asleep." Mehmet looked away again and gazed out the window.

"I looked at her lying there and imagined how I would feel, what I would do to save her." He looked back at John, his expression soft, the hardness gone from his eyes. "I could not stop thinking about it, John. Every time I looked at her face, I remembered you and your friends. That is why I helped you."

A movement below interrupted John's thoughts. He looked down to see Steve walking out of the house and across the gravel pathway onto the lawn. He took a swig from the beer in his hand, then crouched down and called out to Malak. The little girl squealed with delight and ran across the lawn into his arms. He hugged her and picked her up. Holding her in his arms, she giggled and wriggled to get free, so he lowered her down to the ground, and she ran back to the women sitting on the grass. Steve watched her run off, then, as if knowing he was being watched, turned, and looked up at the window. He saw John and smiled. Raising the beer bottle in a toast, he mouthed, "Thank you."

EPILOGUE

The young man dabbed his face dry, then leaned closer to the mirror, angling his face to check each side. It had been a long time since he had seen himself without a beard, and it felt like someone else was looking back at him. Satisfied, he stepped back and moved to the shower cubicle. He pulled out a stool and sat down, turning on the tap.

"Bismillah," he said, then started to wash his hands. He washed them three times, then with his right hand, scooped water into his mouth and gargled. He spat the water out and repeated the process twice more. He cleansed his nostrils, then washed his face, followed by his arms up to the elbows. He wiped his head front to back, then cleaned the inside of his ears with his index finger. Finally, he washed his feet and between his toes, then recited the *dua.*

His *wudu* completed, he stood and walked into the living room of the small ground-floor flat and stood at the foot of his prayer mat.

"Allahu akbar, allahu akbar..." he began to pray.

. . .

Fifteen minutes later, he stood in the hallway and pulled on his leather jacket. Facing the hall mirror, he adjusted it and turned from one side to the other to make sure the Glock tucked into his waistband remained hidden by the jacket. Satisfied, he took a deep breath to calm his nerves, opened the door, and stepped outside. It was a typical crisp and cold London morning, and he turned up the collar of the jacket to protect his neck. Stepping off the front step, he winced as a twinge of pain shot up through his left leg. A memory flashed before his eyes, followed by a tiny hint of regret, but he shrugged it off. He had been chosen, and it would all be over soon. At the end of the path, he hesitated for a moment, then turning left, headed up the street and turned right on the main road, joining the crowds of commuters thronging toward the entrance to the Tube station.

END #

ACKNOWLEDGMENTS

This book wouldn't have been written without the generous assistance of others and I would like to take the opportunity to thank them here.

Chris McGrath for his detailed insights on working in the region as a journalist. Without Chris, there would have been a lot of factual errors in the story, something I discovered only after forty thousand words, prompting a frantic re-write.

Anthony Wallace for his incredible array of contacts.

My Iraqi Habibis, Warka, Fay, and Shams who serve as my living translation app for the Arabic language as well as providing insight into the many different cultures in the Middle East.

David Gaughran, Fabiane Cidade, and Roberta Ferrias, for their assistance with the Portuguese scenes.

I also took advice from various ex-Police and Armed Forces personnel, who taught me about weapons and what it is like to be under fire. Ray DeVere, Ron Turner, James Rangno, thank you. Your input was invaluable.

My editor Sandy Ebel, who despite being handed a

manuscript weeks late, still managed to edit and polish the story in time for release.

Of course none of this would have been possible without the support of my wife, K. This story was written during the COVID Lockdown, when we were confined to an apartment for nine weeks, a time when I struggled to be creative, and she struggled with having me moping around the house all day. Thank you, K.

ALSO BY MARK DAVID ABBOTT

Vengeance - John Hayes #1

When a loved one is taken from you, and the system lets you down, what would you do?

John Hayes' life is perfect. He has a dream job in an exotic land, his career path is on an upward trajectory and at home he has a beautiful wife whom he loves with all his heart.

But one horrible day a brutal incident tears this all away from him and his life is destroyed.

He doesn't know who is to blame, he doesn't know what to do, and the police fail to help.

What should he do? Accept things and move on with his life or take action and do what the authorities won't do for him?

What would you do?

Vengeance is the first novel in the John Hayes series.

Available now on Amazon

A Million Reasons: John Hayes #2

John Hayes is trying to move on but it's not easy.

Haunted by nightmares after the death of his wife he attempts to start a new life in Hong Kong, but the excitement and glamour of the city soon wears off and he finds himself deep in a rut. A mental state bordering on depression, a job he hates, and a salary that fails to last til the end of the month.

Until one day he finds a million dollars in his bank account!

It could change his life forever, but.....it comes with dangerous strings attached. Once again he is tested. Should he keep the money, break the law and potentially turn his life around, or should he give it all up and continue with his unhappy depressing existence?

Just how far is he willing to go?

What would you do?

What people are saying about "A Million Reasons"

"A great read, definitely worthy of 5 Stars. Written by a true wordsmith who knows how to draw his readers in to an exciting story with a number of unexpected twists."

"The second book in the John Hayes series is even better than the first!!"

Available now on Amazon.

A New Beginning: John Hayes #3

A chance meeting with a fascinating woman has the potential to change John's life. Could she be the one to bring him the happiness he lost after his wife was brutally murdered?........ Will it be that easy?

Newly wealthy John Hayes is living an idyllic life in the exotic city of Bangkok. He spends his days keeping fit, exploring the city and enjoying the wonderful food but he is lonely,........and when a beautiful woman walks into his life he thinks he has a chance to start afresh.

But with John life is never simple.

A penniless young girl desperate to start a new life..........a high flying foreign businessman with a murky past.......an alluring woman....... all come together to test John once again. Should he get involved and potentially risk his life and the lives of others? Or should he walk away and lose the woman he is growing to love?

"Great Book. Captivating. Well written and with enough suspense along with a bit of romance that keeps you turning the pages."

Available now on Amazon.

ALSO BY MARK DAVID ABBOTT

No Escape: John Hayes #4

After a chance encounter in the lobby of a Dubai hotel, someone from the dark corners of John's past comes back to haunt him, threatening to sabotage an idyllic holiday and to annihilate everything John Hayes holds dear.

No Escape, another fast-moving page-turning thriller in the **John Hayes Thriller Series,** takes you from the glitzy hotels of Dubai to the vast desert sands of Oman, where once again John has to dig deep and call upon all his wits to fight evil and save the woman he loves.

"These books are very difficult to put down! Like any truly good book, this thriller feels very realistic and I ride the suspenseful roller-coaster of emotions with every page turn. I look forward to seeing what's next for John Hayes..."

Available now on Amazon

ALSO BY MARK DAVID ABBOTT

Reprisal: John Hayes #5

Everyone knows revenge is a dish best served cold and no-one knows this better than John Hayes.

After dealing with the mercenaries sent to kill him in Oman, John realizes he can never live in peace knowing the man who sent them, the man ultimately responsible for endangering the woman he loves, is still roaming free. To hunt him down John must draw on all his courage and will power, and return to where it all began.

India.

Reprisal is another exciting, nail-biting adventure once again starring John Hayes, an ordinary man in extraordinary situations.

Available now on Amazon

READY FOR THE NEXT ADVENTURE?

The next book is currently being written, but if you sign up for my VIP newsletter I will let you know as soon as it is released.

Your email will be kept 100% private and you can unsubscribe at any time.

If you are interested, please join here:

www.markdavidabbott.com
(No Spam. Ever.)

ENJOYED THIS BOOK? YOU CAN MAKE A BIG DIFFERENCE.

First of all thank you so much for taking the time to read my work. If you enjoyed it, then I would be extremely grateful if you would consider leaving a short review for me on the store where you purchased the book. A good review means so much to every writer but especially to self-published writers like myself. It helps new readers discover my books and allows me more time to create stories for you to enjoy.

ABOUT THE AUTHOR

Mark can be found online at:
www.markdavidabbott.com

on Facebook
www.facebook.com/markdavidabbottauthor

on Instagram
instagram.com/thekiwigypsy

or on email at:
www.markdavidabbott.com/contact

Printed in Great Britain
by Amazon